Wilhelmine von Hillern

The Hour Will Come
Volume 1 , 2

Wilhelmine von Hillern

The Hour Will Come
Volume 1 , 2

1st Edition | ISBN: 978-3-75238-330-0

Place of Publication: Frankfurt am Main, Germany

Year of Publication: 2020

Outlook Verlag GmbH, Germany.

Reproduction of the original.

THE
HOUR WILL COME
BY
WILHELMINE von HILLERN
VOL. I.

PROLOGUE.

ST. VALENTINE'S ON THE HEATH.

The heath or moorland plateau of Mals lies wide—spread, silent, and deserted where the lofty head of the Grossortler towers up, and overlooks it in eternal calm. It is five centuries ago—a mere moment in that world of everlasting snows; the keen autumn wind, as at this day, is rushing through the grey halms of the charlock, woodrush and heathgrasses, that have caught a doubtful, golden gleam reflected from the glaciers which are bathed in the glow of the sinking sun; as at this day, the gale packs the driving white clouds together in the still highland valley, as though to rest for the night. They heave and roll noiselessly, spreading a white, misty sheet over the withered heathgrass. The mirror-surface of the moorland tarn lies lead-coloured and dull, wrinkled by the night-breeze, and its icy waters trickle in tiny rills over the bare plain and down to the valley. All is the same as it is to this day! Only life is wanting, life warm and busy, which in these days is stirring in the villages and homesteads that dot the plain, and that have brought the dead moorland into tilth and fertility. Profound silence reigns over the immeasurable level, throughout its length and breadth no living thing stirs; it is as if this were indeed the neutral space between Heaven and Hell—a vast, eternal void! Only the monotonous murmur of the Etsch—that cold artery of the desolate heath—and the roar of the winds that sweep at night across the plateau; these are the eerie voices of this realm of death.

Woe to the lonely pilgrim who is wandering through the night in this boundless desert, in storm and snow, in impenetrable darkness; he is lost in nothingness, owned by neither Heaven nor Hell, and the earth knows him not! No ear can hear his cry for help, it is lost in vacancy; the raven and the wolf mark him down, but they tell no one of their mute prey.

It is true that pitying love has penetrated even to this wilderness and realm of death, and spreads her arms so far as they may reach; but they are but human arms, weak and inadequate for the great divine mind that animates them. Every evening, above the howling of the storm and the roaring of the highland lake, as dusk creeps on, the Vesper bell rings softly out like the beat of some metallic heart. Then a dull-red, flaring blaze is suddenly seen, which parts into wandering storm-blown flakes of flame that disperse themselves about the moor till they vanish in the mist and darkness. The shepherd and lay-brethren it is, who go forth with torches and biers from the Hospice of Saint Valentine in the moor, which pious faith has erected for the lost traveller

2

here in the wilderness. Defying the warring elements, they seek in silent and fearless devotion the strayed, the perishing, and the hungry, and bring them in to the warm hearth of humanity. Happy is he whom they find, he is rescued—but the moor is wide, and they are but a forlorn little handful of men, not all-knowing nor all-seeing.

The sun went down early in angry red; it grows darker and darker. Heavy clouds are packed over the evening sky, the last glimmer of starlight is extinguished, all is as dark as though no light survived in Heaven or earth; for a moment even the howling, shrieking winds are silent, which nightly carry on their demon-dance round and across the heath; but from the distance looms a nameless, formless something, a thunder roll is heard, soft at first like the sound of slow, heavy wheels, then nearer and nearer—a terror, invisible, intangible but crushing, shakes the earth to its foundation. Slowly it surges on, like a deep groan of rage long controlled only to break out all the more fearfully in raving, annihilating fury. The snow-storm, the first of the year, sweeps down from the Grossortler over the bare trembling heath—a mighty, moving mass rolls on before it that breaks incessantly into powder, and is incessantly renewed—as if the winds had torn the eternal mantle of snow from the shoulders of the numberless glaciers, and were flinging it down from the heights. A giant wall reaches from earth to sky; snow, snow everywhere. Touched by the icy breath, the shapeless mists over lake and river curdle and turn to snow, the light evening-clouds form compact masses of snow—whirling pillars that bury everything in their wild dance; the very air is turned to snow, there is no tiniest space between sky and earth that is not filled with snow. The whole moor is overwhelmed in it, and is one vast, white bed, where the storm and night may work their wild will.

But hark! a cry of distress, from a spot between the two lakes and far, far from the sheltering Hospice. It is the cry of a human being that shares that fearful bed with the night and the storm—a woman who lies sunk to the knees under the cold, crushing coverlet of snow, and on her breast a newborn baby-boy, closely clasped in her stiffened arms and wrapped in her cloak. The milk which flows from the young mother's bosom to nourish her infant has frozen above her fluttering heart, and the tears on her closed lashes are turned to ice. There she lies. "Poor feeble mother, who has thrust thee out in this night of storm and tumult for your child to be born under the open sky?" Thus ask the storm and the wild uproar of the elements; and as if even they had pity for the wretched soul, the wind carries the mother's cry of anguish over her starving infant, bears it on its wings to the scattered party of seeking, rescuing monks. "Be quick, make haste before it is too late."

And they hear it, these bold wrestlers with death, themselves half-buried in the snow, and they set out, wading, digging, shovelling, till the sweat of their brows runs down on their frozen beards, ever listening without a word, without a sound after that tremulous wind-borne cry.

And these storm-proof hearts quake with dread and pity for the hapless wretch to whose help they are hastening; they go forward painfully on their deadly and toilsome way, heeding neither danger nor difficulty, with only one purpose and one aim before their eyes—a struggle for life with Death.

At last—it is close by—at last they hear a faint cry; even the death-stricken woman hears them approaching, she collects her remaining strength and once more opens her eye-lids, on which the restless whirling snow has already dropped a white shroud; a red gleam meets her sight, she hears the scraping of iron shovels, the burden that weighs on her breast and on her feet gets lighter and lighter—here are light and human voices—a shout of deliverance—of joy. Round her opened grave stand the snow-whitened storm-beaten group in a flood of red light from the flaring torches, their eyes shining with the divine light of devoted love which has triumphed over danger and death. And they raise her in their rough hands, they lift her out of her cold tomb, they wrap her and the naked child in warm hair-cloth coats and carry her home under the sheltering roof of holy Valentine.

"Salve, Frater Florentinus! we bring a precious prize," says one of the brethren triumphantly to the silver-bearded old man who opens the heavy creaking door. "A young mother and a new born boy—snatched from death."

"Deo gratias!" murmurs the old man in a voice husky from age. "The Lord will bless your labours. Come in quickly, the wind is blowing the snow in."

They step in and the door falls to with a groan. The storm outside snorts and rages and hurls against the door, like some wild beast robbed of its prey, but the door is tight and fast, and within all is quiet and warm; a smoking pine torch is burning in an iron bracket fixed to one of the pillars of the entrance hall, and throws wavering shadows and red lights on the grey stone walls and the black wooden crucifix which spreads out its arms to welcome all who enter.

"Come, hapless suffering mother, here you may find rest," says the old man compassionately, and he opens a low, iron-plated door at the farther end of the hall, through which the procession passes in silence into a room which is at once the guest-chamber, the kitchen, and the refectory of the pious brotherhood, and the only warm room in the little Refuge, whose walls are thicker than its rooms are wide. A vast chimney-place like a roof projects into the half-dark hall, its broad shadow cast on the vaulted roof by the crackling fire that burns beneath it. From the ceiling hangs a small iron oil-lamp covered with cobwebs and giving too dismal and dim a light to illuminate the whole room. Over the fire hangs a cauldron in which a warm mess is stewing for the brethren and for any one they may bring with them on their return, half-frozen, from the desert outside; the roughly hewn seats stand round an octagon table, which is immoveably fixed in the middle of the room on strong supports. The only decoration in the whole smoke-blackened hall is a picture of St. Valentine, who, himself of gigantic proportions, stands preaching the gospel on the open heath to a crowd of very small devotees; the thick clouds of smoke which, all the winter through, are puffed back from the chimney by the stormy gusts, have blackened this picture also; yet it is the most treasured possession of the brotherhood. It was painted by Father Columbanus of the monastery at Marienberg, and Father Columbanus was an enlightened and inspired man, to whom the saints were wont to appear in nightly visions that he might depict them. This picture of Saint Valentine was the last vision that he saw and painted, for he died shortly after; so it is of double value! Under the picture hangs a holy-water vessel of terra-cotta.

On the heavy, rough-hewn table there are wooden platters in which each man receives his share as it is taken out of the cooking pot, and a wooden spoon lies by each. This is all the furniture of the bare room; but such as it is, to the suffering, storm-lashed woman it is full of unspeakable comfort—a city of refuge from the raging wilderness without. She is silent, but her eye rests with an unearthly glitter on the rough, weather-beaten figures, who carry her at once to the chimney and with clumsy hospitality press her to take a little of the warm mess. Then, with a quiet bustle, they make her a couch by the glowing fire; a sack of straw, a pillow filled with white moss, and for coverlet a woolly sheep-skin—this is all the house has to offer, but it is a delicious couch after the fearful bed out on the moor—a couch prepared by careful and kindly human hands. With bashful awkwardness they untie the band of her tangled golden hair, take off her wet outside garment and wrap her in a warm, dry monk's frock, then they lay the frail and trembling form carefully on the bed and put the pale, half dead baby on her arm. The frozen fount of the mother's breast thaws under the warm wrapper, the child finds its natural food, and breathes and lives again. The brethren stand aside in silence, and tears run down their lean cheeks.

"May the holy mother of God protect thee—poor young mother!" says the grey-haired brother Florentinus, laying a little metal image of the Virgin on the suffering woman's breast. "We are unlearned men, unskilled in serving sick ladies and ignorant of what may comfort you in your suffering; but this image is of great virtue and famous for many miracles. It will bestow its grace on you too if your past life has not rendered you unworthy to receive it."

The young woman looked him calmly and frankly in the face.

"Holy brother," said she, "I am miserable and poor, and have not where to lay my head, but in that shelter which Heaven provides for the wretched under the sacred convent roof. But I was faithful, reverend brother, faithful and obedient at all times!" She pressed the image long and fervently to her lips, and silently told her sorrows to the All-pitying Mother.

"Most times when a young wife's first-born is brought into the world a loving grandmother bends over her bed and takes thought for everything, and a young father rocks his first-born tenderly on his arms. But I, O Mother of Grace! am cast off and homeless, and have no one but Thee."

And as the nourishing fount flows freely for her sucking child, the frozen fountain of her soul thaws too, and overflows from her closed eyelids in hot but restful tears. The Heavenly Mother bends lovingly and soothingly over her; the worn out woman rests her weary head on the unseen but omnipresent and ever-merciful bosom, and overcome by deadly exhaustion she falls asleep. The brethren slip off their wooden shoes, and walk barefoot on the stone flags so as not to disturb the exhausted woman. She looks to them like a martyr as she lies there—so calm, with the baby that has also gone to sleep looking like a glorified angel. The flickering fire throws changing lights and shadows on her crisply curling hair, making it seem like a crown of thorns; the brethren observe the resemblance, and point to it in silence.

Old Florentinus meanwhile does not forget temporal interests for the sake of eternal ones. He busily steals about the room on tip-toe, and carries the stranger's garments to the fire to dry, and for the first time he sees that there is a richly embroidered border at the hem of the dress, which glitters in the fire-light, and that the tattered shoes are embroidered by a skilful hand; he silently shows these ornaments to the brethren, and they shake their heads in astonishment. Then he lifts the cauldron from the fire, and dispenses the steaming contents into the platters with a sign to his companions; they obey the signal with but small alacrity, they are in no mood to eat. Noiselessly they draw up to the table, offer up a grace, and take the simple meal of barley and water standing. The thoughtful old man puts by a little of it for the sick woman. Then they cross themselves before the picture of St. Valentine, and withdraw each to his own cell, carefully closing the clumsy doors behind them. The old man only remains to watch the sick woman, and he seats himself in silence on the stone window-seat at the farther end of the room, telling his beads. The storm still roars round the house in long and violent gusts, but it can do it no mischief, for poor and bare as it is, it is built of strong masonry, a fortress against wind and weather, and the narrow air-openings are so deeply imbedded in the thick walls that no draught can pour in through them; only now and then the wind rushes howling down the chimney, and flings the crackling flames and smoke out into the room, so that the sick woman is startled from her painful slumbers; then all is still again. The child sighs softly in its sleep as if dreaming of future sorrow; the mother's breathing goes on in regular rhythm, and even the old watcher leans his weary head in the niche in the wall, and falls asleep. Only the gigantic saint on the wall preaches unweariedly on to his dwarfed heathen in the light of the dying lamp, and the little figures seem to move and dance dreamily in the growing darkness.

Suddenly a cry of pain broke from the lips of the sick woman; the old man rose and went to the bed-side. She lay there quite changed, almost unconscious, her eyes sunken, her lips blue; the hand of death had passed over her face. She was seized with a violent trembling, and the bed quaked under her.

"What is the matter?" asked the brother in alarm. "Will you have a little food? It is standing here by the fire—or shall I make you a drink of warming herbs?" and he hastily threw some more wood on to the embers.

"Good brother," she replied, and her white teeth showed below her upper lip like those of a corpse, "neither food nor drink can help me any more. As it must come, let it come—I am dying; and when I tell you that I walked with my unborn child from Görz as far as this, and that the boy was born on the heath where I was all alone and helpless, you cannot wonder at it. Hear my confession, and grant me extreme unction."

The old man's eyes overflowed with tears. "Alas, poor flower, who can so pitilessly have plucked you, and flung you away to wither, and fall to pieces in the winter-storm. And we are so unskilled in all medical knowledge, and must see you die so miserably when we would so willingly rescue you!"

"Do not weep for me, reverend father," she said calmly; "all is well with me, I am going to rest in the lap of our Blessed Mother. But my poor child— he loses his mother just as I am finding mine. Take charge of him, I beseech you, he has no one in the world—he is wholly forlorn!"

"It shall be as you wish," said the old man. "You may rely on that in perfect confidence—you may die in peace on that score."

"Then take my boy without delay to the venerable Abbot Conrad of Amatia at Marienberg. Tell him that the outcast wife of Swyker of Reichenberg sends the child to him as her last bequest, that she dedicated him to the church in a sorrowful hour, and the venerable man will help a poor soul to keep her vow."

"In the name of all the saints!" cried the monk. "You, the most noble lady of Reichenberg? You, the guardian spirit and good angel of all the country round! Married only nine months since, if we were rightly informed? How, tell me, how come you here in this wild spot without one of your friends, cast out like the poorest beggar or like some criminal!"

"You say rightly, reverend father," she said quietly, and a gleam of the reviving fire fell like a glory on her pale brow, "I was banished like a criminal, and thrust out to be a prey to the fowls of the air, I and the child, the son of a noble house. And yet I am not guilty of that of which I was accused, although God himself was pleased to bear witness against me." A fresh shivering fit came over her, and shook her as the autumn wind shakes the faded leaves from the trees.

"My time is short—I will make a short story," she said in a failing voice. "It is nine months to-day since the noble Lord of Reichenberg, as you know, married me from the house of Ramüss, and soon after we went to Görz, the gay court of Albert, the count of Tyrol and Görz.—Egno of Amatia, the companion of my childhood, went with us. Oh! would we had never gone there—I have never had an hour of happiness since! The countess of Eppan, a beautiful woman of courtly manners and accomplishments, stole my husband's heart and with it his confidence in me; I had to look on while it happened, helpless and with no one to counsel me, a simple woman, having grown up in a quiet town in the Lower Engadine—ignorant of the world and of its wickedness. And then—how can I say it—she whispered to my husband that I and Egno of Amatia—! Oh! reverend Brother, spare me, spare me—If death had not already frozen my blood with his cold breath I should blush purple with shame!"

"I understand you, noble Lady," said the old man.

"My husband believed the falsehood and—oh! that I should have to say it —disowned his child. He challenged Egno of Amatia to ordeal by combat. Reverend Father, the ways of the Almighty are inscrutable and wise—why He, who proves the heart and reins, abandoned the innocent, I cannot understand; but it was His holy will—and so it fell out. Egno fell, slain by my husband's hand. God himself was witness against me—and so my deluded husband cast me out—me and my child. 'Go—bring your child into the world to be meat for the birds and wolves, and if tender hands take pity on it, may it be accursed and they who rescue it also. It is the fruit of sinful love and by sinful love may it perish!' So he spoke and put me out of his house, and in order that the curse may not take effect, worthy father, I dedicated the child to the cloister before it saw the light, for where can it be safer than within convent walls. I was trying to reach St. Gertrude's, the convent in the

Münsterthal—a well-beloved home.—There I thought to have given birth to my child. If it were a girl it was to belong to St. Gertrude—if a boy, I would take it to Marienberg. My brother is there and the Abbot is well known to me, and kindly disposed towards me—he is of the house of Amatia and will receive the child, who is an outcast for his relation's sake, and will bring it up to a holy life in the Lord, so that it can incur no curse and fall into no sinful love. Swear to me that you will report all this to him, faithfully—as I tell it to you—!"

"I swear it by this picture of the Blessed Virgin, who henceforth will be a mother to your son, born in sorrow. You have dedicated him to Heaven, and Heaven will accept him—because the gift is pure. I promise you in the name of the brethren of Marienberg that they will keep and cherish your child so that the curse may not be accomplished." And the old man sprinkled the baby with holy water and laid his withered hand in blessing on his head. The mother suddenly stretched herself out with a wonderful smile of peace. Her child was safe now, she could die content.

"Make haste, give me the last sacraments, I am near my end!" The old man went to wake the brethren—startled, they hurried out of their rooms and gathered round the dying woman's bed. She still breathed, but with difficulty, and speech had failed her; but her lips could still receive the sacred viaticum and smile.

All was still as death in the room; the brethren prayed softly, the old man concluded the sacred office and made the sign of the cross. Yet three more feeble breaths—and all was over. The old man closed the sightless eyes and gently took the sleeping infant from its dead mother's side.

"Come, poor little one, there is no home on earth for you—you belong to Heaven."

He wrapped the boy in a warm lamb-skin and lighted a torch at the sooty lamp.

"Where are you going, brother Florentine? Are you going out in this stormy night, and with the tender infant?" asked one of the brethren. "Shall we not accompany you!"

"No! the child's guardian spirit is with me—I need no human aid. You stay here to pray by the corpse."

"Wait at least till the morning," said even the rough shepherd, the secular Superior of the convent.

"A vow will not bear any postponement!" said the old man, and with the new-born child in his arms he quitted the room where its mother's body was lying. The baby was torn from its mother's breast, torn from the source of its life; and as if the unconscious child felt the sorrowful parting it struggled and cried and fought against the bony, masculine arm that carried it. The old man stepped out of the convent; once more the heath received the outcast and homeless infant with wild cries from the storm; the snowfall was over and an icy blast had frozen the endless expanse of snow quite hard. The old monk's steps crunched upon it, and the evanescent crystals sparkled with a million rays where the flare of the torch fell, so that he made his onward way through the darkness, in the midst of a glory of light. He felt as if it were Christmas Evening, and as if the angel who guided the three kings were leading him too on the way, to conduct the child to his Holy Companion in the manger—to the Child above all children and the city of salvation. The star on the angel's brow threw a soft light in his path, he felt the mighty fanning of his wings on his hoary temples, and he sang joyful praise to the Lord in his heart while he marched stoutly forward through that stormy, glorious night of wonders.

BOOK I.

UNDER A CURSE.

CHAPTER I.

High up on the rocks above the village of Burgeis stands a watch tower of faith, the monastery of Marienberg, with heaven-reaching towers and pinnacles, proudly looking far out and down into the night. Torn, and as though weary, the clouds hang about the mountain peaks that surround it, and the snow storm beats its exhausted wings against the mighty walls; it has spent its rage over night and its power is broken. Now and again between the parting clouds glimmers the pale crescent of the setting moon; below, in the valley, a cock crows betimes to announce the coming morning, but up in the convent as well as down in the village all are sunk in sleep, no ray of light illumines any one of the numberless rows of windows, with their small round panes set in lead; only in the porter's room on the ground floor a feeble light is burning and keeping watch for the sleeping door-keeper. Three blows of the huge iron ring on the back door are suddenly heard. The porter starts up, his lamp has burnt low, warning him that it will soon be morning. He goes out with his clattering bunch of keys in his hand; meanwhile the knocking has been hastily and imperatively repeated.

"Who is out there at this early hour?" He asks cautiously.

"The beginning and the end—an infant and an old man," is the answer.

"What am I to understand by that?"

"Open the door and then you will know."

"I must first fetch the Superior. At such an unwonted hour I cannot open to any one without his sanction." And he goes back into the house and wakes the Superior, who glances with alarm at the hour-glass thinking he has overslept himself. It will soon be the hour of matins.

"Come out quickly," cried the gatekeeper. "A stranger asks to be admitted —I dared not open the gate without your permission."

The Superior threw on his frock and cowl and stepped out.

"An old man and a child—as he says—" continued the porter, as they crossed the courtyard.

"Open the gate," said the Superior, as the wail of an infant apprised him that the stranger outside had spoken the truth. The porter obeyed and at the door, with the infant on one arm and in his other hand the torch, stood the old monk from St. Valentine's.

"Blessed be the Lord Christ! Brother Florentinus! How come you here this wild night—and what have we here for a whimpering visitor?" cried the Superior, admitting the old man.

"Aye, you would never have thought that my stiff old arms would be bringing round such a fragile, wriggling thing.—But take me quickly to the reverend Abbot that we may take counsel in the matter—for the child is hungry and needs womanly care."

"The bell will soon call to matins," said the Superior. "Wait here in the court-yard till the first stroke, and then you will be sure that no bad spirit crosses the threshold with you. Meanwhile I will go and announce you to his reverence, the Abbot."

"Aye, you are right, brother, the child must enter the convent at a lucky hour, for he must stay in for ever."

The Superior asked no more—the brethren were accustomed to suppress all curiosity and to accept inexplicable occurrences in silence. He went in and the gate-keeper remained outside with the old man. They stood there expectant, till the first stroke should sound that should scare away the hordes of bad night-spirits.

Florentinus extinguished his torch, for the light from the porter's window lighted up the narrow court-yard.

"To-day is a great festival, and the fathers were making preparations far into the night," said the porter. "You did not think of that?"

"I do not know what you mean," said the old man. "To-day is no saint's day?"

"This day, a hundred years ago, anno Domini 1150, the edifice of this godly house was begun by Ulrich of Trasp, and a great thanksgiving service is to be performed in honour of the noble founder."

"To be sure I might have known it. Your house is ten years younger than ours and we too, ten years since, had a thanksgiving to our founder, Ulrich Primele."

"But you must not let our reverend brethren hear you say that our foundation is younger than yours, for they may take it ill in you. You know of course that our holy house was built two hundred years ago at Schuls, and was only transferred here because at Schuls and at St. Stephen we were so often visited by fire and avalanches."

"I know, I know," nodded the old man. "I did not mean to cast any reflection on the venerable antiquity of your foundation. God grant it may increase and prosper. It is still a sure bulwark against the decay of all conventual discipline in these days—God save us—the rule of St. Benedict is often followed in outward semblance only, but your severity is everywhere famous."

"Now!" said the guardian, opening the door for the old man. Solemnly and with silvery clearness, the bell for matins rang out. Inside the convent, all was alive at once. One after another, the windows were lighted up but without noise, as in a magic lantern. Brother Florentinus stepped into the hall. Door after door opened, and the dark figures of the monks slipped out in their soft sandals, and glided noiselessly down to the chapel along the long corridor. The deepest "silentium" reigned in the dusky passages and halls—that sacred silence by which the still dormant soul prepares itself to wake up to prayer. But the crying of the hungry baby disturbed the solemn stillness, and the fathers paused in astonishment, and gathered full of wonder and bewilderment round the screaming child. The guardian called the old man to come into the refectory with the infant, and the brethren went in to matins, shaking their heads over this strange visit. The Abbot, a reverend man of near seventy years, was standing in the refectory when Florentinus entered.

"What is this strange story that our brother, the Prior, tells me? You, Florentinus, bring us a child—a new-born infant. Where, in the name of all the saints, did you pick it up, and what have we to do with the helpless baby?"

"Most reverend Abbot, kindly lend me your attentive ear, and then your questions will be answered. But first of all I beseech your grace to allow that a woman may be fetched out of the village to suckle the child, for it has been starving these three hours."

"That cannot be, Brother Florentinus; a woman in the convent! What are you thinking about? You know very well that our order allows no women but princesses to come within our walls."

"Your reverence, it *must* be," said Florentine fearlessly; "I promised the babe's dying mother in your name that it should be received this day within the sheltering walls of Marienberg, and 'he will help a poor soul to keep her vow,' the dying woman said. He is the child of the noble Lady of Reichenberg."

The Abbot clasped his hands.

"What—where did you see her?"

"We found her at night on the heath, where her child had been born out in the snow. She is now lying in our house at St. Valentine's—dead."

The Abbot grasped his forehead with his hand as if he thought he was dreaming.

"The Lady of Reichenberg, the angel of Ramüss! What has happened to her?"

"She was repudiated by her husband on account of your relative Egno of Amatia; he fell in trial by combat. But the wife was innocent nevertheless, the child is Swyker of Reichenberg's child; but he cast it out to the birds of the air, and loaded it with the heaviest curses. In order that the curses might not take effect, she dedicated it to the cloister."

The Abbot Conrad took the child tenderly in his arms.

"Yes, poor orphan, you shall find a home here; none on earth are motherless to whom the church opens her sheltering bosom."

Then he went to the door, and called the Superior.

"Hasten without delay down into the village, and find some good woman who will undertake to care for the infant's bodily needs; the convent will reward her richly. She may live in the Lady Uta's east turret-chamber; there she will be hidden from the eyes of the brethren; and you may also open the Lady Uta's chest for her use and the baby's. Make the room ready so that it may look comfortable and habitable, and that the woman may not feel as if she were a prisoner."

The guardian brother hurried away.

"The church must give to each severally that which he needs, why should she let the suckling starve that wants a mother's breast—she, the All-bountiful, the Mother of all," he went on, giving the child back to the old man. "In such an unprecedented case it is allowable to make an exception to the rule, to save a soul for the church."

"You are great and wise, my Lord Abbot," cried Florentinus with grateful joy, and rocking the child on his arm to quiet it. "It is strange how soon one gets used to a little thing like this. I have quite set my old heart on this little brat, it is so helpless and forsaken!"

"It is no longer helpless nor forsaken," said the Abbot gravely. "When matins are over, and the child has been properly attended to we will baptise it. Meanwhile tell me in detail all that has happened, for it must all be recorded in the chronicles of the monastery, as is fitting."

He seated himself in the deep arm-chair at the upper end of the table, supporting himself on the monstrous dragon's heads which formed the arms of the seat.

Brother Florentinus conscientiously narrated the melancholy occurrences of the night.

"The body must be fetched and interred in the church," said the Abbot, "but without any inscription, for if we are to carry out the dead lady's vows we must efface every trace of her. Nay, the boy himself must never learn who his parents were, so that none of his family may dispute our right to him."

"You are always wise and choose the right, most reverend Abbot," Florentinus again declared.

They heard a sound of hasty steps on the stone floor of the corridor, and the Prior knocked at the highly ornamented door.

"Come in, in the name of the Lord," cried the Abbot.

The door opened, and a handsome young woman entered, whose fine, tall figure was poorly clad in miserable rags. She remained standing timidly at the door.

"Here is a woman who will be a mother to the child, if your reverence thinks proper."

"What is your name?"

"Berntrudis."

"Only think, after the pious waiting maid of the Lady Uta of Trasp, our noble foundress."

"She was my great-grandmother's sister."

"You come of a good stock, so I hope the fruit too is of a good sort," said the Abbot kindly.

The woman was modestly silent.

"I know you already by sight. You are the wife of the fisherman whose business it is to catch fish in the lake for the convent."

"Yes."

"How old is your child?"

"Two weeks."

"Is it a girl or a boy?"

"A girl."

"And you feel that you can nurse another child as well?"

"Six, if you like," said the woman smiling, and showing two rows of dazzling white teeth.

"Good, healthy and strong," said the Abbot to the Superior; "but," he added in Latin, casting a thoughtful glance at the blooming figure before him, "the brethren must not come in her way, you must be answerable for no scandal coming of it." Then he said to the wet-nurse,

"Take the child then, in the name of the Lord. The Prior here knows where your room is, and will see that your own child is brought to you. You may go at your pleasure into the convent-garden so long as the brethren are at vespers or at their meals, but you must never on any account go outside the convent-walls. You are henceforth under the rules of the order, and must submit to live like a nun. Will you?"

The woman hesitated a little, but then said,

"Well—yes; it will not last for ever."

The old white-bearded men looked at each other and shook their heads,

"Oh women—women!"

"Take her away," said the Abbot to the Superior, laying the child in her arms. "Now do your duty, and the convent will give you a handsome reward."

The woman pressed the child compassionately to her bosom and was about to kiss him. But the Abbot checked her severely.

"You are never to kiss the child—do you hear? under the severest penalties; so that the boy may not be accustomed from his cradle to foolish caresses and wanton tenderness, for they are not seemly for a son and future servant of the Church. No woman's lips may ever touch him—not even those of his nurse."

The woman looked at the Abbot half-surprised and half-indignant.

"Oh! you poor, poor little child!" she murmured in her Rhætian dialect. "But—when no one sees us I *will* kiss you, all the same," she thought, and followed the Superior out of the room. The two old men looked at each other and again they shook their heads.

"Who would have thought of telling us, brother Florentinus, that at the end of our days we should be inspecting a wet-nurse?" said the Abbot laughing. "So it is, the unclean stream of life penetrates even the strongest convent walls and fouls the very foot of our sacred altars."

"It is the duty of the strong to help the weak," said Florentinus simply, "and such a humble labour of love disgraces no one, be he ever so high!"

The Abbot nodded assent.

"Now come to the chapel, brother Florentinus, else we shall miss the mass."

With slow steps they passed along the corridor and into the choir of the darkened church, which was lighted only by the scattered wax-lights of the brethren who were deciphering their manuscript breviaries. A grateful fragrance of pine-wood pervaded the consecrated place and, so far as the scattered tapers allowed, a number of festal garlands were visible, made of pine-branches and red-berried holly twisted round the pillars and carvings by the brethren who, during the night, had thus decorated the chapel for the coming anniversary; and with hearts lifted up in praise the two old men knelt down to perform their deferred devotions.

Meanwhile the Superior had conducted the wet nurse through the spacious building to the eastern tower. A shudder came over her as she felt her way up the narrow spiral stairs, while the pine torch held by the Prior—who let her pass on in front of him—threw her gigantic shadow on the steep steps before her, and the solid masonry on each side. It was so damp and cold, so uncannily still, so painfully narrow—she felt as if a weight lay on her breast. "Where am I going? How high will this take me?" She begins to get giddy. Turning after turning—always one turn more—till she turns round with the stairs, and the stairs with her—she feels as if she were spinning round and round on one spot and yet she gets higher and higher, farther and farther from mother earth on which till this day she has always walked, which hitherto she has tilled with her own hands, in poverty and want, but happy in her labour and free!

She climbed wearily up with the child, frequently treading on her gown, for she had never before mounted steps in her life; she had lived in a humble hut under a scanty straw-roof, or in the fields and meadows. She had never thought it possible that men should build such tall high dwellings, and she was seized by a secret terror, a real anguish of fear, lest she should never be able to get down again.

The Superior spoke to her. "Only a few steps more, and it will be done; we shall be at the top directly—in a moment." But the steps seemed to grow before her, and her guide's "directly" was half an eternity to the poor frightened soul. At last she almost hit her head against some wooden beams and rafters; she was under the roof, and before her was a small low door covered with curious iron-work; this was the turret-chamber which she was to inhabit. She stood despondingly in front of the door, but her guide opened it, stooped and went in before her—she too had to stoop in order not to hit her head as she entered the room. However, she was used to low doorways, that did not scare her, and inside the room it was not so inhospitable as on the dark, stone, spiral stairs. A first glimmer of day-light shone in through the lens-shaped panes of the turret window; it was only a narrow opening, high up in a deep niche in the wall, but three stone steps led up to it and a stone seat was built at the top of them so that one could look out at the distance or down into the valley according to fancy. A homely bedstead, brown with age, stood by the wall with a heavy wooden sort of roof, like a little house by itself, and curtains of faded Byzantine silk. Old and clumsy as it was, to the poor woman who was accustomed to sleep on nothing but straw, it appeared strangely magnificent, and she felt as if some one must be hidden in it—some grand personage, before whom she must bow low and speak softly so as not to disturb the sleeper. Puffy-cheeked cherubs were carved on the four bed-posts, just like round balls with wings attached to them. The walls were whitewashed and painted with saints; the little ivory crucifix over the embroidered but faded praying-stool seemed to greet her as a friend, and a cheerful fire crackled in the chimney. It was an ancient and venerable little room and it had an oppressive and solemn smell like that of a reliquary— partly of dried rose-leaves and partly of mould. The Prior showed her a large worm-eaten chest full of costly linen; as he opened the heavy lid the dust flew off in a cloud and little spiders scampered away.

"Look here," he said kindly, "You are in the room which was formerly occupied by the Lady Uta of Trasp, the wife of our blessed founder, when she came here on a visit from St. Gertrude's. She had this trunk full of linen clothes brought here for her use and desired that whoever might stop here as a guest should have the benefit of it for their use and comfort. So now you may wrap yourself and the baby in it; it will bring you a blessing, for it was spun by the innocent hands of the Lady Uta and her maids, and many a fervent prayer has been said over it." Berntrudis looked thoughtfully down at the linen garments; it touched her to think that her ancestress, the pious Berntrudis, should have helped with her hands to spin the web in which she, so long after, might clothe herself. But she would not waste time in unpacking the treasure, she pitied the hungry child.

"Go now, Brother Superior," said she, "while I give the child a drink, and when my husband comes with my little girl, send him up at once."

But the Prior put on a considering face. "What—" he said, "your husband up to you? That is not feasible; you heard—you are now under convent rule!"

The woman started up in horror.

"What! my husband may not come to see me! I shall never see him again? Then take your child back again. I will not stop. I will go away on the spot."

"Oh! what a wild fury!" exclaimed the horrified Prior, "to fly into such a passion at once; think of the sacred place you are in—would you cause a scandal among our chaste brethren by your foolish worldly affections?"

"That is all one to me. Only I must see my husband once more, else I shall die of heartache—if I had known it I would never have come—never, never."

"Think of the high wages—you will be made rich by the gratitude of the convent, your house will be raised, your husband freed most likely, absolved from his bondage to the convent—"

"That is all one to me," repeated the woman with increased vehemence. "If I can never see my husband I will not stop—do as you will," and she laid the baby on the bed and was hastening past the Prior and out of the room, but he held her back.

"In the name of all the Saints—stay; will you leave the poor child to starve? There is not another woman in the village who can nurse it and take care of it. Can you be so cruel?"

The woman burst into tears, and turned to the bed again.

"No, you shall not starve, poor little orphan—you cannot help it!" and she seated herself on the edge of the bed, took the child pitifully in her arms and unheedful of the monk clasped it to her breast; the child drank eagerly while her tears ran down upon it. The Prior turned away and stood puzzled. He remembered how in his childhood he had never dared to vex his mother while she was nursing his little brother for fear the baby should not thrive, if the milk were turned by her anger. What should he do now to soothe the wet-nurse?

"Listen to me," he said at last, "I know of another way out of the difficulty for you; I will allow you to see your husband again, outside the convent gate, now and then for half an hour; that I will take upon myself. If that will satisfy you, we are all content—the child, ourselves and you."

The woman sighed, but she nodded assent in silence. It was better than nothing, and she felt she could not let the child starve, she could never be happy with her husband again, if she had loaded her conscience with such a dreadful sin for his sake.

"Are you content with that?" asked the Prior again, for he had not seen her nod. The child had drunk till it was full and had gone to sleep; she laid it on the bed, she could not speak, but she went up to the Prior and kissed his hands in the midst of her tears.

"That is all right then," said he, glad of this happy turn, "I will see whether your husband is already waiting with the child and then you can speak with him at the little gate while we baptise this one. You shall be allowed to do so once every week. And I will get our brother, the carpenter, to carve you out a cradle that you may lay the baby in it, and you will see that you will not want for anything."

The monk closed the door behind him and the woman went up to the little loop-hole and pressed her hot brow against the small round panes. In the early dawn she could hardly see the roofs of Burgeis deep down in the valley and the scattered huts around it on the declivity and on the opposite side on the mountains freshly covered with snow. Hers was down there too, she could distinguish it quite plainly, for her sturdy, industrious husband had built it better and bigger than the others, and had loaded the thatch with heavy stones. The crowing of cocks from far and near came up from the depth below—so homelike! and hers among them—she knew his voice! She pressed her hand over her eyes—it was like a dream that she should be mounted up here in the lonely turret-chamber—so lonely; so high, high up, as if she were in prison.— Oh! if it were but a dream, if only she could wake up again in her husband's arms, in her own humble hut; never again would she follow any one who might come to tear her away from her husband's fond heart. How could she have done it—how ever could she have done it.

CHAPTER II.

Mass was over. The whole brotherhood had assembled in the underground founder's hall, to offer up a special thanksgiving before the effigies of the founders. This hall was the most ancient part of the whole building, and in it a hundred years ago the brethren had performed their devotions until the convent-buildings were complete. Bishop Adelgott of Chur had consecrated it, and remained there still in effigy. Since then it had been the custom to perform a thanksgiving-service every year on the founder's day, in honour of the venerable bishop and the noble patrons of the house, whose portraits were preserved there for the safe keeping of the subterranean vault.

Here also the pious feelings of the brethren had expressed themselves in beautifying care, and had clothed the damp walls down in the earth, where only roots can live, with the fresh green of the tree-tops that wave gaily in the upper air; the bright gleam of wax-tapers in two tall seven-branched candlesticks was reflected from the dark walls, as if the sun-shine, under which the busy convent-bees had gathered their store, had laid hidden in the wax itself, only awaiting its release. The natural incense of aromatic pine-wood filled the heavy underground atmosphere; thick translucent tears of resin hung yellow and sparkling from the freshly broken boughs, like drops of limpid topaz. The portraits of Ulrich of Trasp and his veiled wife Uta looked down with a gentle smile from thick wreaths of heath-plants and rue; and the text, "They only live who die to the world," which proceeded from the mouth of the founder on a golden ribband, shone in the light of the tapers like letters of fire. Over these the two shields of Ulrich of Trasp were displayed as precious relics; the shield of faith with a gold cross on a white field, which was presented to him by his companions in the faith in the Holy Land, and the shield of his house bearing a rainbow.

The thanksgiving was ended; but the Abbot detained the brethren for a hasty consultation. The fathers sat silent in a circle, and listened attentively to the Abbot's story of the fate of the hapless Lady of Reichenberg.

They are a circle of proud faces that look thoughtfully before them; proud of superhuman victories, proud of the consciousness of belonging to a band of men who by their iron strength of will have upheld the dignity of humanity, and have preserved the thoughts which can govern the world from the ruins of the decayed Roman Empire, from the horrible subversion of all social order; through the migrations of peoples, and the irruptions of barbarians; have saved them, and given them a sanctuary for the benefit of later and riper generations. Only one face accords ill with the quiet scene and its solemn

22

setting; a good-humoured, crafty, smiling, Epicurean countenance with fat cheeks and piercing, sharp, glittering eyes under grey, bushy brows. It is brother Wyso, the registrar and historian of the monastery; the laughing philosopher who knows everything, and lets everything go its own gait. The world lies below him in a bird's-eye-view—so small, so insignificant—all humanity is to him like an ant-hill, and altogether amusing and comical; how they build, how they fight, how they marry, and at last are buried! he looks on at it all complacently, without love and without aversion, as at a colony of ants or a hive of bees. He never troubles himself with any enquiry as to how it began, and how it will end; he satisfies himself with the knowledge that it is. They dislike him in the cloister for this lukewarmness; then too he is "foul of mouth," and now and then gives utterance to loose speech that scandalises the brethren; for the rule of St. Benedict prohibits useless and gay discourse, unless it be to cheer the sick or the sorry; but they cannot accuse him of anything, for his conduct is irreproachable in all important matters, and much may be excused in a man of his learning. He needs must read of many unclean things and evil deeds of men, which are hidden from the other monks.

Brother Wyso is a man of between fifty and sixty years, stout and somewhat short of breath; for although Saint Benedict forbids the use of meat there are many other excellent gifts of God, and brother Wyso is very ready to give his attention to all permitted delicacies. On this occasion he makes a by no means cheerful face, for the Abbot has assembled them with fasting stomachs, and has not allowed them their morning-meal after the cold early mass. He pushes his short fat hands with a rueful shiver under the sleeves of his hood, and slaps the back of his left hand with the fingers of his right, casting a side-long glance meanwhile at his neighbour, brother Correntian, with a sort of mischievous curiosity as to whether any trace of the weakness of the flesh could be detected on his stony countenance; but he seems not even to perceive this, and his passive face is turned to the Abbot with unmoved attention. This brother is the strongest contrast to the smug little monk by whom he is sitting. A noble countenance is his, but furrowed by many a moral struggle, and set to stoniness by an assumed calm; a tall, lean form mortified by hair-cloth, scourging and chastisement; deep-set, dark, reproachful eyes—reproachful of the patience of Heaven that never falls on the sinner to smite him; of the light that shines alike on the evil and the good; of rosy cheeks and white arms, such as are often to be met in the village; in short of all that they gaze on, of all that thrives and rejoices or that is cherished or enjoyed. It seems as though it were darker just round him, as though he cast a deeper shadow than the others; and there is a wider space between his seat and those of his neighbours than between any of the rest. On his left hand sits Conrad of Ramüss, the brother of the deceased Lady of

Reichenberg, a handsome man of about twenty. He has only lately come into the monastery, for he was a secular priest, and an eloquent speaker to the glory of the Lord. But his handsome person and the sweetness of his voice served the arch-enemy as weapons to turn against his pious efforts, and to turn all good into evil. There were too many foolish women who sinfully fell in love with him, and thought more of the sweet lips whence flowed the sacred lore than of the teaching itself; more of the servant than of his Lord. Such scandals vexed Conrad's honest zeal. It had too often occurred that ladies in the confessional had made him the confidant of their affection for himself, and had made the chaste blood mount to his cheeks for shame. So he fled from the world, laid these attractive gifts of nature in all humility on the altar of the Lord, and hid himself in cloistered solitude. Now for a year he has been a monk, and has never quitted his cell but for the services of the church and general refreshment with the brethren. Now all is peace in his soul, and though he knows that he is still very far from perfection, he strives towards it cheerfully and hopefully—his duties are his highest happiness, and what are all the joys of earth to him compared with this consciousness?

While the grey haired Abbot is speaking, his eyes linger with peculiar satisfaction on the high pure brow clustered round with fair curls, which rests thoughtfully on the slender white hand; and old Florentinus, standing behind the Abbot's throne, is involuntarily reminded of the still, peaceful corpse lying up there at St. Valentine's. Even in death the likeness is striking, and the tears which spring from the monk's eyes as he hears of his sister's hapless fate, confirm the relationship.

But many another grave and noble face is visible among the sombre circle in the light of the low-burning tapers, and with them many dry, hard and angular ones—as the same soil may bear very different fruits. There sits Bero, the oldest of the brethren, a modest and enlightened man, but of the severest principles; he has already been privately chosen to be the successor of Abbot Conrad I. when the old man should be gathered to the Holy Fathers of the Church. There is Conrad, surnamed Stiero or the bull, to distinguish him from Conrad the Abbot and Conrad of Ramüss; a man worthy of his surname,—a bull with a thick neck, and a broad, angular forehead moulded much as the heathen figured that Jupiter Ammon whom the Church overthrew after such a severe and bloody struggle. He is a man of no subtlety, but a strong bulwark of the faith and of the convent. So long as Conrad the Bull is there, no enemy will venture near, for his fist and his wrathful temper are everywhere known and none would brave them without good cause. There is brother Engelbert, the painter, who writes the exquisite illuminated manuscripts, Candidus the precentor, Porphyrius the sculptor, who chisels out the crosses and tombstones of the deceased brethren, Cyriacus, the Latin—and many more; Josephus, too, the lean brother-carpenter, sits modestly in the background little dreaming that his next task will be to make—an infant's cradle.

The Abbot finished his melancholy tale and ended with the words,

"You see, my brethren, the surges of the wicked world, rolling blindly on, have cast a young life on our sheltering shore. Yet, let us not say blindly—no, it is doubtless through some high purpose that this child has been brought to our house on the very anniversary of our founder's day. I have called you all together to take counsel with you as to whether we shall take him in or cast him out on the wild ocean of life?" "Take him in! take him in!" the majority of the brethren hastily exclaimed; but the sinister Correntian said, "Stay."

The brethren looked at him in surprise.

"If our venerable father, the Abbot, wishes to hear our opinion he may perhaps listen to my warning; reverend father, do not do it—my Brethren, do not receive this child within your walls."

The brethren muttered indignantly to each other, but he went on undisturbed. "It is accursed—it will bring the curse under our roof."

"A poor, innocent child!" murmured the circle of monks.

"Innocent or no it must expiate the sins of its parents, for even the mother is not free from guilt. She revelled in the dazzling levity of worldly joys, she consented so long to the courting attentions of the playmate of her youth that she excited her husband's jealousy, and who knows—if things had gone so far —how much farther—"

"Be silent!" thundered out a clear full voice. "Do not dare to calumniate the dead; her brother still lives to avenge her." Conrad of Ramüss stood before him with his fist raised and his lips pale and trembling. "I knew that chaste and lofty spirit as well as I know my own—she is dead—she died like a saint, and no stain shall come near her so long as my eyes are open and have tears to weep for her."

The scowling monk looked at him with a calm, cold, piercing gaze.

"What is this woman to you?"

"You have heard—my sister."

Correntian turned to the Abbot with an indescribable gesture of his head.

"I ask our venerable father—I ask all the brethren here in conclave—Has a Benedictine a sister?"

"No!" was the slow and soft reply—as if reluctantly spoken—from every man.

Conrad of Ramüss struck himself on the brow, and a bitter, burning tear forced its way from under his drooping lids. One minute of deep agonised silence, one brief struggle, and then the proud young head bowed humbly before the Abbot—"Punish me, my father—I had indeed forgotten myself."

"Ask your brother's forgiveness on your knees," said the Abbot sadly, "and for not having yet quite torn your heart free from all the earthly ties that hang about it, so that the evil demon of wrath could stir you up against your spiritual brother for the sake of an earthly sister—this you must expiate by a fortnight's nightly penance."

The young man kissed the Abbot's hand. "I thank you, father, for so mild a punishment." Then he knelt down before the offended monk and pressed the hem of his robe to his lips, "Forgive me, Brother."

The inflexible man raised him with the usual formula, "May God forgive you even as I do."

The brethren stood round in silence; not a face betrayed what one of them thought, but the culprit sank back on his seat as if exhausted, and cold sweat stood in drops on his forehead. Correntian went on, as if nothing had happened.

"And so I say the child must expiate the folly of a mother who thought more of her amusements than of God and her solemn and happy position, else would the Lord never have visited her with such a judgment. This child was dedicated to the Evil One ere yet it was born—it is his prey—we cannot snatch it from him, we shall only incite him to strive with us for its possession."

Then rose Conrad Stiero, the broad-browed: "Shame upon you, brother Correntian! How long have we Marienbergers been afraid of the Devil? In truth such cowardly counsel ill becomes you who boast of such a stony heart. Have we come to such a pass that we shall shut ourselves up in convent walls to pray and stuff in idle piety? Do you call that fighting for God when, so soon as we have to rescue a poor soul from the fires of hell, we put our fingers to the tips of our ears like burnt children and cry out, 'Oh!—it is hot—we will not touch it!' Give me the boy and I will go out with him into the wilderness, if you are afraid to keep him here—and wrestle for him with all Hell let loose!"

"You use too rough and uncouth a tongue, brother Stiero," said the Abbot. "But it shall be forgiven you for the sake of your good motive. Yes—brother Correntian, it seems to me that he is right and that it would be the first time if we now were to shrink like cowards when we have to snatch a soul from hell. How would God's kingdom prosper—of which we are the guardians—if it were not stronger than Hell."

"Aye, it is stronger," replied Correntian with eyes raised to heaven, "and it will and must one day triumph; the light must conquer the darkness; but as often as on earth the night swallows up the day, so often will the kingdom of darkness triumph over the kingdom of Light till the day of Redemption is come—the day when God's patience has an end and he destroys this earth."

"And shall we therefore withdraw from the fight like cowards?" asked the Abbot again.

"Nay, never could I think of saying such a thing," said Correntian. "But I ask you, what is the price of the struggle? Is this wretched child of sin and misfortune, whom the Devil already has in his power—is this I say a trophy worth struggling for with those evil spirits that every one would fain keep at a distance from his threshold? Besides a single handful may succumb, even if it belong to the victorious side; and so while the Church triumphs, churches and cloisters may fall; nay, even this our own convent, for they too are accursed who succour the child! If the blessing of the father can establish the childrens' houses and the curse of the mother overthrow them, will a father's curse be impotent think you? And how can you believe in the efficacy of a blessing, if you do not believe in the power of a curse?"

"God is righteous and does not punish the innocent," Bero was now heard to say. "And why have we been awakened from the darkness of heathenism to the bright light of the Holy Spirit, if like the ancients we persist in believing in a blind fate, conjured up by a curse?"

"The Devil—the Devil is the Fate of the ancients, and is at all times the same!" cried Correntian. "A parent's curse tears a rent in the divine order and in human nature, in which the seed of hell at once strikes root and, like a poisonous fungus, feeds its growth on all around it."

"Well—" said Bero with a bright look. "May be you speak the truth, brother Correntian, but if we were not fully capable of extirpating the brood of Hell by the power of the Holy Ghost and pure resolve there would be no such thing as guilt! We should be the helpless sport of Satan without any guilt or responsibility, and at the last judgment the Lord could not ask us, 'Why did ye this or that?'"

The Abbot and the brethren murmured assent; only Wyso and Correntian were silent.

"I ask you," Bero went on, "since God gives us the power to choose our own course of life and whether we will follow the path of virtue or of sin, can we prove incapable of guiding this boy into the way of righteousness if we all gather round him to watch every thought of his brain, every impulse of his heart, every glance, every breath."

"And yet it must come."

A voice like the breathing of a spirit spoke in the farthest corner of the hall; every eye turned towards the spot. A very small monk was leaning in the deepest shadow against a projecting pillar; his little grey figure was as inconspicuous as that of some little gnome, but his eyes were keen and bright, as if they could pierce the depths with their gaze, and their genial glance shone through the gloomy hall.

"What, is it you, brother Eusebius?" said the Abbot. "It is an event indeed when you quit your turret-cell to assist at the council of the brethren, and the occasion must have seemed to you a serious one for you to open your lips. Speak on—what do you mean? Who or what must come?"

The old man looked at him with a smile.

"Do you not understand me?" said he, and his eye rested thoughtfully on the excited circle. "There are only two sorts of just rights—the rights of Heaven and the rights of man. Man's rights are his share of the joys of Creation. If he casts them away of his own free impulse for the sake of the rights of Heaven he makes the highest effort of which man is capable, and the angels sing Hosannas over him. But never ought you to steal them from him —as in the case of this infant—for they are bestowed on him by his Maker, and it is Him whom you aggrieve. Bring the child up, but bring him up free; and leave him to choose, when he is ripe to make the choice. If he is called he will remain faithful, but let it be without compulsion. For if he is not called, better let him withdraw than that he should remain among you against his will, with a divided heart, half attached to the world and half to the Church— a tool with a flaw in it that shivers in the hand, and recoils on him who would use it. For the hour will come upon him which none can escape. Do you what you will—it must come upon him as it has come upon each of us. You know it well—only those that are called can triumph, and the weak fall in the conflict between pleasure and duty. *Divisum est cor eorum, nunc interibunt*— their heart is divided and they perish. And to you it can bring neither glory nor reward; for it depends upon the Spirit and not on the number of the servants of our Church, and never can an unwilling sacrifice be dear in the sight of the Lord."

Then Conrad Stiero struck his fist a mighty blow on the arm of his chair.

"What spirit, what human right?—'called' or 'not called!' We need strong arms to protect our venerable house, for we have fallen on evil times, and the nobles covet our goods and our authority. It is time to protect them as best we may. Shut him in and keep him close, then he will be ours and no one's else."

"I know of only one really sure way," said Correntian quietly, "and that is to blind the boy."

A cry of horror broke from every one.

"Shame on you, brother Correntian! are you a man?" cried Bero in wrath.

"You see how you start at an empty word! Ye feeble ones! Do you call the physician cruel who by one swift cut obviates future—nay eternal suffering? If any one had released me from the torment of sight and its myriad temptations while I was still slumbering in the cradle, I would have thanked him as my lifelong benefactor. However, fear nothing; I know well that no shedding of blood beseems us, and it was only an idea, suggested by the truest pity."

"You are a great man, Correntian, but fearful in your strength," said the Abbot, and the brethren agreed with a shudder.

But the little gnome leans unmoved and silent against his pillar; he feels no astonishment, no horror—he knows that there are many different growths in the Lord's garden; deadly poisonous plants by the side of wholesome and nutritious ones, and that each has its use and purpose. This brother Eusebius knows right well, for the hidden properties and relations of things are clear to his penetrating eye. He is the herbalist, the astronomer and the physician of the convent. He watches the still growth of roots and germs in the bosom of the earth as well as the course of the blood in the human body, and that of the stars in the immeasurable firmament, and in all he sees the same ordering, the same great inexorable law against which the creature for ever rebels, and which ever works out its own vengeance. But he says no more at present, for he sees that it would be in vain.

But Conrad Stiero would have no mistake as to his meaning,

"I say walls—they are the best security! Let Heaven and Hell fight for him, our walls are thick, and we will not let him go outside them."

The little man by the pillar folded his hands.

"Oh! human wit and human wisdom!" thought he.

"Allow me to say a few words," said Wyso, addressing the whole conclave, "and do not take what I say amiss. You are all dreamers, thrashing empty straw. The small thread of one's patience is easily broken when one has to listen to such idle talk on an empty stomach. What have we to do here with the Almighty and the devil? or which of them we may least offend? This is above all things a matter for the law, a trifle which it seems to me that you have all forgotten. If you have a mind to receive the child as a guest, and

29

make a nursery of the old house, well and good, no one can prevent you; it is not forbidden either by canon law or by the rule of St. Benedict to give shelter to the homeless so long as they need it. But if you think of receiving the boy into the order—and your solemn talk seems to imply it—one of these days we shall find ourselves laid under ban and interdict, so that not even a thief on the gallows will ask absolution at our hands."

An uneasy movement ran through the conclave.

"Aha! now there is a stir in the ant-hill. But is it not so? Do you not remember that in the tenth canon of the Council of Trent under Pope Clement III. the Order was forbidden to receive as members children under years of discretion without the express consent of their parents? What? Have you any fancy to defy pope and bishop, church-law and interdict for the sake of this infant? I fancy that would be somewhat worse than a compact with the devil."

"Guard your lips, brother Wyso! remember Duramnus of Predan, who, as a punishment for his scandalous talk, was burdened for ever with a hideous, foul snout," threatened the Abbot. "You can never keep yourself from abuse and scoffing; what you say is good, but the way you say it is bad. Brother Wyso speaks the truth, my brethren," he continued, turning to the monks, who were ashamed of their own ignorance. "It appears that our senses are still clouded by sleep, or we should have thought of the new law. We cling too naturally to old usages, and it is difficult to accustom ourselves to such newfangled ways. However we must submit to them if we would not bring evil consequences on ourselves. It is true that the mother has given the child over into our keeping, but the father's consent is wanting, and so we cannot receive him. I say it with pain, for I would fain have held the vow of a dead woman as sacred. And I am grieved to thrust the child out among the wild waves of life. Still, so it must be, and we can but resign him to the mercy of him who clothes the lilies of the field."

At this point Conrad of Ramüss rose modestly.

"Pardon me, father, if I, though in disgrace, once more take part in your discussion."

"Speak, my son, only in a more becoming manner," answered the Abbot. Then the young monk went on,

"It is indeed true that we may receive no child without its father's will. But this child has no father. He who is called its father has cast it out and denied it; it is an orphan. Who—by the laws of the world—who takes its father's place, brother Wyso?"

"Its next blood-relation on the father's or the mother's side," replied Wyso.

"Well then," continued Ramüss, "I myself am its nearest relation, the boy's uncle, his mother's brother; I now am his father, and I dedicate him to the cloister."

A shout of joy from the brethren answered him.

"Amen, my son," said the Abbot. "I receive him at your hands, and I hope that we have acted rightly."

He turned to the pictures of the Tarasps. "Give him your blessing, noble and glorified masters, whose memory we this day keep holy." The conclave was over, they all crossed themselves before the pictures, and then went up into the light of day. They hastened to the sacristy to baptise the child, for the solemn tolling of the big bell was already calling the inhabitants of the valley to high-mass.

. The morning-sun shot its bright beams through the tall arched windows, and scattered the mists and shadows that Correntian, the sinister friar, had conjured up.

"The light must be victorious!" This was the happy promise with which it filled all hearts.

The folding doors sprang open; the Prior entered with the child. It was prettily wrapped in the Lady Uta's white linen, and lay there flooded in a ray of morning sun-shine as if transfigured. And drawn by a strange and tender human emotion the younger monks gathered round the tiny brother that Heaven had sent them, and pressed a kiss of welcome on his sweet and innocent lips. And the celestial Mother of Sorrows smiled down on them from the wall as if she were indeed the mother of them all, and rejoiced to see her elder sons welcoming the new-born child as a brother.

No—this is no gift of hell—this heart-winning, sun-lighted child that rouses so pure and harmless a joy in every breast; and the Abbot lifts his hands in blessing, and says, "Donatus we will call him, my brethren, for he is given to us, and his name shall mean a gift."

"Yes, yes—he shall be called Donatus," cried the monks in delight.

"And now swear to me," continued the Abbot, "before we proceed to the sacred ceremony—swear to me on the innocent head of this infant—that you will help to preserve him for Heaven; that you will watch over the boy at every hour, and protect him from every temptation that may alienate him from us—and above all from that which is the devil's most dangerous weapon, to which many a youth has fallen a victim—from earthly love."

The brethren raised their hands in solemn asseveration and, like a pillar of sacred sacrificial incense, the steamy cloud from thirty throats rose to Heaven in one united breath, "We swear it!"

The brethren gathered round the child like a wall—stronger than those walls of stone of which brother Stiero had spoken, and brother Correntian towered above the rest like an invincible bulwark. But brother Eusebius silently shook his head and said to himself, "And yet it must come."

CHAPTER III.

There is an old story of a king of the dwarfs whose wife died in giving birth to the heir to the throne. This king chose a poor woman from the human race to be his son's wet-nurse, and as the woman would not come of her own free will the little dwarf-folk fetched her one night and brought her by force into the underground kingdom of the gnomes. The woman was not to be allowed to return till she had fulfilled her office of nurse to the little dwarf prince, and she lived a year in exile far from her people under the spell of the strange uncanny folks in their realm of ore and earth. She had to surrender all of her human nature, that gave joy to her heart in the fountain of life, by which the child was nourished—mother's milk and mother's love—but otherwise she might never be in any way human and her reward was barren gold. But she persevered, not for the sake of the gold only, but because motherly-love is so good a thing, a thing that grows with rapid increase, throwing out aerial roots that cling blindly to any support that is offered them. As the hen loves her changeling duckling, so the human foster-mother clung to her dwarf foster-child, and so the cloistered wet-nurse loved the child of the Church that had been forced upon her although she also felt that she was in a strange realm; in a realm between the grave and Heaven, quite other indeed and higher than the kingdom of the dwarfs, but inhabited too by uncanny beings outside and beyond all natural relationships, and having nothing in common with flesh and blood; and that the child to whom she was as a mother belonged to the same strange race. And the more deeply she felt this, the more painfully did her heart cling to the child to whom she had no right; that might never be truly human and that yet was nourished by the milk of a human mother. She knew not what her feeling was—it was a strange pity for the boy, so that she loved him almost better than her own child. Her own child had its natural belongings—a mother and a father—but this poor child had no one in the world. The cold and strong church-walls were its home and no human lip might ever touch it, nor its head ever rest on a soft warm human breast. And as if to compensate to it for all future privations she loved and kissed it with double fervour, and cradled it with double tenderness in her bosom.

Almost seven months had passed since the child was received into the monastery; a long time for the young and ardent wife who, as if it were a sin, could only slip away from time to time and by stealth to meet her husband behind the door where for months together the bitter wind blew the kisses away from their lips.

The cloistered nurse was sitting with her nursling at the dim little window in the east turret-room. It was a mild spring evening and death-like stillness reigned all round. Deep shadows fell on the bed of Lady Uta; one star threw its pale rays into the lonely room and they fell and were lost on the silk hangings, which Lord Ulrich had brought from the gorgeous East on his return from a pilgrimage. High up by the window something whisked by; it was a swallow flying home to the nest she had built at a giddy height on the ridge of the roof. The swallow was no better off indeed up there than Berntrudis herself—but she was free. So Berntrudis thought, and a deep sigh broke from her breast on which the children lay slumbering. In the corner, in Lady Uta's chest, she could hear the soft and regular sound of the death-tick, and the white linen hanging in the room—the linen woven by the chaste hands of the penitent Berntrudis of old—was stirred by the draught through the room to a ghostly flutter. But the warm living soul that sat by the window, looking longingly out to the distance—where human hearts might beat and not count it a sin—she was thinking neither of death nor of penance, but her pulses throbbed while she wondered how late it was and whether her husband would tap for her to-night at the convent gate? She closed her eyes and threw back her head while her full lips breathed a kiss upon the air—a message of love sent out to meet her looked-for husband. But he came seldom, he had quite run wild during this long separation; he was wandering about unsettled and discontented, she knew it well; and bitter anxiety gnawed at her heart.

Thus she waits evening after evening till her head-aches, and she throws herself wearily into bed. Then the soul of the heart-sick woman is nailed as with iron clamps to two opposite points—the present and the expected moment, and the farther these two points recede from each other the more the poor heart is torn—an invisible rack of which the tension almost cracks her heart-strings.

Out on the other side in the western wing brother Correntian was leaning his hot brow against his window panes and gazing out on the falling night. He had closed the window, for the evening breath of spring wafted up the sweet perfume of half-opened flowers, which soothed his senses—so he flung the window to. He who cannot resist the temptations of Satan in small things will never conquer him in great ones! So there he stood in the soft spring evening shut in by walls damp with the chills of winter, and he cast a reproving glance across to the eastern tower where the wet-nurse was housed. He hated this woman, he himself knew not why, but he hated her with a deadly hatred; as often as he met her—when occasionally she went down into the court-yard to fetch water or walked in the little garden with the child—he turned his eyes earthwards with horror and aversion, as if in the poor, sweet, blooming woman he beheld the snake that destroyed Paradise. He would have poisoned her with a glance, have torn her up like a root of sin if he could; he had to endure her presence, that he understood; but he could not leave her in peace in his thoughts, his hatred must needs pursue her even into her quiet turret-chamber—it dragged him nightly from his bed and forced him to go to his window, and watch and spy the strong walls that sheltered her, as the foe spies out in his antagonist's harness the joints through which he hopes to give him his death-blow. And he could see through those walls as though the stones were glass—he could always see her and loathe himself for doing so; see her wake in the morning and hold the children to her young and innocent breast—comb her long and waving hair—all—everything—he saw it all, whether he would or not. At this very moment he could see her, as she flung herself on her bed—and the kiss that her unguarded lips breathed into space.

But stay! what was that? was it a trick of his senses—the very spirit of his hatred that had taken bodily form and glided across the star-lighted court-yard to the eastern tower? He held his breath—he checked the beating of his heart.

A second figure stole along by its side and cautiously knocked at the little turret-door. The first, a sturdy, manly figure in a short tunic such as was worn by serfs, disappeared into the tower; the other—quite unmistakably the gatekeeper—glided back again and returned to the gate-house. It is the fisherman—the nurse's husband. He has bribed the gatekeeper and has stolen in to see his wife. Now—now he is up stairs, they are clasped in each other's arms.—Oh! shame and disgrace—that this should happen within the sacred precincts of the convent!

The monk was shivering as in an ague fit, all the suppressed fire in his blood broke out. Loathing, aversion—he knew not what—all the furies of hell were lashing him. He rushed raving down the rows of sleeping brethren.

"Up—get up—the cloister is defiled, do not suffer such disgrace. Up! holy Abbot—the nurse up there is receiving stolen visits by night from her husband. Is this house to be the abode of love making and shameful doings?"

The brethren flung on their cowls in hot haste; the Abbot came out in high wrath. "She promised me that she would obey the convent-rules and she is doubly guilty, if she has let in her husband and broken in on the peace of the cloister."

"We will soon have him out!" snorted Conrad Stiero, delighted that for once he should have a chance of fighting again.

"Are you possessed by the Evil One that you come screaming us out of our sleep like this?" said brother Wyso, bustling breathlessly up and treading on his untied shoe-strings as he went.

"Shame on you, brother Correntian," whispered he in his ear, "to spoil the poor woman's sport so—that is envy." Correntian started as if stabbed by a dagger—he threw a glance of flaming rage at Wyso and raised his hand threateningly. But he as quickly let it fall again, his face turned as pale as death, and his old stony calm suddenly overspread his wildly agitated features.

"That," said he, "is so base as to be unworthy of reply."

"A hypocrite even to yourself!" muttered Wyso between his teeth while the Abbot signed to the brethren to follow him. Then Conrad of Ramüss came modestly forward. "Most reverend abbot, permit that we—I and the younger brethren—remain behind. It seems to me that it is no scene for our eyes."

"True, you are right, brother Conrad," said the Abbot. "Accompany me alone, you elder brethren! but come softly, that we may not warn the evil-doers before we visit them with the penalty of sin."

So the stern judges went noiselessly across to the eastern tower with a lantern.

Up in the turret-room, there is whispering, soft laughter and crying, and silent happiness; the wife, taken quite by surprise, is folded in the arms of her husband intoxicated with delight. He has not told her why or how he has come, but the storm of joy in the poor soul that has thirsted so for love is so wild that she can only caress him and kiss him and will neither hear nor know anything, but that he is there—a lovely fulfilment of a spring night's dream.

But—voices on the stairs! coming up! A beam of light falls with fearful brightness through the crack of the door. Husband and wife start from their blissful dream; there is a loud and threatening knock, "Open the door to his reverence the Abbot," cried Conrad Stiero. There could be no delay.

"Be easy," said the man to his trembling wife, "am I not your plighted husband? What have you to fear?" and he went forward with a determined manner and let in the brethren.

"God and the Saints preserve us," said the Abbot as he went in. "Berntrudis—unworthy daughter of your pious ancestress, how dare you carry on such unseemly doings?"

"And what is the harm, reverend father," said the fisherman boldly. "If a wife makes love to her husband? I never heard any one call such doings unseemly!"

Correntian, who was carrying the lamp, lifted it up and let its full light fall on the undaunted speaker's face. It was a handsome, bold, manly countenance, not free from the traces of a wild life. The deep lines on the forehead showed that it was long since a woman's loving hand had smoothed it, his neglected doublet of frieze plainly told of wild wanderings in wind and weather. Correntian took it all in at a glance, he understood in that instant as if by inspiration all that the man had suffered, and, instead of pitying him, he longed to thrust a dagger into that broad breast where just now the woman had lain—the eager, loving woman that he scorned and hated. And as if some suspicion, some comprehension of this hostile glance had dawned upon the man's mind he answered with a wrathful flash from his large eyes, and for all at once the humble serf was turned into a raging fiend checked by no sense of bashfulness.

"Ay, you may look at me, monk," he exclaimed threateningly in his broad Rhætian accent, "I am what you have made me. Am I not smooth and fine enough for you great lords? You take away the dearest thing a man has—take it away as you did from me, so that he wanders alone about the fields and woods, and then do you think he will care to smarten himself up and streak himself down?"

"Woe upon you! what are you saying!" cried the Abbot. "You break in like a thief on the peace of the convent, you bribe the gatekeeper, you are guilty of such dreadful sin, and then you dare to speak like that?"

"I speak like one whose measure is full, and overfull. I have nothing but this woman and you take her away from me—take away a man's married wife and his heart out of his body, to suckle a strange child. What is the child to me that I am to sacrifice all that is dearest to me to him? Seven months have I borne it patiently and that is enough. The brat there can do without a wet-nurse now. My own child has shared its food with him long enough—look here what a stunted plant it has grown, while the strange brat has thriven and got strong; my heart ached in my body when I saw the poor little thing again! —I tell you plainly, for I am not clever at lying, I came to steal my wife away, my sacred property. But now I ask you—as you have found me out—give me back my wife and my child. I desire neither reward nor thanks, but I will have back what is my own."

"Spare your words, we have shown you too much favour in listening to you so long. What if we did take an impure and sinful woman within our sacred cloister walls against all law and usage, do you think we did so without any necessity and simply for our pleasure? The sacred vow of a dead woman which we were bound to honour was the solemn duty which compelled us to such an abominable proceeding. And when we received your wife we hoped that the sanctity of the place and the sacredness of her office would purify her vain heart so that she would not succumb to the temptations of sensual pleasures and base impulses and would cause no scandal to our chaste brethren. This indeed she solemnly vowed, and oh! Berntrudis, how badly you have kept your word! Alas! that the pure child of the Church should be compelled to drink from so impure a vessel. Willingly would I spare him this, of that you may both be very sure. Still, so it must be, we cannot yet dispense with your services, and if you had remained true to your duty, at the end of your probation we would have rewarded you and raised you up in the sight of God and man. As it is we must force you to do that which you do not do willingly. And you," he continued to the husband, "you who have broken into our house like a weasel into a dove-cot, in contempt of our prohibition under the severest penalties—you may thank us for the mild punishment we impose —you are under a ban not to come within a mile round the convent so long as we need the offices of your wife. You must go up to the moorland lake and catch fish for us there till the winter-storms next sweep down on the heath."

A cry of horror from the husband and wife answered this frightful sentence, the gentle Abbot had no conception of its cruelty. What could he know—a calm old man whose blood ran so sluggishly in his veins—of the passion and longing and torment of two hearts that have grown into one, when they are torn asunder?

Only one there present understood it; he who stood silent, his nails dug into his crossed arms—and yet of pity he knew nothing, that unsparing zealot who had no mercy on others because he knew of no mercy on himself. "I am suffering—you may suffer too" was the frightful thought by which, in his self-torment, he released himself from the duty of loving his neighbour. There he stood, the stony man, with an unmoved stare—the chaste and stern Correntian.

But Wyso shook his head and said to the Abbot in Latin, "Go no farther."

Berntrudis had fallen crying into her husband's arms and hid her face on his broad and labouring breast; but Correntian stepped forward with a hasty gesture, "Stand apart!" he said with pale lips. "Do not offend our eyes by such a sight."

The man lifted his sturdy head and the words he had kept between his teeth with so much difficulty broke out, "This is too much! Who is to forbid me kissing my wife—who can force me to believe that it is a sin when husband and wife make love to each other? You—you make a sin of it by forbidding it. By what right do you forbid a man and his wife to see each other—by what right do you put asunder those whom God and the Church have joined together?"

"The Church can bind and it can loose," said the Abbot wrathfully. "Do not call us to account."

"Why waste so many words?" muttered Correntian between his teeth. "He is the convent's bondsman—he and his wife; you can do what you like with him."

"You—with your gloomy corpse-face—" cried the infuriated man. "You are my enemy—even if you said nothing I could see it in your face. What have I done to you that you pour gall into the poor serf's little drop of happiness?"

"Now—come away, we are tired. Do you think we are going to spend the whole night arguing with you as to whether or no you will do the Abbot's bidding?" Conrad Stiero now threw in.

The veins in the fisherman's forehead were swollen with rage and he raised his fist threateningly.

"I am going," he said, "but not without my wife and child," and he put his arm round Berntrudis. "Let me pass or mischief will come of it!"

The Abbot drew back terrified, even brother Wyso started back, only Correntian remained immoveable. Stiero set his broad back against the door, but with a heavy lurch of his shoulder the fisherman pushed him almost off his balance, as if lifting a door off its posts.

"Oho! is that what you mean?" cried the monk, eager to fight, "then you do not know Conrad Stiero!" And with a mighty blow of his fist on his opponent's forehead he sent the strong man staggering back with a heavy fall on to the floor. "I will teach you to behave yourself, you clown!" said Stiero, kneeling on the vanquished man, and he bound his hands with the cord which he took from round his own waist. The woman had sunk on the ground by the side of her husband, and Correntian made a movement—only one—as though he would raise and support her; but he started back in horror of himself and left her lying there.

Stiero desired the man to rise. "You have found out now that we are no women under our cowls, to be frightened by violence. Now kneel down, poor wretch, and crave for mercy, for your life is no safer than that of a mad dog."

The man, with his hands tied across each other, stood silent in a stupor of despair; he knelt down as Stiero bid him, but he did not utter a word, he fixed his sullen gaze on no one, he knew his fate and had lost all hope.

"What do you think, my brethren," said the Abbot turning to the others, "shall we give him up to the provost to be judged?"

"Yes!" replied Correntian.

"Then his sentence is pronounced; he has lifted his hand against a priest, his life is forfeited," said the Abbot.

The woman gave a piercing shriek of anguish and fell at Correntian's feet.

"Pity—mercy!" she sobbed out almost mad with terror, and she clasped his knees with all the strength of despair, for she too felt that her ruin was lowering in those sinister eyes. A scarlet flush lighted up the monk's pale face —as the northern lights flash across a winter midnight-sky—he flung her from him and clung to the bed-post for support.

"If you do not have some regard for the nurse you will kill the boy," said a voice suddenly in Latin, and father Eusebius was seen standing by the unhappy woman as if he had sprung out of the ground.

"God be thanked!" muttered brother Wyso. "Here at length is a reasonable man."

Eusebius had looked on at the proceedings, silent and unobserved till it was necessary to speak; he raised the trembling woman from the floor, and kindly comforting her he led her to the bed on which she sank down powerless. Correntian let go the bed-post he was clasping, as if it had suddenly turned to hot iron.

Eusebius' gaze, which he could not evade, fell upon him with a strange smile; Correntian hated that gaze, and from that moment he remained silent as if spell-bound by the gentle power of those clear eyes.

"What do you mean, worthy brother Eusebius?" asked the Abbot, unskilled in such matters.

"He means," interpreted Wyso in Latin with an impatient yawn, "that the woman's milk will fly to her brain or turn to poison, if you torment her so. Brother Correntian may fatten the brat with an extract of his doctrines of asceticism, but he will then probably not become a man but an angel at once," he added spitefully.

Correntian trembled with rage, but the eye he feared still rested upon him and kept him within bounds.

Meanwhile the Abbot had turned to the fisherman.

"We will let justice give place to mercy—for the sake of your wife, our child's foster-mother. We stand by our first decision; till we release your wife you are banished as well as the gatekeeper who let you in. Henceforth no lay-brother shall guard the convent gate, but our brethren shall have the charge of the little gate-house in turn. Hope for nothing more and do not attempt again to penetrate our sanctuary—a second time will be your ruin."

He turned to the Superior who stood in confusion in the background, for though he was innocent of this intrusion he had good-naturedly permitted meetings outside the convent walls, and so had made the gatekeeper too lax in the performance of his duty.

"Lead the prisoner up to the moor; there hand him over to the shepherd and our lay-brethren at St. Valentine's—they can release him from his bonds. The shepherd will provide him with nourishment and other necessaries and will be answerable to me for his not quitting the moor.—Come now, brethren, we will not waste another hour of our deferred night's rest."

The brethren followed him in silence.

"I am sorry for the poor creatures," said Stiero to Wyso in an undertone. "It was Correntian who stirred up all the mischief. Why in the world can he never sleep?"

"That he and God alone can tell!" said Wyso, shrugging his shoulders.

"Take leave of your wife," said the Prior as the monks disappeared. "I dare not give you any farther respite, for the stern father Correntian will assuredly watch us from his window up there."

The husband and wife fell into each other's arms in bitter grief, but they suddenly started apart again, for a monk still remained behind—are they not to be allowed to press heart to heart before parting?

But the monk who has stayed behind is brother Eusebius; his face is radiant with mild dignity and sweet compassion. He signs to them with his slender withered hand that they need have no fear of him, for he has stayed to be a comfort to the miserable wife and not as a spy.

"Do as your heart bids you," he says. "Nature is sacred—woe to those who violate her rights!"

All was as still in the room as in a church, and he who had spoken these words stood there in calm grandeur, in divine unselfish peace, and looked on pityingly while the couple held each other in a close embrace and could not bear to tear themselves asunder, till the Prior separated them almost by force. A stifled scream from the woman—and the door closed, shutting her husband out for ever. The cloistered nurse was alone with the old monk, the gnome, who lived only between the grave and Heaven. She threw herself sobbing at his feet and he whispered words mighty to comfort in her ear, in a tongue as it were from another world that she but half comprehended; but they quelled the wild outbreak of her sorrow and lulled her soul, as if it were rocked by spirit-hands, filling her with strangely melancholy and yet glorious presentiments.

Dawn was already breaking in the lonely turret-chamber, the bell was ringing for matins. The mother sat pale and weary on the edge of the bed and held her child to her breast. She had taken it in her arms unthinkingly—it had waked before the other child—never remembering that after this night's work the milk might be poison which her frail baby was drinking in eager draughts. Father Eusebius had left her to attend the early mass. She had not yet slept at all; but now she sank back on the pillow, nature asserted its rights—she fell asleep—while the poison was slowly but fatally coursing through the veins of the infant which, in her slumbers, she still held closely and tenderly to her breast.

CHAPTER IV.

A scream of anguish rang through the still convent court-yard from the eastern tower; it rang out to the clear spring sky and through the open turret-window, following the glorified infant soul that had taken its flight to Heaven up, up into the eternal blue; it startled the brooding swallow from the roof, and fearing some mortal evil she fluttered round her nest; it roused the grey monk in the western tower from the books and writings among which he sat day and night poring over his little desk and imbibing living food for his soul's roots from the dead parchment. He closed his book and rose. Meanwhile someone was already knocking at his door. For father Eusebius was the sick nurse of the whole convent; whenever any one was ill in the Abbey or in the neighbourhood he was sent for.

"Come quickly, brother Eusebius," cried the messenger. "The nurse's baby has died suddenly."

Brother Eusebius was not in the least surprised, he had foreseen it; since that night of terror three days ago the little girl had been ill and had defied his utmost skill. Some of the brethren it is true were of opinion that the child was possessed by the devil, because the mother had been snatched from her wicked pleasures, and that it ought to be exorcised; but the wise Eusebius knew better—he knew that the feeble infant had drunk its death at its mother's breast.

He went up to the little room which was lighted up by the brightest sunshine; the poor woman lay stretched over her child's body, her wild sobs betraying the agony which was rending her heart. The other child lay smiling in his cradle and playing with a wreath of blooming cowslips[1] that his uncle Conrad of Ramüss had brought up from the valley where he had been tending a sick man. The poor little corpse had its eyes still open and they were fixed on the unconscious boy as if she had something to say to him which her little silent lips could not utter. But the mother understood—at least she thought she understood—and she gave that look a cruel and terrible meaning; for her it had no other interpretation than this: "You have killed me."

Eusebius silently laid one hand on the mother's head and the other on the child's, and with a practised touch he closed the dead, fixed eyes. The sobbing mother was pressing her aching head against the cold little breast as if to break through the icy crust laid over it by death, but he raised her head with a firm hand, and without a word pointed to the open window. At that moment a white dove flew through the clear ether, shining like silver in the sunshine—

rising higher, growing smaller, as it soared on rapturous wing through immeasurable space; soon seen no more but as a fluttering speck, higher and still higher—till lost in the blue distance. That was the soul of the dead child —so the mother believed—nay knew for certain. She sank on her knees and with folded hands worshipped the miracle that had been accomplished before her mortal eyes. And so once more the wise old man had been able to triumph over death and misery in that hapless soul by an alliance with Nature which he alone understood—Nature who would utter her divine wisdom to none but him.

But the measure was not yet full.

Out on the moor the lonely outcast husband was rocking in his canoe by the shore of the lake; his nets lay idle at the bottom of the boat and he sat sunk in sullen brooding; it was growing dusk, the lake bubbled and foamed; there was dumb rebellion in its depths—as in the depths of the exile's soul. Cold gusts dashed frothy, splashing waves on to the banks which were as bare—up at this height—as if it still were winter, and which were so sodden with the melting snows that they could absorb no more of the superfluous moisture; the dry scrub that grew about the place sighed and rustled softly as the wind swept over it. The fisherman started from his dreaming, unmoored his bark and pushed away from the shore; but hardly had he got a yard from the bank when he heard a voice calling. He stopped and listened; it was a messenger from the monastery to tell him that that morning his little daughter had died.

The man let go his oar and hid his face in his hands sobbing aloud like a child.

The convent servant called out to him compassionately to "come to shore, to compose himself; that the holy fathers had desired him to promise the afflicted man all kindness, and good wages for the future—" the stricken man rose up in the rage of despair.

"Spare your words," he shouted across the roaring of the waves as they tossed round the frail canoe. "Take yourself off with your hypocritical convent face or I will choke your false throat with your own lying promises. Why should I believe you—how have you kept your word to me? You have stolen my wife and murdered my child. I curse you—I curse the day when you enticed my wife and child within your dismal walls, I curse the day when that boy was born who is the cause of all the mischief. Be advised while still it is time—kill the child before he does any farther harm—an evil star guides him and he will bring ruin on all who go near him. And now get you gone if you value your life."

The convent servant crossed himself in horror and hastened to obey the warning; he was frightened at the infuriated man, standing up in his bark with his fist clenched, with his tangled hair and flaming eyes like a "Salwang," one of those most fearful giants, before whom not mortals only, but even the "phantom maidens" fly.

And as soon as the messenger had disappeared the unhappy man threw himself on his face again and abandoned himself to his sorrow. The canoe drove over the waves—rudderless as the boatman's soul. He did not heed the spring-storm that blew in deeper and deeper gusts across the lake, nor the waves that ran higher and higher as though Nature were dreaming uneasily in her sleep—till suddenly a swift current caught the boat and carried it on with increasing rapidity down the lake. The man started up, and his aroused consciousness made him clutch sharply at the oar, for he perceived with horror through the darkness that he was driving towards the spot where the Etsch[2] rushes out of the lake with a considerable fall. But alas! the oar was gone—it had slipped away, escaping him in his anguish without his being aware of it; the loop of straw which had served to fasten it was hanging broken to the hook. For an instant he was stunned, then he gave an involuntary shout for help—then came the knowledge of the danger, the certainty that he was lost. He went through a brief struggle of vigorous healthy life against the idea of destruction—a short pang of terror of death— and then came the calmness of despair, and a still heroism that none could see but God! The lost man sat with his arms folded in the boat, driven down the stream beyond all hope of rescue, with one last prayer on his lips—a loving prayer for the wife he was leaving behind. Far away on the shore he sees the lights of the brethren of St. Valentine—they call to him—signal to him—the boat rushes on, in headlong haste, to its fate. There—there are the falls—a thundering roar—the canoe tips up on end—then it shoots over head foremost, turning over twice in its fall, till it lies crushed and smashed among the stones in the bed of the cataract. It is all over—the swollen spring-flood of the Etsch carries a mangled corpse and dancing fragments down into the valley on its sportive and roaring waters.

"Now indeed, poor woman—you have lost all!"

Father Eusebius was sitting in the nurse's little room, which during the last three days had been to her a cell of torment; he held the unconscious woman's head between his hands and rubbed her forehead and temples with strong spirit of lavender; but her mind was wandering far away in the twilight of oblivion and must return to a consciousness of nothing but horror—torment and to suffering. Her hands moved with a feeble gesture to push him away, her dumb lips parted as though she would say, "Do not be cruel—do not wake me—I am at peace—leave me, leave me."

But though his heart seemed to stand still for pity, he must call her back to life.

At last she was roused; she looked round enquiringly, for all her world was in ruins and she knew not whom she could turn or cling to. Before her on the floor lay her dead husband's clothes—there stood the cradle out of which they had carried away her baby only yesterday to the charnel-house—what was left her in the world? There still was one! Father Eusebius took the living baby from the bed and brought it to her. "It is a stranger's child," he said. "But it is yours too!" and the bleeding heart-strings, torn up by the roots, clung to the strange child as if he were her own—the poor beggared soul accepted it as the last alms of love bestowed upon her by the Creator; for she was humbled in her misfortune, she did not strive, she did not contend, nor did she bear any malice to the child, for all that it had unconsciously been guilty of. "The child is yours," spoke comfort to her heart, and she believed it as father Eusebius himself did when he spoke the words.

"What is yours? Who within these walls may venture to boast that anything is his own?" said Correntian's stern voice at the door.

"Oh! that man!" shrieked the terrified woman and she fled with the child into the remotest corner of the room from the sinister monk who now came in.

"I spoke of the child—to comfort the poor soul, and if you are a man you will leave her that comfort," said brother Eusebius.

"In this house nothing is ours—but suffering and the hope of redemption," the dark man went on pitilessly. "Know that, woman; and remember it at every hour—The venerable fathers have sent me to tell you that you must now wean the child, that the shock of the last few days may do him no harm."

A flood of tears burst from the nurse's large and innocent eyes as she heard this, and she asked with white lips,

"Must I go away then?"

"No, not so long as the child is still little and needs a woman's care. Now, you know the fathers' determination—act accordingly."

And without vouchsafing her a glance he quitted the room.

Calm, clear and gentle, like the moon in the high heaven when the sun has set, father Eusebius stood before the poor woman whose sun of life had set, and in half-inarticulate words she made her lament to him, telling him her sorrow; to him she dared to weep out all the unutterable anguish that would have driven her mad if she had had to bear it alone.

Day after day passed silently away in the lonely turret-room; in a few weeks the fresh handsome woman had grown pale, thin and old—no longer a scandal to the chaste eyes of the brethren. Not a word, not a smile ever came to her lips—she lived only for the child that throve joyously on her crushed affections.

Every day the little one grew stronger and more blooming; a child as sweet and winning as if angels came down from Heaven from time to time to play with him. He was like a ray of sunshine in the gloomy convent and in the closed hearts of the brethren. He could entice a smile from the sternest lips— hardly any one could resist giving him a flower in passing, throwing him a spray, or bringing him some tempting fruit from any more distant walk—a bunch of wood strawberries, an empty bird's-nest, a sparkling pebble— whatever came to hand. "Our little brother," they called him, and the words were repeated here and there in the early morning, when the nurse would sit with the boy in the little cloister garden for him to play on the soft grass-plot while she went on silently with her work, for the little one had begun to run about quite prettily and she could leave him to himself for hours. But indeed he never remained alone; hardly was he down in the garden when all the younger monks gathered round him like bees round a newly opened flower. And they played with him like children and made him all sorts of toys; chains of bird-cherries and little parchment wind-mills and ships—downright waste of time the older brethren called it. The rigid old brother carpenter carved him out little sheep and cows and a little manger with a baby Christ in it. Brother Engelbert, the painter, painted him all sorts of lovely pictures in the brightest colours—the whale swallowing Jonas and Saint Christopher carrying the infant Christ through the water; and was delighted with the child's shouts of joy when he showed some comprehension of one and the other. Brother Candidus, the precentor, cut him out sweetly tuned pipes and was never tired of admiring the boy's good ear.

Thus each did what he could for the "little brother." The hour of recreation was their play-time with the boy and the older men would look on smiling and observe with satisfaction how such innocent and childish amusements could please the younger brethren.

The child grew up in bliss—as if in Paradise. Loved by all, affectionately taught by all, he developed rapidly in body and mind. One above all others bore him in his heart and cared for him with his hands—to one above all others he clung with increasing devotion; this was Conrad of Ramüss, his uncle. However deep the child might be in some new game, however close the circle of monks around him, when he heard Conrad's voice he flung everything aside, got up on his tottering little feet, and trotted jubilant to meet him. It was a striking picture when the tall, handsome man stooped down to lift the boy; when the fat baby arms were clasped round the proud neck with its golden curls and the small round cheeks were pressed caressingly against that noble, spiritual face.

"My sweet angel, the flower on my cross!" he would often say to him, and the child would listen almost devoutly and look before him vaguely with his large brown eyes, as though he already could know the significance of the Cross which stood in the midst of the convent garden to the honour of the Most High.

He would sit for hours in the quiet little garden with the child on his knee and his breviary in his hand; so long as he felt the little heart beating against his own he was content. Now and then it struck his conscience that perhaps he clung too closely to the child as an earthly treasure; and then he would raise his eyes imploringly to Heaven, "Forgive me for loving him—I am bringing him up for Thee—my God." And as the child grew bigger and learned to speak, it was Conrad who with inexhaustible patience taught him his first little prayer; to fold his baby hands and kiss the wooden Christ in the garden when he lifted him up in his strong arms. The little one knew every wound as a cruel torment and would lisp out, "Holy! holy!" while he pressed his rosy lips to the blood-stained wooden hands and feet. But he who inflicted these torments on the Redeemer, to the child's fancy was none other than Correntian; the brethren might do what they would, they could never get it out of the child's head that "the cruel man" had nailed the Saviour to the cross.

"The brat has more wit than all of us put together," said Wyso when he heard it. "If Christ were to come again Correntian would be the first to crucify him."

From that time Correntian hated him if possible more than before, and the child was so much afraid of him that he fled from him crying when by any chance he approached him. Never had he favoured the child with a single word but one of rebuke, nor a look but one of reproach. The merriment of the brethren was in his eyes an outrage and a crime against the rule of Saint Benedict which did not allow of speech "with gesticulations, nor with showing of the teeth, nor with laughter and outcry."

But the others who set the spirit above the letter, and who better understood the rule of Saint Benedict, did not care, but loved the child all the more. Correntian was like a seceder from the rest of the brethren, and the unacknowledged breach between them grew daily more impossible to heal. Here again it was the child that was guilty. "The seed of hell that I pointed out is beginning to germinate," said the implacable man.

Three summers had passed over little Donatus and the autumn wind was once more blowing over the stubble-fields though the midday sun still blazed with much power. The nurse was sitting with the boy in an arbour of blossomless juniper; the brethren were busy in the house with their prayers and duties. She was quite alone; as often as the autumn winds blew, the old wounds broke out again in the saddened heart and bled anew; it was now near the season when, four years ago, she had first left her husband and her lowly home, which was now empty and ruined. "You—you took everything from me—and yet I cannot help loving you, you child of sorrow," said she to the boy, who was playing at her feet at a burial, and was just then placing a cross he had made of two little sticks on the top of a mound he had thrown up. It was a delightful occupation and the child was eager at his play; he decked the grave with red bird-cherries as he had seen done in the grave-yard when one of the brethren took him there; then he swung his little clay mug over it by a string for a censer and sang an edifying litany in his baby way as he had heard the brethren do, and he was so absorbed in his pretty play that he screamed and struggled when his nurse suddenly caught hold of him and took him up. But he was easily pacified and, well-pleased with his foster-mother's caresses, he clung closely to that faithful breast. It was long since she had forgotten the prohibition to kiss him. She clasped him again and again with melancholy fervour and pressed a thousand kisses on his sweet baby-lips.

At this moment, as if it had sprung from the earth, a dark shadow stood between her and the sun, which threw a golden light on the grass-plot in front of the arbour. She looked up startled—again it was Correntian who stood before her. And as if that most sacred feeling, a mother's love, were a sin, she blushed and set the child down on the ground. She was suddenly conscious that she ought not to kiss him—a look of loathing from the monk told her all and she trembled before him. But he only shook his head and said,

"This must have an end. Stay here!" he added in a tone of rough command and quitted her with a rapid step.

The woman sat still as if spell-bound and dared not move from the spot. What misery would he bring upon her now? All at once it had grown cloudy and chill, and yet the sun was shining as before; the grass, the trees—though still green, the sky—though still blue—everything was all at once autumnal and sere as if metamorphosed by a touch. And the child looked to her so strange, so distant, so unattainable, and yet she need only put out her arms to clasp him.

So she waited with folded hands, motionless.

At last she heard returning steps over the path; it was the Abbot and a few of the elder brethren. The Abbot hurried up with unwonted haste.

"You are an incorrigible woman," he scolded out. "We have shown more than due pity for you, we have kept you here longer than was fit although the boy has long since ceased to need you; there was no way left for you to sin—so we thought—and now I hear that even this child is not sacred to you! Why, have I not forbidden you to kiss the boy? 'under heavy penalty,' I said; and you—you despise our orders, you compel the child to submit to your caresses although he struggles with vague misgiving, and you teach his innocent mouth, which is consecrated to God's service, to kiss a woman's lips; you outrage the sight of the brethren who betake themselves to the garden for devout contemplation? It must come to an end, brother Correntian is right. There," he added, drawing a little bag full of gold coins out of his frock, and laying it in her hand, "there is your honest pay. I think you will be satisfied with us, it is a donation worthy of a prince. You may buy yourself a farm and land with it down there near Nauders or wherever you will, but take yourself off out of the sacred precincts of our cloister, for ever."

The nurse made no answer, she stood there pale and dumb; tears dimmed her eyes as if she had been plunged into a lake, and saw everything through water. Her clenched hands trembled so that she had let the purse fall, the wretched price of her life's ruined happiness. Now the last treasure was taken from her, the only thing left—the child to whom she had sacrificed all; this too! "Within these walls nothing is our own but suffering," Correntian had said, she remembered that.

"Take the child with you at once," said the Abbot, and Correntian's bony fingers grasped the child; but the boy cried so heart-rendingly, and clung with such deadly terror to his foster-mother that he had to be torn away from her, and his screams brought out the younger brethren. The nurse leaned helplessly against the pillar of the arbour, and a deep groan broke from her. The younger monks, looking on, were filled with blind fury; their hatred for Correntian, which had been growing for many years, could be no longer contained; they forgot all discipline and obedience, all the rules of their order. They crowded round Correntian like a pack of hounds.

"Leave the child alone, you blood-hound, you spy, who can never leave any thing in peace."

"For shame, reverend Abbot, for listening to him, the wolf."

Thus shouted the angry mob who would listen to no farther commands; it was open revolt. The Abbot and the elder brethren ran about in confusion, not knowing what to do, when above the tumult they heard the voice which had so often restored peace and calm; father Eusebius had just come down from his tower-chamber, and with a rapid glance had taken in the state of affairs.

"You are forgetting your obedience, my brethren. We could not keep the woman here for ever; so it is my opinion that Conrad of Ramüss should take the child into his cell, he loves it, and it clings to him."

"Yes, yes, let Conrad of Ramüss take him," they cried with one voice, and brother Conrad was fetched out from the chapel.

With a glance of infinite pity at the poor trembling woman he took the child in his arms. "Be easy, I will take good care of him for you," he said kindly, and she gratefully kissed the hem of his robe. She took one last long look at the child, the beloved boy that she had nursed so faithfully in those arms which might never clasp him again. She dared not give him any parting kiss, his little hands might never touch her more. The tall monk carried him away high above the crowd of brethren, as if he were borne along on a dark stream; now, now the doors close upon him—it is over!

The woman sat alone under the withered arbour; it was evening, the dew was falling, the wind rustled in the dry branches, and warned her that it was time to make up her bundle, and to find her way—out into the world where all was dead or strange to her. Whither should she go? She knew not, she must wander about alone and helpless so long as her feet would carry her, till she dropped and lay down somewhere or other. She pulled herself up, for so it must be, but she must go upstairs into the empty room whence they had taken the child, just to fetch a few wretched garments. No, she could not do it.

She stole away, just as she stood, her knees bending under her, taking only one thing with her: the little cross with which the child had been playing at his mimic grave-yard. She pressed it to her lips while she shed hot tears. Thus she glided like a criminal through the mist and darkness, out of the little gate where she had so often watched for her husband. But now no loving arm was waiting to clasp her; the Prior called out a compassionate farewell; that was all. One more glance up at the turret-window, and then she went down into the misty valley—a lonely beggar.

Up in the convent a great conclave was held by the elders in judgment on the younger brethren and their criminal outbreak against all discipline. Father Eusebius would willingly have hurried off after the poor forsaken woman, but his duty to his Order kept him here.

"It has all happened just as I said and prophesied," said Correntian. "All the mischief comes of the child. It is the child of a curse, and it will bring the curse under our roof."

Then Eusebius rose, his voice sounded sharp and stern as it never had before, and his eyes flashed round upon the assembly with an eagle-like glance.

"I will tell you," said he, "the cause of the curse that clings to the child. All the conditions of its life are unnatural. Its father's rage was unnatural that made the child an outcast before it was born; your demands on the nurse were unnatural, and the husband, wife, and child have come to ruin in consequence; and the child's life here in the convent is unnatural. That is the seed of hell of which you spoke, Correntian, which you have cherished, and which you will reap—the revenge of outraged nature."

BOOK II.

MARTYRDOM.

CHAPTER I.

Joy, joy in all the fields! for it is harvest-time. In all the fields up hill and down dale; down in the valley and up on the heights they are cutting the last swathes, the last Rodnerinnenlocken are sounding—so they call the old traditional cry with which the hay-maker calls upon the blessed phantom-maidens to come and help him. He strikes three times on his scythe with his whet-stone, so that it rings over hill and valley; the phantom-maidens hear it, and hasten down from their cliffs to help the mowers, so that they may get in the harvest in dry weather. For they are kind-hearted and well-disposed to the peasant who contentedly tills his field, and many old folks are still living who have seen with their own eyes that they were not too proud to work in peasant's dress, helping those who were industrious. But since a rude lad once seized upon one of the "good women," and kissed her by force, they no longer show themselves to mortal eyes; only their kind handiwork can be traced. The more industrious a man is, the more they help him, for they never come to any but the industrious; the idle call on them in vain. But this year there must have been more of them than ever, for it is a splendid harvest, and has been got in quicker than usual. Singing and shouting resound on all the meadows, and the long lines of hay-waggons with their intractable teams of spanned oxen seem endless. Children are romping among the odorous hay-cocks in the meadows, or lie on the top of the soft piled up heaps stretching their weary limbs luxuriously; lads and lasses together teazing and joking each other in exuberant merriment.

Up at the window of the eastern tower of Marienberg a pair of large melancholy eyes were gazing longingly down on this glorious, smiling scene. A pair of wonderful eyes they were; deep, dark, and yet full of light as though glowing with some inward fire, so that even the white seemed to take a ruddy tint, like an opal held against the light. They gazed down from the tower with a fixed regard, drinking in all the splendour in one long look.

The gay, social doings of men—the silent, all-powerful day-star that was riding at its noon-tide height and shedding its rays over all the wide landscape, so that every roof and turret of the thirteen hamlets that lay strewn around were distinctly visible up to the very edge of the gleaming snow-fields and glaciers, which were the only limits set to the roving eye—the wide verdant plain, like a garden with softly swelling hills and tufted woods, and traversed by the silvery streak of the murmuring Etsch—all this was mirrored in those hungry, dreamy, far-gazing eyes. They followed the course of the wild, swift rivulet that tosses itself so impatiently over rapids and falls as it

54

leaves the lonely mountain-tarn on the moor, rushing on to the all-engulfing sea. And those eyes sent forth a message of enquiry up to the blue sky, down to the smiling plain, beyond the majestic heads of the great Ortler-chain—a dumb, burning question.

But no answer came back to him; it vanished, wafted away by the winds, like broken gossamer-threads.

The eyes, the anxiously enquiring eyes, belonged to a youth so nobly formed, so full of graciousness, that it seemed as if nature must have formed him for a world of perpetual Sundays, and not for a world of weariness, labour and duty—those grim destroyers of the beautiful.

"Oh! sweet child of humanity; here you sit imprisoned and bemoaning your living death between cloister walls and among pale disfigured faces. Forgive me, O, God! if it is a sin to regret that all that is beautiful should be rejected by pitiless asceticism in these rough times—that it must wander through the world misunderstood and unprized, and either perish like flowers on a cross or sink in the pool of perdition."

Father Eusebius was standing behind the young man's chair and his eyes rested sadly and thoughtfully on the young head, with its thick crown of dark curls that waved rebelliously round the prescribed tonsure. Eusebius had grown old and feeble, he was now ninety-three years old. His hair was like snow, and his body frail and bent, but his spirit was perennially young and his glance had the same power as of old. The youth turned his head. "What, Father Eusebius," said he in surprise. "Are you there? I did not hear you come in. What has brought your weary feet up here?"

"I knew that you would be up here and dreaming again."

"Are you vexed with me?" asked the boy, and a pleading smile lighted up his face as sweetly as when a crystal pool reflects the sunshine.

"Who could be vexed with you?" said Eusebius, and his old eyes lingered with undisguised delight on the beautiful face of the boy, "I only fear lest the brethren should take it ill in you if you keep apart in the recreation-hour."

"Ah, reverend brother," answered the youth, "you cannot know how happy I am up here; I can see out into the wide world, far over hill and valley! This was my first home, here stood my cradle, here a kind voice sang me to sleep and in the little nest up there on the roof I first heard the twittering of birds. I cannot tell you how content I am here. I feel as if when my time comes I must die here and fly straight out of that window into eternity after my little foster-sister—as if there could be no other path-way to Heaven."

Eusebius laid his hand on the boy's shoulder.

"I do understand you, my son. It would be well for you if so it could be and you need only fly away to reach eternal bliss! But a long and weary and thorny path lies before you, a path which you must tread with bleeding feet; and many a heavy cross awaits you that you must bear on aching shoulders ere you may rest in God!"

"Oh! brother—why may I not die at once? Why may I not depart at once and be with the Father, for whom my soul pants?"

"Because we must live—live and work, my son; work for our neighbour and for future generations. Thus only can humanity ripen into perfection; each must do his duty in his own way by word and by example and none may escape his task."

"Why must we first be men if we proceed from God and are his children?" asked the boy with a sigh.

"We do not proceed from God—we shall only go to God! Of dust were we born and out of dust we shall be raised and purified by the Spirit—to the Spirit."

The lad rested his head upon his hand and looked out again. "By the Spirit, to the Spirit—yes—yes—we must cast off this flesh with all its longings and weakness and yet—Oh! Eusebius, it is so hard! It would be so much easier to throw off this whole miserable body at once and die once for all than slowly to crush this throbbing, longing heart. Eusebius, a feeling comes over me as if I must fling my arms wide open and embrace the desert air—as if I must throw myself down on the grass and rest my head on the lap of earth—as if somewhere—in the earth itself or in the warm summer-air—a heart must be beating towards mine on which I might fling myself and weep out all my pain. Ah! Eusebius, it is true you all love me—and I love you; and I love God too and my Holy Mother Mary above all—and still it is not enough and my soul still thirsts for some love—for something—that shall be my own—wholly and solely mine. 'It is not good for man to be alone,' was said by the Lord himself—and I am alone—so utterly, absolutely alone."

And the youth raised his glowing eyes with such fervent entreaty to Eusebius that it cut the old man to the heart. Then he passionately grasped Eusebius' hand.

"Eusebius," he said, "you are wiser than they all. Tell me why must it be so? Why must we love nothing but God? Why is that a sin for us which is permitted to all the rest of mankind?"

Eusebius was startled by this unexpected question. He himself had once upon a time purchased his salvation with his very heart's blood and the wounds had healed. But would that which had cured him work a cure in another? Would the idea that rules the world damp this fire also? Eusebius looked thoughtfully before him and there was a pause as if he were seeking the right words; then he said,

"The great mass of people are struggling upwards by degrees—working, toiling, producing—step by step to the throne of God; but the steps are centuries and it is only after long centuries that the goal is ever visible to them. But there are solitary souls that feel a more powerful impulse towards Heaven than others do and that can separate themselves from the common herd and by great acts of self-denial attain to that perfection, for which centuries are needed by mankind as a whole. Such a soul can tread the direct road to God;—but he must walk alone—for he is shut out from all community with nature as soon as he sets forth upon that road. He no longer belongs to the toiling, producing mass, seething with perpetual reproduction of itself from itself—his life must be one long death. It demands the noblest heroism, the highest effort; for one single glance backwards—one false step on his lonely way to death; and omnipotent nature clutches him again and drags the lost soul back among her blindly-working wheels. But in the last judgment God will judge those presumptuous ones who undertook that which they could not carry through, more hardly than all the others, and will say, 'Why wouldst thou fain be better and greater than these, if thou hadst not the strength to achieve it?' Therefore, my son, we live apart from the world behind these sheltering cloister-walls, that nothing may tempt us from the path of holiness which we have chosen."

Eusebius paused and watched Donatus, who was leaning against the window and breathing hard.

"Eusebius!" he exclaimed, fervently grasping the old man's hand, "God will be merciful and give me strength to carry through that which I have begun—will he not?"

"Who can tell? What we ourselves undertake we ourselves must carry out. Therefore prove your heart, my son, before you swear the great irrevocable vow; you yourself wished to be a priest—you have obtained your wish, in a few days you will be consecrated to God's service. But if in your heart you bear such earthly longings will you be strong enough for such a sacred calling? If not—renounce it rather than some day break a double vow and so be doubly sinful. Better, better that you should fly away into the wide world than that you should be false to your own and to our plighted truth, and so fall lower in the eyes of God than those who never purposed to be more than men among men."

"I fly! I not be a priest!" cried the youth vehemently. "Nay, nay, my brother. You only wish to try me—you cannot be in earnest. If I said anything to make you doubt my truth, forgive me. Never, never has such a thought crossed my mind. And what should I do out in the world? If you drive a bird that was hatched in captivity out of doors it will starve in the midst of plenty —and so it would be with me. Only sometimes I suddenly feel as if the convent were too narrow for me, as if you ought not to keep me here like a prisoner! Look out there—is not that glorious! Must I not long to be out there in the blue distance? Must not the plain below tempt me down there, down to the delicious verdure which affords nourishment and refreshment to all? Must not those solitary heights tempt me up to the everlasting snow, so high, so near to Heaven? Or over there, near the bed of the silver stream, out on the heath where I was born? Is not God everywhere—over there as well as here? And is it not He whom I would seek down in the valley or up among the frozen glaciers? You—all of you—go in and out; you strengthen and refresh your souls in wood and field, why may I only never quit these walls?—why must I, so long as I live, be rooted like a dumb motionless plant within the narrow limits of the little convent garden?"

"My son, I have long expected you to question me thus. I will take upon myself to tell you the reasons why the fathers shelter you so anxiously— against my advice—for so far as I am concerned you should not be a monk nor take the vows of priesthood. I have read many books, old heathen chronicles and histories as well as Christian ones, and I have always found that human wit and human cunning must fail when anything was fore-ordained, and that what must be must. And if it must be, you will be torn from us even if we keep you within seven-fold walls. You must know then that a curse of interdicted love rests upon you; that is why your dying mother dedicated you to the cloister, and the reason of their keeping you so strictly, in order that the last will of the dead may be faithfully carried out. The fathers dread lest every step beyond these walls should entail the accomplishment of the curse; nay, Correntian even proposed that you should be blinded when you came to us as a new-born infant, to secure you for ever from all temptation."

"Dreadful man!" said the lad with a shudder. "But—one thing more— solve, I beg of you, the mystery of my birth. Why was I born out on the heath, who was my mother, and what crime had she committed that my father should cast her out?"

"We all took a solemn oath to our Abbot Conrad—the Abbot at that time— never to breathe the names of your parents either to you or to any one else, so that every tie between you and the world might be broken. Your mother died as a saint, and it was her wish that you too should live and die in an equally saintly manner. You are the child of the church; ask after no other parents. This was the answer we were to give you when you should ask, and so I answer you now, as is my duty."

"Oh! now I understand it all!" said Donatus, his voice trembling with deep agitation. "Woe is me! a curse rested on my innocent head before I saw the light! Aye, it is true; I was the death of the mother that bore me, I made the foster-mother that reared me miserable; she lost her husband and child for my sake. I was born to misfortune, and misfortune will pursue me wherever I go. Yes, you are right, there is no road for me but that to God, not a hope but Heaven! and I will keep three-fold watch over myself now that I know this! I will quell my rebellious heart even if it must break. I will not dream up here any more; no more shall the soft breath of the morning-breeze caress me, no more will I inhale the aromatic fragrance of the limes beneath this window nor let my gaze wander round the smiling distance—all these things rouse my longing! And perish the wishes even which may tempt me away from the step of the Altar to which I am dedicated! I am yours henceforth body and soul, and the world shall never more rob you of a single thought of my mind!"

"God grant it may be so!" said Eusebius, and his eyes rested sadly on the transfigured countenance of his young companion. Did he shake his head? no, he was only shaking off a startled moth. And Donatus rose.

"Let us go down," he said, "and leave this ensnaring spot which too much befools my senses! For I feel I had said things that I ought not to have said, and that it was not God who lent me such words."

So saying he closed the little window with its panes, obscured by dust and its worm-eaten frame. At this moment a cheery blast from a horn rang in the distance. "Oh look!" cried Donatus, "a procession of riders is coming up the mountain!"

Eusebius went to the window.

"It is true," said he, "a riding party—they are coming here; we must hurry down to announce them to the Abbot; come."

It was eleven o'clock, the hour when the brethren walked in the garden for recreation. Abbot Conrad of Ramüss, for it was he who now wore the mitre, was just then walking under a shady alley of trees and discussing with one of the brethren the preparations for ordaining Donatus a priest; for his favourite's festival must be kept with all the pomp of which the rules of the order allowed. Noonday silence lay on the peaceful little garden. The apricots and pears on the walls swelled their ruddy cheeks under the hot rays of a July sun and the brethren rested at their ease, stretched out in the shade of quiet arbours and trees. The pigeons cooed on the roof, and at the foot of the Crucifix, where the sun shone hottest, lay the lazy old convent cat, her green eyes sleepily closed.

Suddenly a wild noise was heard at the gate, the neighing of horses and barking of dogs, blasts on the horn and confused shouting; the brethren sprang, up in alarm. Donatus and Eusebius hurried up. "For God's sake, venerable Abbot—there is a splendid riding party at the gate, desiring to be admitted," they called out, "What shall we do?"

"What we cannot avoid doing—give them what they require."

"Oh, dear!" lamented fat old Wyso, who had been brought out by the alarm and who could hardly walk for old age and swelled feet. "Oh, dear! they will eat us up like the Egyptian locusts—do not let them in—or ask first who they are. We are not bound to harbour any one but the lords of the soil and they have already left us poor."

"Good brother Wyso," said the Abbot smiling, "if it pleased the Lord to let a swarm of locusts fall upon us, should we not be obliged to submit? so submit to these and act cordially with us in showing hospitality."

Thus speaking they had reached the gate and the Abbot himself opened it and met the impatient troop with a dignified demeanour.

High above him on horseback sat a number of nobles with a crowd of followers. The gay robes of silk and velvet, trimmed with costly furs, shone splendidly in the sun. Men and beasts were bathed in sweat from their hot ride up the steep hill.

"*Deo gratias*, noble gentlemen," said the Abbot. "If you are satisfied to accept what a poor, out-of-the-world mountain-convent has to offer, step in and be welcome in Christ's name."

"Come in, as many as there is room for," said the foremost horseman with a laugh, urging his prancing horse through the narrow doorway. "God save you, my lord Abbot, I do not think you good folks here starve?" he added with a merry glance at Wyso, who was trying to keep his gouty feet in safety out of the way of the crowd of horses.

The knight guided his horse under a shed, in order to alight in the shade; as many of the others followed as could come in; the silent convent yard was like a bustling camp, the mass of horses and men were pressed so closely together in crowded confusion. The horses kicked out in every direction, not liking such close quarters; the hindermost forcing their way in, the foremost unable to go any farther in the narrow space. There was pushing and screaming, prancing and stamping. Wyso escaped into the house, not without abusing the visitors, and even the other monks were frightened and startled out of their quiet life by the rough incursion of this high-handed party.

"Oh—locusts! locusts! you would be a lovely sight compared to these monsters!" Wyso lamented as he looked out of window.

At last all the horses were put up, some in the cattle stalls and some tied up in a row all round the walls, nay some—and this cut the brethren to the heart —some to the beautiful promising fruit trellises—the toil and care of many years all undone in an instant! And the brethren looked with consternation as they saw great horses' mouths with rolling tongues and sniffing nostrils poking about in the trees and eating what they took a fancy to, pending the arrival of better fare.

"What is to be done?" said the Abbot in a low voice to the brethren, "We must submit! And this is a friendly incursion—think what it would be if it were a hostile invasion—God preserve us!"

Meanwhile the marauding visitors had without farther ado overrun the hay lofts and brought down fodder for their horses, and to facilitate the beasts' enjoyment of it they stuffed it between the bars of the fruit trellises, for there were no mangers in the convent. The pack of dogs let loose in the little garden tore with wild howls across the flower beds in chase of the convent cat, who had little expected such visitors.

"Now, my lord Abbot," said the foremost of the riders good-humouredly enough, but in a tone of rough command. "Where are your cellarers? They should have appeared long ago to present us with a bowl of wine! True hospitality does not delay till the rider has his foot out of the stirrup."

"You shall be served at once, my lords!" said the Abbot. "You must take the will for the deed, for we are inexperienced and unaccustomed to receiving so many guests."

"But if I am well-informed you have occasionally received your seignior, the Count of Matsch—or Amatia, as they prefer to call it, with all his following?"

"We are the vassals of the Count of Matsch; it is an old right of our liege lords to visit us once a year," answered the Abbot.

"Then you cannot refuse to your sovereign prince what you grant to your liege," said the knight. "I am Meinhard the Second of Görtz and Tyrol and the Duchess is following me immediately."

The Abbot bowed to the very ground in pleasure and respect, "Happy is the day that procures us the honour of seeing your gracious countenance! Hail to Duke Meinhard!"

"Hail to Duke Meinhard! our powerful protector. Hail!" rang from all lips, and even Wyso came hobbling out again, panting and perspiring, and made his way with unwonted courage among the horses to testify his respect for the powerful Duke.

"Now the ducal horses might be welcome to eat all the apricots and pears, and the dogs to trample all the vegetables and flowers—this is quite another matter!"

"Make way—make way for the Duchess and her suite!" was now the cry of the marshal at the gate, and all made way for the litters of the Duchess and her ladies.

"Oh, dear! Oh, dear! Women in the cloister! And we cannot keep them out, for our wise rule allows princesses to enter!" lamented Wyso slily and winking with secret delight at Correntian, who was standing near him. "What do you say to such doings, Correntian?"

The Duke and the Abbot went to meet the procession and receive the noble lady. Foremost of all on a quiet horse rode the marshal, then followed the panting and sweating beasts that bore the Duchess' litter, each walking between two poles which hung from their backs from strong girths; one went in front and the other behind, each guided by a driver with a large cracking whip. Between them swung the tall palanquin with light rustling curtains of red silk, blown about by the hot south-wind, and inside it, wearily stretched out on soft crimson cushions embroidered with gold, lay a pale, delicate woman, closely veiled and so simply dressed that it was visible at the first glance that her mind was not set on the royal splendour with which her proud husband loved to surround her. But the ladies of her suite looked all the more haughty as they followed her on horseback. They rode behind the litter between the rows of monks, laughing and chattering, swaying their slender bodies carelessly on their broad-backed palfreys and looking curiously at the shorn heads around them, from under their broad hats, adorned with peacock feathers. Suddenly one of them drew her embroidered rein and whispered to her neighbour, "Look, there is a handsome one!" And all eyes followed hers to where Donatus was standing with downcast lids, grave and silent.

"Forwards!" cried the marshal, for a troop of riders were still behind as an escort for the ladies.

The Abbot had taken the leading-rein of the foremost horse in the litter and guided it with his own hand through the court to the inner gateway; here he paused and went up to the lady, "May it please you, noble lady," he said, "to alight and to put up with the accommodation of our humble roof."

At a sign from the marshal the squires and pages sprang forward. In an instant the horses were unharnessed, the litter let down on to the ground, the ladies lifted from their horses and litter and horses all led on one side. The Duchess, a lady of middle age and apparently afflicted by severe illness, bowed her head humbly before the Abbot. "Give me your blessing, reverend Father," she said softly.

The Abbot blessed her and led her with her ladies into the cool refectory.

"Will you condescend to rest and cool yourself here for a time, noble Lady?" he said, "while I see to providing some farther refreshment."

He conducted the men of the party into a large dining hall which he himself had built and which was only just finished; here the brother-cellarer had set large goblets which were all dewy outside from the coolness of the wine they contained; that was a drink after the frightful heat! hardly could the thirsty lips part with the bowl till the last drop was drained; there were rich cheese and fragrant rolls too, to stay their hunger till the noon-day meal was ready. For the Abbot would fain do everything that the resources of the house admitted, and its resources were many, for it had long been in a flourishing condition, and the labours and tillage of the monks had been blessed. He sent new milk to the ladies and little wheaten cakes with limpid golden honey, as might beseem fastidious ladies' lips.

Thus he cared paternally and tenderly for his guests, rejoicing at the evident satisfaction with which they enjoyed it. Even the grooms in the court-yard had heavy loads of bread and mead carried out to them, and soon there was such riot and jubilee as if they had entered into the land of Canaan. Nay the thoughtful host had remembered even the dogs; they stood in a circle round a great bowl of cool butter-milk and were lapping it with their hot tongues. Through the railings of the underground windows there rose up a mighty steam and reek of roast and stewed. The choicest fowls and fat joints of hastily slaughtered mutton sputtered on the rarely-used spits, for such a dainty meal was never prepared but for strangers, and the unusual savour of meat pleasantly tickled brother Wyso's nostrils. He could not omit this opportunity of saying spitefully to Correntian,

"Hey! what is that smell?"

"The devil's roast!" said Correntian with a burst of anger, for the whole occurrence was an abomination to him, and he could hardly control his indignation. He muttered the words of the prophet Isaiah, chap. 22: "*Et ecce gaudium et lætitia, occidere vitulos et jugulare arietes, comedere carnes et bibere vinum*—they slaughter oxen, they slay sheep, eating flesh, and drinking wine. *Comedamus et libamus, cras enim moriemur*—let us eat and drink, for to-morrow we die."

"Come, come," said Wyso chuckling. "It is not so bad as all that—we shall not die quite so soon as to-morrow, unless we may enjoy ourselves too freely to-day, and eat and drink too much—"

"*Et revelata est in auribus meis vox Domini: si dimittetur iniquitas hæc vobis, donec moriamini*—and in my ears was the voice of the Lord of Sabaoth: Verily this sin shall not be forgiven thee till thou die!" continued Correntian, but Wyso was not to be silenced.

"If the reverend Abbot grants us a dispensation, God too will forgive us the sin. Not that which goes into the mouth defiles the man, but that which proceeds out of the mouth. Do you understand? Well, why are you staring at me like that with your martyr's face?" he added in a tone of good humoured scolding to Donatus. "When I was your age, would I have girded my hungry stomach with rough haircloth, that I might ride lighter on the road to Heaven? Good Lord! they would have to haul me up with cords now, if I had to take all my earthly ballast up with me. But as we must leave to the earth all that is of the earth, earthy, it is all the same what we stuff ourselves with—that is my view."

Meanwhile the guests within had satisfied their first hunger and thirst, and Duke Meinhard had informed the Abbot of the reason of his visit. His wife Elizabeth of Bavaria had so long felt herself ailing and feeble, that before her end came she would fain do some good deed for the welfare of her soul, and with this end in view she had founded a House of God at Stams in the Ober-Innthal. The building was now far advanced, and she had made up her mind to undertake a journey, in order to inspect all the most distinguished foundations in the country, and thus to inform herself as to what arrangement of the building, what system and preparatory dispositions would be most advantageous to the newly founded religious house. When the noble lady was rested it was her wish that the Abbot might conduct her round the monastery, so that she might see everything for herself.

The Abbot declared himself most ready to aid in so Christian a work, and he designated Donatus, as his favourite and most promising disciple, for the high honour of conducting the Duchess, as the Duke took possession of the Abbot himself, to confer in manly fashion about the neighbourhood, the customs of the inhabitants of Vintschgau, and all sorts of things ecclesiastical and temporal.

Donatus coloured with surprise when the Abbot informed him of his good-fortune; nay his imploring look seemed to convey a remonstrance; but that was impossible, the brethren of the order might never say "no."

Next to the Duke sat a broad-shouldered, dark man, sunk in sullen, brooding silence. His hair was grey, but before its time, his brow morosely wrinkled and marked down the middle with a strong angry vein. He took no part in the conversation, and from the moment when he had taken his place he never once had moved his eyes from the end of the table where Donatus was sitting.

"Well, Count," said the Duke, pushing him to rouse him, and nodding to him over his glass. "You are staring fixedly at that one spot; does that young fellow remind you of your own youth?"

"It is strange, but do not you think that the boy is like me?" muttered the Count.

"He certainly is, to a hair; and if you had a son I could believe it was he. Only you never looked as gentle and sweet as he does; do not you agree with me, Count Reichenberg?"

"Count Reichenberg!" For an instant every face turned pale as the monks heard that name; Donatus only remained quite unconcerned, for he knew not as yet who and what Count Reichenberg was to him.

"By my soul!" cried another of the gentlemen, "you are as like each other as young and old, tender and tough can be."

Count Reichenberg sprang up. "My Lord Abbot," said he, "a word with you."

The Abbot turned paler than before; he exchanged but one rapid glance with the brethren, but they all understood him; then he rose and followed the Count into a deep window-bay.

"My Lord Abbot, I am a connection of yours, do you not know me?" said the knight without farther preface.

"I never saw you," replied the Abbot. "For since my sixteenth year I have lived out of the world as a monk. But if you are the man who married my sister and then repudiated her, you are no relation of mine, there can be no friendship between that man and me."

"I am the man," said Reichenberg defiantly. "I ask you—where that boy came from to you?" He pointed with an angry expression to Donatus.

"He was bequeathed to us," said the Abbot calmly.

"By whom?" The Abbot looked at Reichenberg, measuring him from head to foot with a steady gaze.

"That," he said, "is a secret of the confessional."

"I will pay you for it," the Count whispered in his ear. "Your convent shall benefit largely, I will make over to you by deed a manor and an alp above Taufers with glebe and pasturage, and all rights secured to you—only tell me the name of the boy's parents."

"No, my lord—not a word; did you ever hear that a Benedictine sold the secrets of the confessional?"

The Count stamped his foot.

"Then I will find some means of making you speak by force—at a more opportune moment."

The Abbot looked at him quietly and proudly. "You may kill me, but you can never make me speak."

"Then one of your herd will, who is less steadfast that you."

"I will answer for my brethren, man by man," said the Abbot with dignity.

The Count raised his hand threateningly, "Woe to you if I discover what I suspect—"

"Ho, ho! Count Reichenberg, what are you making this noise about?" and the Duke suddenly stepped between them. "What am I to think of you for thus disturbing the peace of this quiet hour?"

"I will inform you presently, my lord Duke. Just now grant me one word with the young monk there." He signed to Donatus to approach, and the boy rose and came modestly forward.

"Will you tell me who you are?"

"I am a monk," said Donatus, shortly and firmly.

"I see that—but who were you originally—who were your parents?"

Donatus looked calmly at him—"I do not know."

The Count cast a glance of hatred at the Abbot, "Oh, you priests, you priests; who ever got behind your tricks?"

"Pray be easy, Count Reichenberg," said the Duke soothingly. "I did not come here to torment peaceable monks who entertain us hospitably.—Do not take this to heart, my lord Abbot—nor you reverend brethren!" he signed to a servant who was standing by a large chest in a corner. "Look here, I have something to show you!" He opened, the coffer, which the man carried with difficulty, and took out of it a magnificent chalice of pure gold encrusted with garnets and chased with artistic reliefs representing the Passion, a work so fine and costly that the monks had never seen the like.

"Look here, this is the work of master Berthold, the goldsmith of Ulm," said the Duke.

Then he took out a little golden tube with a mouth-piece of amber, such as were in use at that time, in order that, when the Cup was presented, clumsy or greedy partakers might not imbibe too much of the costly wine. Next he produced a heavy golden Paten; this was in the same way set with garnets round the edge, and had two finely chased handles, while on the ground of the dish a cross was engraved. This he set on the table by the side of the Cup that all the brethren might rejoice in the sight. Finally he brought out a dozen of pure silver apples of artistic pierced work and called Calefactories; these were hand-warmers for the monks. They were filled with glowing charcoal and held in the hands to prevent the monks' fingers from being frozen at the early mass in winter.

"Well! how do you like them?" asked the lordly donor, well pleased at the astonishment and admiration with which the monks gazed at the costly treasure. "Do you think they will pay you for our dinner?" The Abbot looked at him enquiringly.

"I do not understand you, my lord!"

"No?—that is my offering in return for your hospitality. You shall have cause to remember the day when you entertained your Duke under your roof."

The brethren, with the exception of Correntian and Donatus, sprang up with confused cries of delighted surprise, "Oh! can it be!" and, "It is too much!" and the Abbot said with moistened eyes,

"You are magnificent in your favours, my Lord, and may God reward you, for we are only poor monks and can make you no return but by blessings and prayers."

"That is all I ask," said Duke Meinhard laughing, "only pray for me stoutly —I am sure to want it, for I hope to commit many more sins, and I shall have great need of the intercession of pious folks with the Almighty." He threw the treasure back into the heavy chest and slammed down the lid.

"There!" he exclaimed, "now take all the property away into your treasury and let us have dinner brought in as soon as possible, for we must proceed today to Münster and pass the night there. The Duchess wishes to spend some time in the convent of St. Gertrude, while we men ride to market and hunt in the neighbourhood."

"If it please, your lordship, to wait until we have shown her highness your wife the extent and arrangement of the monastery as she wishes—"suggested the Abbot.

"Aye—pray do so, my lord Duke," urged Wyso anxiously. "It will be to the advantage of your teeth if you leave the fat sheep, which were running about only an hour ago to sweat a little longer in front of the fire."

Reichenberg looked sharply at the fat monk with his thick lips and sensual grin. "You are not the man to die for the sake of keeping a vow," thought he. "When you have well drunk you will make a clean breast of it."

"Very well," said the Duke. "Then we will wait—less for the sake of my teeth than of yours, old gentleman—if indeed you still have any left. You will grant a dispensation this day in our honour, my Lord Abbot, will you not?"

"I will do so, my Lord," said the Abbot smiling, "they may enjoy themselves to their heart's content. And so, Donatus, my son, come now with me that I may conduct you to her ladyship, the Duchess, if she will accept you as her guide."

Donatus rose with simple dignity, and followed the Abbot. The two gentlemen, Meinhard and Reichenberg, looked after him in silence.

"Tell me, Count, what passed between you and the youngster that you got so angry about it?" asked the Duke, pushing back a little way from the table that the others might not overhear them.

"It is a mere whim, if you will," replied Reichenberg in a low voice. "But the boy's resemblance to me struck me amazingly. I—I might have had a child who would have been of just his age, and if it had been a son he might have looked exactly like that, for not only is the lad like me, he has just my wife's eyes and soft voice."

"Your wife's?" said the Duke, and he shook his head.

"My first wife's," said the Count, "whom I repudiated just about the time when my first child would have been born. You were then only a boy, and you were not at the court of your grandfather Albert. My wife was a Ramüss, and hardly were we married when that venomous serpent, the Countess of Eppan, poisoned my ear and heart. Not till last year, when the wretched woman was on her deathbed and sent to me in her last agony, did she confess that she had accused my wife falsely, in order to obtain her place. The name and wealth of the Reichenberg family were an eyesore to her, for she was both poor and haughty; the castle of Reichenberg, as you know, formerly belonged to the house of Eppan. She longed to restore it to them by a marriage with me—her heart was never mine as I saw very plainly later on. Now for a year past I have been wandering about the world, seeking in vain for some trace of my outcast wife. God in Heaven alone knows what may have become of them both, mother and child; my race ends with me, and I myself have driven out the heir that God perhaps had granted me—an outcast—to die! And that boy's eyes struck me like a thunderbolt. He looked just as my wife looked when I drove her away. Duke, if it were he—" The Count was silent, and his lips quivered.

"What good would it do you? It would be too late; he has taken the vows, and you could not break them."

The Count looked darkly before him, and made no reply.

"Your second wife never had much joy of her treason; you repudiated her too if I remember rightly?"

"Yes; at the end of two years the Pope gave me permission to announce that my first wife was dead, and to marry again; my mind had already wandered from the Lady of Eppan, but I had to keep my word—she held me to it hard and fast—and so she became my wife; but I was always away from home in battle and danger, for the world was spoilt for me, and so was all my liking for that false woman. When I returned from my four years' expedition to the Holy Land I found her carrying on an intrigue with Master Friedrich von Sunburc, the minnesinger and chronicler of your father's court. Nay more, a faithful waiting-woman of my first wife who could never get over the loss of her former mistress, betrayed to me that the shameless woman had not long since had a daughter, and had concealed the child with a strange beggar-woman whom she had met gathering berries and simples in the woods; as soon as the news of my return was known, the woman and the child had disappeared, leaving no trace behind. How I punished her, how the minnesinger was expelled from the court by Meinhard the first, and how she died, abandoned to remorse in her own ruined castle, all that you know."

"She was an intriguing coquette," said the Duke shaking his head, "and ensnared all men with her gold-gleaming owl's eyes and her auburn hair. She had something of the witch about her, and I could almost believe that she was one, for you know the common people say that you can tell a witch not by her feet only, but by her eye-brows that meet above her nose; she had such eye-brows you may remember?"

"I do not believe in such things," said Reichenberg sulkily.

"Nor I either," said the Duke laughing. "But there was something not quite canny about her, say what you will."

The Abbot meanwhile had taken Donatus to the Duchess.

"May it please you, noble Lady," said he, "that this youth, my favourite disciple, should have the honour of guiding you in your walk round the convent."

The Duchess glanced at Donatus with condescending kindness, and the court-ladies exchanged meaning glances, "That is the one we saw just now." Donatus stood in the door-way with downcast eyes.

"Come then," said the Duchess rising. "Two of you accompany me; you, Emerita, and you, Countess Hildegard."

The two chosen ones sprang forward with pleasure; one of them, Hildegard, was the beauty who had previously pulled up her horse in her admiration of Donatus' fine figure. She wore a light blue upper-garment or cappa of a fine and almost transparent woollen stuff, and under it a dress of heavy yellow silk rich with gold and bordered with white fur. She had laid aside her broad hat, and her very light hair was bound with a golden circlet, and crowned with fresh Alpine roses that she had gathered on the way. Her handsome dress hung round her slender form in soft folds, and was gathered in round her waist by a girdle of red velvet embroidered with gold. She was fair to see, that haughty maiden! Her brow was as white as marble, and the roses in her cheeks were heightened by a faint touch of the finest Florentine rouge. Her flashing eyes seemed to ask: "Where is there one fairer than I?" Nothing was to be got out of the simple God-fearing monks in the cloister, which she now must explore with the Duchess, nothing but looks of disapprobation of such worldly court-fashions, and if she could not ere long produce some sort of sensation, she felt she must die of tedium.

The other, Emerita, the Duchess' favourite, was dressed no less splendidly though less elaborately; her hair was modestly fastened up in a fine net of silver-threads tied with white, and a black velvet cap embroidered with pearls; her robes of soft white silk and woollen stuff were bordered with dark fur, and fell heavily and simply to her feet.

The Duchess herself was the most plainly dressed of all; deeply veiled in matronly fashion, and enveloped from her shoulders in the broad folds of a brown silk mantle fastened over her bosom with a single gold clasp; the rest of her dress consisted entirely of grey woollen stuff.

These three figures—so unlike each other—followed their monkish guide through the cold, damp, musty corridors of the vast building.

He led them first to the library; the Duchess found here a rich harvest for her craving for pious learning, for sacred books and parchments of inestimable value and splendour were amassed in it, and she was soon greedily absorbed in these treasures. Hildegard was almost in despair. The dust of books and rouge! these have little in common! And no one by but the coy saint with a head like a heathen god, as fine as any to be seen in Rome— living, breathing, and yet of marble! A secret revulsion to spite and hatred sprang up in her soul. Tedium is the parent of all kinds of crime. But to her great joy just then it occurred to the Duke to accompany the Duchess on her tour round the convent, and, conducted by the Abbot, he at this instance entered the library.

"Well, Countess Hildegard, how do you like yourself here?" said he, laughing and threatening her with his finger. "How fine you are! Come, come, do not be bewitching the poor young monk with your charms."

"Do not be alarmed, my Lord," said Hildegard mockingly, "he has not vouchsafed us a single glance; I believe his eyes have grown fixed to the ground."

The Duke looked at her with a smile. "That is a sad grievance for you, is it not, Hildegard? If it is but a monk he ought to admire you."

Hildegard coloured and was silent; but the Duke, good-humouredly carrying on the joke, said to Donatus, "Tell me, pious brother, why do you keep your eyes so immoveably fixed on the ground; are our fair maids of honour not worthy to be looked at?"

Donatus was standing before the Duchess, holding a heavy folio which she was turning over. "It does not become a servant of God to gaze at anything but the earth, which will be his grave, or Heaven, which is his hope," he replied with serene gravity.

The Duchess looked at his guileless countenance, and deep compassion filled her soul, she knew not wherefore. She could have loved this youth as a son.

"You are right, my child, and may God give you strength to hold to your principles," she said benevolently.

"Ah! you see," said the Duke in a low voice to tease Hildegard. "Your arts are wasted on him, pretty Countess; here at length is a man who can resist you."

"What do you mean, my lord?—I will bring him to look at me this very day—or I will go for a year in sack-cloth and ashes and break every looking-glass," whispered Hildegard smiling and showing two rows of brilliant teeth to the Duke's admiring eyes.

"Aye, aye," he said laughing, "that would indeed be a conquest for you. You have Princes and Dukes at your apron strings—and now a poor monk's soul must burn in eternal fires for your sake."

The Abbot suggested that they should proceed; the Duke gave his arm to his wife, the Abbot went on in front, Emerita followed; Hildegard hung behind a little.

"You take your vows in the strictest sense, and that no doubt is right," she said. "But it seems to me, worthy brother, that you must have very little confidence in your own strength if you have to guard your glances so strictly. Are you afraid lest a single look should bring you to ruin?—If so—forgive me, but I cannot help saying it—if so, your virtue is in a very bad plight." Thus she teased and tried to pique Donatus who walked by her side in silence.

"Whether I am strong or weak—I do not know. But it is written in the first epistle of Paul to Timothy, that women shall adorn themselves in modest apparel, with shamefacedness and sobriety; not with braided hair, or gold, or pearls, or costly array, but with piety and good works. And your dress is against this commandment—you are scandal in the eyes of the Lord—and the eyes of men should avoid seeing you."

"Bless me! That sounds very terrible! Such a severe speech would better become a father confessor than your youthful years; but even stern words sound soft from your lips, and I would sooner obey you than any old lenten preacher." And without pausing to consider, she took off her golden chaplet with its pearls and preciously wrought trefoils, she took out the broad gold clasp which held her robe together over her full bosom, so as to uncover her white throat—and she laid them both in the young monk's hand.

"There," she said, "take these for your poor; I offer them willingly, and I will give up everything that I usually wear if you will only give me one friendly look to repay me." The inexperienced boy stood speechless; was she in earnest? Was it true that she was so submissive to his words, so self-sacrificing, so ready to repent? And he involuntarily raised his eyes and looked at her—a wide, questioning, admiring gaze. She caught his glance and fixed it with a magic spell, entangling him in a net, woven as it were of the radiant glances of her own eyes.

"Oh!" she sighed softly, and her voice fell caressingly on his ear like the faint whisper of the limes under the eastern turret-window, "You see, you too can smile. Believe me such a smile on your lips has more power than a whole epistle of St. Paul."

Donatus was alarmed and his lids dropped again. "God forbid! You were joking and I thought you were in earnest. Take back your golden ornaments—they burn my hands as though they had been forged in unholy fires."

But she pushed the things from her and said with an air of sweet earnestness, "Nay—you do me an injustice. If I talk the language of the world teach me a better one. Look at me! your gaze has a purifying power; look at me, look me in the face and see if I can lie?" And once more he raised his eyes and drank the sweet poison of beauty such as he had never dreamed of.

"Come, come!" it was the Duke's voice, "my coy brother; you are already over head and ears in contemplation of our maid-of-honour! It seems to me she has converted you more quickly than you have converted her.'"

Donatus started, as from a dream; he blushed deeply, and casting down his eyes, he turned to the Abbot to present him with the jewels, which he still held in his hand. The Abbot, much surprised, thanked and blessed the generous donor.

But the Duchess paused and called Hildegard to her side.

"Why did you disturb us?" whispered Hildegard angrily in the Duke's ear as she passed him. Her breath came quickly and her cheeks glowed more scarlet than their rouge.

"You are a perfect fiend, Hildegard," the Duke whispered in return.

"I am much displeased with you, Countess," said the Duchess. "What have you to do with that innocent young monk? Try your arts where you will, only not here on these saintly men and do not destroy the peace of these chaste souls. I fear we shall never suit each other, Hildegard."

Hildegard set her teeth, then she said, "Very well, my lady Duchess, when we reach Munster I will ask you to grant me an escort to conduct me back to my father's castle, if my service is no longer acceptable to you."

"That will be best for you and for me," said the Duchess calmly, and she passed in by a door which the Abbot unlocked, and which opened into some steps that led down to the subterranean hall.

"In a few days," said the Abbot, who had not observed what was passing, "we shall celebrate in this crypt a requiem for the wife of our noble founder, who died in the Holy Land. Our youngest brother Donatus will then preach his first discourse, for on the following day he is to be consecrated to the priesthood." Thus speaking he led the way down the steep damp stairs, and the sanctity of the spot struck them all involuntarily silent.

Meanwhile Reichenberg was waiting in the refectory, sunk in gloomy brooding, and the hungry monks, who had long passed their usual meal-time, stood about listening if the footsteps of the company might not haply be coming nearer. At last the brother who was in control of the kitchen sounded the dinner-bell, and at the same instant the Duchess entered the refectory with Donatus, the Duke following with the Abbot. The Duchess was deep in conversation with her companion; presently turning to the Abbot, she said kindly,

"I thank you, my Lord Abbot; I have seen a great deal that has both delighted and instructed me. Particularly the library—I could spend whole hours there, for you have inestimable treasures preserved there in ancient manuscripts written by pious, learned, and godly men. But above all, I must honestly confess—nay more than all the books of wisdom—this child has edified and elevated my spirit. In good truth, my Lord Abbot, Heavenly blossoms grow in your garden and this world would be a Paradise if the Lord had many such gardeners."

"Dear me! the Duchess is growing quite young again," said the Duke with a laughing, threatening gesture. "Hey, hey! my Lord Abbot, what sort of monks have we here that turn the heads of all the ladies, old and young?"

"Do not laugh, my lord," said the Duchess gravely. "I assure you, the wisdom of old age and the innocence of childhood are united in this youth. If I had only known sooner, my Lord Abbot, what disciples you could bring up, I should have chosen the monks for my new foundation from your community, and I deeply regret that I have already made an agreement with Morimond, the head of the Cistercian Abbey, for none can have higher qualifications than you possess. But this at least I beg of you, that you will spare me this youth to be my castle chaplain. You tell me he is to be anointed priest; let him exercise his holy office in my service, and God in Heaven will recompense you for the good deed you will do to a poor sick woman."

The Abbot was silent for a moment from surprise and looked at Donatus. "Happy child!" said he, "what honours are heaped upon your head. Shall I grant this gracious lady's wish and give you to her? Speak freely."

"No—Father!" cried Donatus in mortal terror. "You will not cast me out!"

"Forgive him, Madam," said the Abbot smiling. "We have taught him always to speak nothing but the truth. You see, it is not compulsion that keeps him here, and it will not be against his will if I find myself obliged to refuse your request! The boy, in fact, must never leave the convent, a sacred vow binds us and him."

"Nay, then God forbid that I should force you to break it, and since it is so I renounce the wish though with regret. But I tell you—and remember my words—if ever you find yourselves under the pressure of any need, if you are threatened by enemies, or if for any cause whatever you have occasion to crave any favour from me, send this youth to ask it, and, on my word of honour, whatever you ask shall be granted you. My noble husband will help me to fulfil this promise."

"Yes!" cried the Duke laughing. "By Heaven! your will is my will, Elizabeth, but now keep me no longer from my dinner, for I am almost dead of hunger."

Donatus stepped modestly up to the Abbot. "Father, you granted a dispensation for to-day, but give me leave, I entreat you, to keep myself from flesh and wine."

"Do as you will, if you do not wish for meat do not eat any."

"Yes, I wish for it, but for that reason I would deny myself," said Donatus in a low voice.

"You are right, my son," said the Abbot, and his eye rested with unutterable affection on the boy's pure brow.

The serving brother now brought in the first dish, and the Duchess signed to the Abbot to sit by her side.

"Where are your ladies, Madam?" asked the Abbot.

"I did not bring them in with me to dinner, for they are young and vain, and might disturb the grave souls of your younger brethren. So, if you please, you will send them out some of the dishes."

"I am obliged to you for your forethought," replied the Abbot. "You have saved our brethren much scandal. Let us now say grace."

Grace was said and the meal proceeded; the serving brethren could hardly carry the heavy copper vessels with their savoury contents. All enjoyed themselves but Correntian and Donatus, who sat at the farther end of the table, and would touch none of the tempting food.

When dinner was over the Duchess returned to her ladies; the Duke rose from table, and withdrew to rest for a while in the Abbot's cell; the brethren and the gentlemen sought the shade and freshness of the cool arbours in the garden. No one was left in the dining-hall but Count Reichenberg and Wyso. Wyso, flushed with his intemperate enjoyment of God's gifts of meat and drink, was resting his red face on the table, and snoring loudly. Suddenly he felt himself roughly shaken; he looked up blinking, and saw the Count—

Donatus' father—standing by him.

"What is it—what do you want?" said Wyso stuttering, and he lazily sat up. "Oh, Oh—what a thing is man? Oh! for shame—what have I eaten?"

"Can you still understand what is said to you, in spite of your drunkenness?" asked Reichenberg in a harsh tone.

Wyso snorted and wiped his forehead with his sleeve. "Oh dear! eating and drinking is a glorious gift of God!" he stuttered in a lamentable voice. "But all the time there is a little devil at the bottom called Too-much, and he spoils the pleasure of it."

The Count gave him another shake. "You have too much wit to be quite drunk; listen to me, you can and you must."

A glance shot from Wyso's little eyes, all swelled as they were with drink —a glance at the Count so full of cunning that Reichenberg seized him roughly by the shoulder.

"I believe," he said, "you take me for a fool."

"I believe I have made a fool of you, my Lord; so at least it would seem by your not stirring from my side. But take heart, my Lord! Was it not a splendid dinner?"

"You may henceforth have better dinners than you ever get here; you may come with me to Reichenberg, I will give you my chaplaincy, there is not a fatter living in the country; then you may eat all day whatever your heart desires, and I will furnish your cellar;—only say one single word—"

Wyso cast a sly sidelong glance at Reichenberg.

"You are very wise, my Lord, not to stint your bacon when you want to catch your mouse."

"Well, I should think a good broil of bacon would smell better to a sturdy old glutton like you, than the incense they will burn upon your coffin when fasting and prayer have brought your miserable life to a close."

Wyso slowly winked with one eye.

"Ah!" said he. "Is that what you should think?"

"Tell me, whose child is the young monk whom you call Donatus?"

Wyso's head suddenly fell down on his breast again, and he began to snore.

"Do not pretend to be asleep, I do not believe it. You are a cunning fellow; what, is the living not enough for you! I will give you a nag and a sledge, much finer than those of the Bishop of Chur, goat-skins for shoes, and white lamb-skins—what more shall I offer you? Only say what you desire, and you shall have it."

Wyso looked at him with a cunning glance.

"You are a very clever man, my Lord, but you do not know us yet! Do you really suppose that because I do not turn up my eyes, and drawl out the name of God, nor snap in two from sheer fasting and scourging when any one touches me like a starved cockchafer—do you suppose that I am a gluttonous booby who holds his conscience between his teeth, and can wash away all oaths, all honour, and all fidelity to the Church which he has served all his life long in one unwonted drinking bout? No, my Lord, clever as you are, we have not gone so far as that; you may catch mice with bacon, but not Benedictines; do you understand?" And from loud laughter he fell to coughing till every vein swelled, and he had to wipe his face with the corner of the tablecloth.

"You oily priest—you! You mock me, do you? I will see if I cannot find means to make you speak—" and he unconsciously clutched at the knife in his girdle; his blood boiled with rage and he hardly knew what he was doing.

"What do you want, my Lord?" said Wyso coolly. "Would you like to rip my body up? That would do you no good—I have not written the secret on parchment and then swallowed it!"

Reichenberg stood for a moment speechless from astonishment, then his arm dropped as if suddenly sobered. Reflection came back to him and he understood that his efforts were wasted on this half-drunken cynic.

"The devil only knows what you priests are bound by," he muttered and put his knife back into its ivory sheath.

"Take a little nap, Count Reichenberg," said Wyso, smiling mischievously, "when children have not slept they are always ill-tempered. God grant the dinner may be blest to you! it must have cost us at least twenty gulden, everything included." The Count turned away and walked moodily to the window. "Go now, my Lord, and if you do not want to make an end of me, do not disturb me any more in my noon-tide sleep," said Wyso, laying his arms on the table and his red face on them, and pretending once more to be asleep.

"Count Reichenberg," said the Duke laughing, as Reichenberg went out into the courtyard, his spurs ringing as he walked, "Have you any more progeny in these parts? If so pray tell me beforehand, for your humour is enough to spoil the weather for our journey."

"I have given it up, my lord, and must wait for better times to take the matter up again," answered Reichenberg shortly.

The Duchess now appeared walking between the Abbot and Donatus, and ready to set out on her journey. The maids of honour followed, very ill-pleased, for they had been beyond measure dull, and the Countess Hildegard walked foremost with a broad-brimmed hat and trailing peacock feather on her pretty head in the place of the golden chaplet. She fixed her longing eyes immoveably on Donatus, but he did not venture to lift his gaze to her, and the fine Florentine rouge fell off her cheeks that turned pale with vexation.

The sundial indicated four o'clock in the afternoon; the Duke had had the horses saddled and the outriders had already started. The litter was led out and the Duchess got into it.

"Farewell, my Lord Abbot," she cried once more. "Farewell, Donatus. Bear in mind the words I spoke to you and do not fail to apply to me if ever you are in need of help."

Once more the Duke and the Abbot shook hands. The ladies put their gold-embroidered shoes into their stirrups and sprang, ill-satisfied, into their saddles; the whole cortège moved off as it came, amid the cracking of whips and barking of hounds, shouting, trampling, and hallooing, so that it could be heard long after it was out of sight.

The brethren drew a long breath of relief and went back to their daily duties, the convent servants swept the court-yard clean with large besoms; the scared cat sneaked suspiciously back over the granary roof and all was soon as quiet and peaceful as before.

But a shadow had fallen on the Abbot's soul—a secret anxiety which would never let him breathe again so freely as he did that morning—a vague feeling that all was not in fact exactly as it had been before.

CHAPTER II.

The week was ended; it was Saturday, the eve of the ordination. The busy hands were at rest; harvest was garnered, the doors of the overflowing barns would hardly close. And the church too was to reap her harvest; the seed of faith, which the pious monks had sown, twenty years ago, in the heart of the tiny foundling, had grown fair and strong and full in ear. Donatus had just preached his first sermon before all the brethren; with a beating heart he had pronounced the final "Amen," his eyes flashing with sacred fires; his words had seemed to fly over the heads of the assembled brethren as if winged by the Holy Ghost. Nay, even after he had ended, the echo of his words sounded in the building, and they listened devoutly till it had quite died away. Then the Abbot rose and clasped the young man to his heart,

"Marvellous boy!" he exclaimed. "You came to us, a stranger, and we thought that we knew from whence you came, and believed that we should give to you out of our superfluity and teach you out of the stores of our wisdom. But now you give to us of your abundance and teach us by your wisdom so that we are fain to ask, 'Whence are you?' For it was not in the snows of the wild heath where you were picked up, nor between our humble convent-walls that you received such a divine revelation."

Donatus kissed his uncle's hand. "Oh father," he said softly, "I kiss your faithful and fatherly hand in all reverence, for it is the hand that has led me to that sacred fount whence I have drawn living waters for your refreshment. Nothing is my own, I have received everything from you, and to you I give it back, and whatever I am, that I am through you! I thank you, my father—I thank you, my brethren! To-day—on the eve of that sacred day—the day of my new birth in the Lord—let me offer you all in one word the thanks of a life-time."

And all the brethren—with the exception of that one who was always irreconcilable—crowded round him and grasped his hands affectionately. Aye! it was a rich and glorious harvest to the Lord that they were celebrating that day, and they were proud of it—proud of having brought up the boy so well—proud that they had all been so wise, and so good to him. Then the Abbot led him to the chapel that he might there make his last confession before the holy and solemn festival.

Long, long did Donatus kneel before the confessional, and the iron grating against which he pressed his brow was wet with his tears. For a secret sin had weighed upon his soul these three days past. "Oh father, father!" cried he from an oppressed heart, "I, your son, no longer appear before you pure as I did a few days since. Father! I dread to tell you. My eyes have drunk of the poison of woman's beauty and it courses through my veins like a consuming fire. Always—always—I see before me the light curling hair, the rosy cheeks, the white throat as I saw it when her robe fell back, when she took off the clasp—the whole lovely form and figure. Augustine speaks truly when he says, 'the eyes every day cast us into all sin and crime; what has been created that is more subtle than the eye?' My heart was pure, it harboured no thought but of God; but these eyes, subtle to betray me, have cast me into temptation, they have destroyed the peace of my soul, for even now they still bring the sinful image before my mind again and again. They paint it on the blue sky, on the pillars of the church, on my prayer-book—nay, on the altar-cloth. I see it wherever I turn my eyes, it comes between me and my prayers. Oh father, how dare I, with this snare in my soul, bow my head to receive the consecrating oil; will it not hiss and dry up as if it were poured on hot iron?"

"Calm yourself, my son," said the Abbot. "There can be no virtue without a struggle. To be tempted is not to sin, and I know that during the last three days you have mortified and scourged yourself severely, and for three nights have not sought your bed, but have knelt here on the stones of the chapel pavement. He who does such penance for a small fault must certainly win grace and pardon! But it is true that all sin comes of a wanton eye, and it is written in the VIth chapter of Matthew, 'If thine eye be single, thy whole body shall be full of light; but if thine eye be evil, thy whole body shall be full of darkness.' So guard your eye henceforth, my son, and keep it single, that it may not gaze on forbidden things and that you may continue chaste and pure before God and man."

"Yes, father!" cried Donatus, raising his hand to Heaven. "And I here swear in the sight of all the Saints that I will act in accordance with your precepts. Never again shall my eye rest on the form of woman, never shall it be raised above the hem of her garment where it sweeps the ground, never will I be betrayed into a wish or a desire, or else may God's Grace abandon me, and may He cast me into the deepest damnation."

"Hold, pause, mad boy! That is a curse and not an oath," cried the horrified Abbot. "God's grace is far greater than your sick soul can imagine; He pities even the sinner, and judges him after the measure of his strength, not according to his guilt. Would you prevent God's grace and pronounce your own damnation when He in His eternal and fatherly mercies would most likely pardon you? Whither will your youthful vehemence carry you? Man may not purify himself by blind self-destroying zeal, but by faithful and humble submissiveness, by silent fulfilment of duty, by incessant inward struggles. Take this to heart, son of my soul, and may the Lord pardon you your wild mood; for you will fall again, and many a time, and must often need His saving grace."

It was now late; the door of the chapel closed behind the Abbot. Donatus' confession was over; he remained alone, praying on the steps of the altar.

There is silence in earth and Heaven, not a breeze stirs the air, there is not a sound in the valley below. All is at rest after labour accomplished, waiting for Sunday, the day of rejoicing.

For all the human beings down in the valley belong to the Church, literally body and soul, and when the Church rejoices they too rejoice. A church festival is a festival for them, and they know no others; on the eve of such a festival each one lays him down to sleep full of pious thoughts, so that no sinful dreams may scare away the angels which come down in the night to prepare the souls of the sleepers for the sacred day that is about to dawn. Silent, but busy the guardian spirits soar and float from hill to vale all the night through, till the sun rises and its first rays stream through the little cottage-windows, falling on the closed eyelids that open again to the light. Then the wakers rub their eyes with a wonderful sense of rapture. Sanctification lurks sweetly in their souls though hidden as yet and not fully understood, but in a few hours the consecrated lips of the Church will speak the words of absolution; then it will flash into consciousness like a revelation from Heaven.

The young novice for whom the festival was prepared was still lying on his face before his praying-stool, just as the Abbot had left him the evening before. All the night through he had lain there and prayed without moving, the bridegroom of Heaven; he had triumphed through fervent prayer, and overthrown all that was earthly. He had purified himself in the fires of devotion, and his soul burned and glowed whole and undivided for Her, the celestial Bride. His eyes were sunken, his cheeks pale with watching and prayer. For what prayer could indeed be strong, eager, and fervent enough to merit that grace of which no mortal is worthy, and least of all he—he the weak and erring novice who had scarcely mounted the first step towards perfection.

The morning-sun streamed brightly down on the towers and pinnacles of Marienberg, and threw golden disks of light through the circular panes on to the pavement of the silent chapel. The penitent saw them not, it was still night to him, for he lay there with his face closely hidden in his clasped hands.

The bell rang for matins; up flew the angels from the valley to rouse the bridegroom, and he felt their palm-branches waving over his head. He roused himself from his acts of contrition, and hastened to the dormitory to dress, that he might appear in festive attire as a bridegroom, to receive that invisible Bride to whom his whole heart went forth in rapture.

Meanwhile down in the valley all were awake and busy; all souls were purified from sinful thoughts, and water from the sparkling mountain springs served to cleanse all bodies from the soil of labour. Rosy baby faces came out from the fresh moisture under their mothers' busy hands, like flowers after rain, with their bright shining eyes that looked undimmed upon the world. And many a wrinkle of care and weariness was washed from the brow of the old by the pure wonder-working glacier waters; the every day frock of frieze was exchanged for a decent Sunday dress of stuff, camlet or even better material. The maidens put on white linen gowns—the garb of innocence—not without a happy thrill of veneration, for they were to accompany the bridegroom as bridesmaids, when he walked in procession round the church; then they went out into the little gardens, resplendent with the glories of summer, carefully holding up their white gowns in the narrow paths that they might not sweep the dewy borders; they plucked the ever-sacred elder which must never be wanting at any solemnity whether joyful or sad; a few sprigs of hazel because under it the Blessed Virgin once took shelter in a storm, for which reason it has ever since been blest with peculiar and marvellous powers; then the juniper with its blackberries, from which the wholesome juniper-spirit is extracted, that they burn to counteract the evil spring-mists; tall-grown lilies and humble daisies—which blossomed under Mary's tears when she was forced to fly into Egypt; marjoram, rue, and thyme—potent against all devilry; rosemary, hawkweed, and ground-ivy—all sacred blossoms and plants that grow under fortunate stars. Of these the girls made the festal garlands, carefully selecting the flowers according to their emblematic significance. Last of all they clambered up to break off some boughs of the Rosa pomifera, which first sprang from the innocent bloodshed by a pure maiden; which grew luxuriantly, high up on the wall, and when they tried to pull a branch that was too tough to yield, a sparkling shower of dew was shaken down upon them so that they had to take hasty flight with laughter and clamour as though from some saucy teasing companion. Presently the tramp of horses coming from the direction of Mals broke the morning stillness. One of the girls in the garden farthest from the village peeped over the wall at the approaching party. A lady was riding foremost, she had given the reins to the horse and came rapidly onward, followed by two women on horseback and a few men servants; by her side rode a tall knight to guide and protect her. Close to the wall the lady paused and signed to the astonished girl. "Here—are they not going to ordain one of the monks up at the monastery to-day?" she called out. "Yes—

the bell will ring directly," was the answer.

The lady threw her bridle to the rider by her side and sprang from the horse before a servant could come to her assistance.

"Will you give me your linen frock?" she went on. "I will pay you for it as if it were a royal robe."

The girl laughed; she thought the lady was jesting.

"Come round and let me in," commanded the stranger.

"Dear Countess—I beg of you—what have you taken into your head?" whispered the knight.

"I am going to the consecration of this priest," said the Countess laughing. "But I must not be recognised and shall mingle with the peasant girls—do you understand?"

"But consider, I beg of you, such a proceeding is most unbecoming for you," remonstrated the knight.

"I know best what is or is not becoming for myself. You others must ride off by another way, up to where the ruins of the old fortress of Castellatz will afford you shelter against sun or rain; there you must remain concealed till we proceed on our journey."

"Could we not find shelter in the convent itself," said the knight, "as we did lately with the Duchess?"

The Countess laughed. "And do you think those strict old gentlemen would receive a wandering maid-of-honour—particularly on a day so solemn? You little know them. Do as I desire you, my Lord, and your obedience shall meet with its reward," she added with a meaning glance of such promise as brought the blood to her companion's cheeks for joy.

"Oh! what a beautiful wreath," she exclaimed, as she went to the girl who stood waiting for her. "You must give me that too." Her long train disappeared behind the wall and the little door closed behind her. There was nothing left for the knight but to console himself by doing her bidding and to ride slowly away.

"What can she want up there?" muttered he, shaking his head and carefully leading away her horse by the bridle. If the horse could have spoken it might have told him—it had carried her on its back that day when she had entered the convent-yard and had seen the young monk for the first time.—But snort and blow as it would it could say nothing and the little procession moved off in silence, behind the village, and through the dewy woods up to the lonely hill of Castellatz.

The great bell of Marienberg was already tolling, the bell that was the wonder of the whole neighbourhood and whose mighty voice could be heard afar over hill and valley. The boys of the village had long since gone up to help to pull the rope, for the sound of that bell had a particular sanctity, and besides it was excellent fun to fly up and down hanging to the rope. The maidens with their large bunches of flowers walked properly close to their parents, and their hearts beat in their young breasts with high and holy festival joy. Thus they all mounted the hill in devotional silence, and high up over the church door stood troops of angels with seraphs' wings more radiant than the sun, inviting the people who came pouring in from far and near in their holiday dresses, to enter their Father's hospitable mansion where they were welcomed with incense and myrrh and green garlands.

The floor of the church trembled under the feet of the crowds that flocked in, and those who could not find room within knelt down outside; for a long, long way round the church the eye could see nothing but kneeling figures, and as the people could not come in to the church, the Church went forth to the people. Just as in spring-time the streams overflow their banks or as a too full heart overflows in moments of supreme joy, so the Church in her hour of highest happiness outstepped her walls of stone and poured her blessing on the crowds outside. When the ceremony of ordination and the high mass were over the solemn procession came out under the open heaven. "They are coming—they are coming!" cried one and another; and amid the ringing of bells, the roar of the organ and the jubilant strains of flutes, harps, psalteries and cymbals, out they marched with banners flying, in white surplices; first the musicians, then the choristers, swinging the censers, while the girls formed a line on each side and strewed flowers in the way. Then came the standard bearers with the banner with the image of the Virgin, which was embroidered by the Lady Uta; the deacons with lighted tapers in their hands forming an escort for the Abbot who carried the Host, and gave his blessing to all; last of all the troop of priests with the newly ordained brother in their midst, walking under the protection of the sacred banners that had been dedicated to the convent by pious hands. The kneeling people reverently made way on each side so that the procession might pass through and bestow salvation on all sides. A scarcely suppressed cry of admiration trembled on every lip, as the young priest made his appearance. He wore a long white surplice, the Alb, which was girt round his slim form with a golden girdle; a richly embroidered stole was crossed on his breast and from his shoulders fell the black folds of his cope, while on his head, as signifying innocence and purity, rested the festal chaplet and a wreath of white roses—he came onwards, his head modestly bent, as if the honours of this day were crushing him to the earth.

The girls strewed his path with the flowers and plants of good omen that they had gathered in the morning and his feet fell softly on them, so close was the green carpet they made. But suddenly he started as if he had trodden on a thorn. It was only a word that struck him, and with the word a glance. "What a pity!" one of the girls had said to herself, and as he involuntarily looked round, his eye met a glance so appealing, so touching, from such a lovely face —and that face! he knew it so well. And yet how could it be? A peasant-girl and that haughty maid-of-honour, how could they be alike? But the resemblance was so striking that he stood as if blinded by a flash, struck to his inmost core; only for a second, no longer than it takes to draw a deep breath or to snatch a flower as you are passing by, but his foot stumbled as he walked on, as if he were in too great haste to make up for some long delay. On they went, making three circuits round the hill, each wider than the last, till the very last of the crowd of believers had shared the blessing for which he had waited so patiently.

Out at the farthest edge of the hill, almost at the brink of the precipice, knelt a poor, pale woman with grey hair, miserably clad in rags; she looked longingly up at the young priest as if she were gazing at celestial bliss. And close beside her, also clothed in rags, crouched a being of strange aspect— half child, half girl—with a mass of reddish-brown hair, and large round eyes with golden lights in them under dark brows that met in the middle; eyes that looked dreamily out on the world as if the soul behind them were sleeping still at mid-day, and yet moved in its sleep—as a golden owl spreads its gorgeous plumage in the sunshine while night still reigns to its dazzled eyes, "dark with excess of light." But the strange looking little creature started up as if suddenly awakened, and grasped the woman's arm in alarm. "Look there, is that an angel?" she asked, pointing to the slight figure of Donatus who was coming near them—now close to them, and the child trembled and shrank back, as from some dread apparition, behind her companion, who furtively put out her lean hand, and seizing a fold of his robe pressed it to her lips. "Donatus, my son, do you not know me?" she murmured. The young man looked enquiringly at her. She held up before him a tiny cross of rough wood made of two sticks nailed together, and as if by the waving of a magic wand all the long years vanish, and he sees before him the autumn-tinted arbour where one evening—so long ago—he played at the feet of "his mother," as he had always called her—he sees the little grave-mound, and on it the cross that he himself had made; then they snatch him from his mother's arms, the cruel dark man seizes him, he sees her weep and clings to her knee—and a home-sick longing for all that has vanished, for the warm shelter of a mother's breast—the bitter home-sickness of a life-time is reawakened in his heart.

And then—the procession of lofty inaccessible beings moved on, and he with them! One more unperceived glance round, one hasty look; he saw the poor soul stretch out her arms after him, and then fall forward on her face. He had not been able even to ask her the simple question, "Mother, where do you live and where can I find you?" He saw that she was starving and he could not even carry a bit of bread to her who had nourished him so that he had grown to strength and manhood, to her who had given her heart's blood for him! And two bitter tears dropped trembling from his lashes and fell into the daisies, which had sprung from the tears of the Mother of God as she fled homeless into the desert—and the little flowers seemed to look up at him with answering eyes, and to ask, "For which mother are you weeping?" His eyes fell for shame before the innocent blossoms that he trod under his foot. The unutterable sorrows of the Virgin-Mother were revealed to him in all their greatness through the woes of his outcast foster-mother; what must She have suffered who bore to see the God who was her son slain like a lamb! And could he weep over the sorrows of the nurse who had not borne him—who need not see him die as Mary had seen her divine son—nailed to the cross by cruel hands? "Mary, eternal Mother—forgive, forgive that I could forget Thee for the sake of any earthly woman. My tears are Thine alone—and I could weep for another!—forgive, forgive!" Thus he prayed and raised his eyes in penitence to the floating banner which went on before him, waving in all its splendour in the fresh mountain breeze.

This was the blessing that the daisies had brought him and he thanked the hand that had gathered them. If only it were not the hand of the rosy girl with alluring eyes who had made him start and stumble by her resemblance to the lady who had robbed him of his peace? How much fairer too was she in the simple linen frock than the haughty maid-of-honour in her sinful attire! and the two were so alike, so indistinguishable that it might be easily thought that the peasant girl was in fact the maid-of-honour herself.

Oh! Heavenly Mercy! again these earthly thoughts, and on his festal-day—his wedding-day! For the first time in his life he had passed beyond the shelter of the cloister-walls, and he felt already how the world stretched forth its arms to tempt him—fear and trembling came upon him. Could those arms reach him in the midst of all this wealth of mercies? Woe unto him! for the greater the grace the more fearful the retribution if it were not deserved—the greater the elevation the deeper the fall. "Beware, beware," he said to himself, and a cold sweat of anguish stood in drops on his shaven head under the chaplet of roses.

The circuit was over, and it was high time, for he felt that he was on the point of fainting; the night spent in prayer and scourging, the fervour which had fired his blood were taking their revenge and he was exhausted to death. The procession turned towards the church again, the white-robed maidens forming a passage as before; once more he stood in their midst, he the pure and pious youth who of all men could never divine how the operation of a blessing could turn to a curse in the unhallowed soul! Another glance at that sweet face with its blue eyes would be rapture—but he resisted it. With a beating heart and tightly closed lids he walked on, and only breathed again when he found himself once more within the cool, protecting walls of the church.

The ceremony was over, the crowd was dispersing, all was silent again; he was alone, prostrate before the altar and still wrapt in prayer. But the maidens of Burgeis had stayed to pray too—the old folks would go slowly and they could soon overtake them; they would not go away so long as the young priest remained there. At last he rose and they pressed round him, as round a saint; they were eager to lay the few flowers they had left, at his feet on the altar steps—and the first to touch him—on whom his eye unconsciously fell was she—whom he dreaded and yet longed for! She was standing close to him like a bride in her white dress, crowned with a festal wreath of flowers; half-shy, half-forward, her eye full of intoxicating invitation. How happy must the man be into whose hands she would resign that maidenly crown as now she lay the flowers at his feet! And without knowing or intending it, his lips repeated the words she had spoken before, "What a pity!" But as the faint murmur left his lips it seemed suddenly to grow to an avalanche in his ears and to sound like the crashing thunder-roll that follows it. Could he say this— he, and to-day! And his oath of yesterday! Alas! what was sacred, what was sure? The walls of the church tottered, the flames of the tapers danced before his eyes in wild circles, he felt dizzy, he saw nothing but bewitching eyes, glowing cheeks, and white arms stretched out towards him. He must be steadfast, he must not fall or they will reach him, bend over him, ensnare him with their love-spells. If he can only get as far as the door of the sacristy without falling—if he can reach that he will be safe! But it is so far, so much too far, he can support himself no longer—he falls; there—they are there— they fling themselves upon him, he feels soft arms supporting his head—one glance into the dewy blue eyes that are close to his—. And he is lost—his consciousness drowned in a deep blue sea.

CHAPTER III.

Night had fallen, the noise of the festival was hushed; a lamp still burned dismally in Correntian's cell where he was sitting before a large volume—but he was not reading. He leaned back in his chair, brooding gloomily. Suddenly there was a light tap at the door, and he called out in much surprise the usual *"Deo gratias!"* for the rule of Saint Benedict does not allow two brethren to be alone together in one cell. It must be an extraordinary occasion that could excuse such a breach of discipline. The door opened and there entered, divested of his festal attire, and dressed in a monk's black robe, the newly ordained priest.

"What can you want with me?" asked Correntian with a look of contempt. "What can the spoilt darling of the indolent brethren, who can not sufficiently fill up their time with prayers, what can he want of me whom he always was afraid of?"

"Do not mock me, Correntian," said Donatus with much solemnity, "I want your help. Do not forget that we are brothers."

"Brethren of the order, but not brothers in heart. Leave me. You are sinning against the rules of the order, and you gain nothing by it, for I hate you as much as I love God and the Church."

"It is precisely because you hate me that I come to you."

"Do you hope to propitiate me? Do you think you can befool me with the honeyed slaver of your lips as you have the weaker brethren? Never flatter yourself. I am your enemy, and shall remain so."

"But I tell you again it is not a friend, it is an enemy that I seek. And if you could hate me more than I hate myself, all the more would I seek you."

"I do not understand you."

"Listen, and you will understand. I ask you to be my father confessor because you are the only one who does not love me, the only one who has no pity on me; now do you understand? The others love me too much and they show mercy to me. But I ask for no mercy, I desire only stern inexorable justice—that is why I seek you."

Correntian turned towards him at last, and looked astonished at his agitated countenance.

"Are you so much in earnest?" he said.

"In fearful earnest!" cried the young man with a burst of despair, leaning his forehead against the bare wall. "Oh, Correntian, for years I have hated, abhorred you; only a few days ago I was angry with you because one of the brethren told me that you wanted to blind me, when I was first brought here. Oh! would you had done so, it would have been better for me."

"I understand," said Correntian coldly. "The tempter seeks you in woman's form, and you are weak. The curse will run its course as sure as the stars, and you cannot escape it."

"No, no! for God's sake, not that, only not that. Correntian, I will perform any penance you lay upon me, for none can be too great for my sins. The Lord hath loved me, and drawn me to Him as he did Peter, and like Peter I have betrayed Him at the first cock-crow. I was not faithful even so long as I wore the festal robe, not so long as while I stood before the altar, not so long as the breath which wafted my vows to Heaven! Cast me out into misery as my father did, I am worthy of nothing better, unworthy of the compassion of men. I am mere dust, flung to every wind; cast it out and scatter it to the blast!"

Correntian slowly nodded his head.

"It has all happened just as I said it would.

"You are not made of the stuff from which the Conqueror chooses his fighting men. Begotten among the wanton joys of a frivolous court, nourished at the breast of a wanton woman, your whole breeding has been wantonness. The loving glances that you raise to Heaven are wanton, they wanton with the sun and the blue sky that soothe your senses; the last looks you send after your dead brethren in the grave are wanton, they wanton with the roses that the wind bends over it. Nay, even the gaze you fix in devout prayer on the image of our Mother Mary is wanton, as it looks at the fair woman, at the lovely work of the painter's brush. And how then should it not wanton with the first living woman of flesh and blood who comes before you, as the first woman in Paradise appeared to the first man. You are yourself as fair to see as sin, and pleasure-loving women will everywhere run after you; for the doors by which sin may enter into you and go forth from you, are in truth fair and enticing, and those doors are your love-inviting eyes."

"True, alas! too true. But what am I to do? Can I shut my eyes?" asked the youth.

"Yes," was the terrible answer, and Correntian drew the desk with the heavy Latin Bible towards him, and hastily turned to a page where it was written, "If thine eye offend thee, pluck it out and cast it from thee."

The youth turned pale. He stared at his sinister judge as though a ghost had sprung from the earth before him, a figure so incomprehensible and inconceivable that his gaze could not take it in. The monk sat before the big book, his eyes cast down; the uncertain light of the dingy lamp cast two round shadows in his pale face, like the empty eye-holes of a skull. The youth felt as if he were looking at his own face—corpse-like—eyeless! And yet so calm, so sublime!—and the moon-light that streamed in floated round the bald crown with its narrow fringe of black hair, like a nimbus, in strange, livid contrast to the red light of the lamp. The hour-glass ran calmly on, in its even flow neither hurrying nor tarrying though hearts might throb or break. Minute after minute passed—the deadly horror that filled the culprit's breast had paralysed his tongue. The judge leant back quietly in his chair, and gave him time to grasp the idea—even on the rack an interval of rest is allowed. At last the young man said with quivering lips,

"No man ever yet did such a thing!"

"It is because no man ever did it that it is worth doing."

"Correntian," continued the youth, but so timidly, so softly, as if the air even might not hear, or as if he feared that the sound of his words might rouse a sleeping tiger, "Correntian, why did you never do it?"

But the dreadful creature was not roused. Without moving a feature, without raising an eye-lash, Correntian replied,

"Because I was strong enough to triumph though I could see; the harder the fight the greater the prize."

Again they both were silent. The radiant disk of the moon rose higher and higher over the convent-roofs and towers, and looked in with a tender smile. Longingly, eagerly, as if it were for the last time, and as if he must harvest all the light ere it was yet night, the boy's large brown eyes drank in the soft radiance. No, no, things have not gone so far—not yet. He may yet fight and conquer. He covered his face with his hands as if for protection, as if he saw already the dagger's point that was turned against it. No, he will fight with all the strength of his soul; fight not for his eternal salvation only, but for his eyes too.

Well, he will look neither to the right hand nor to the left, he knows well that now every forbidden glance must bring him nearer to the murderous iron that threatens him. "Do not look that way; you are looking at your death," this is what he must say when temptation beckons him, and will not that terror enable him to conquer?

He fell on his knees before Correntian,

"Time—give me time, a respite," he groaned with pale lips, like a man condemned to death.

"Coward!" said Correntian contemptuously.

"No, do not call me so," cried the youth, striving to man himself. "Send me out into the wilderness to fight for my life with the snow-storm and wild beasts, or out to the land of the Saracens to shed my blood for our Mother Church. You will not see me tremble, but do not ask me to turn the knife against my own eyes; it is our strongest instinct to cherish them, even stronger than to preserve our life. For though I have often heard of men who plunged a dagger into their heart, I never heard of one who thrust it into his eyes. Correntian, have mercy. Grant me sight, to see—not the earth—but the heavens only, that eternal home for which we all strive. The wanderer, who is nearing his final rest, feels his strength revived as he sees the metal star that shines on the tower of his home, or the smoke that rises from the paternal roof, and he struggles with renewed vigour to reach the longed-for goal. How much more must we when we are weary, be refreshed by a glance upwards at the real stars, at the distant clouds which look down upon us from our Father's House. Who does not revive after such a prospect, and hasten joyfully forward? Grant me sight for that, and that only, it draws me on and upwards."

"Sensual fool," said Correntian smiling, "Do you think to reach Heaven by roads that are indicated by earthly light, do you believe that you will lose the way by not being able to see—as an earthly traveller might fail to find his home if he lost his eyes? It is from within and not from without that the light shines which must show you the path to Heaven, and the darker all is without, the brighter it is within; that path lies through earthly darkness. None have trodden it on whose eyes death has not first laid its black shroud; and do you not believe that the heavenly light which can irradiate the night of death can also illumine our deepest earthly darkness? Do you not believe that God the Lord is mighty to open in your soul a spiritual eye instead of the bodily eyes you sacrifice to Him, by which you may discern more and fairer things than any mortal yet has gazed on?"

"Oh Correntian—I do understand you—I admire you, but I cannot imitate you—not yet, not yet. If I could, then I should not be the sinner that I am, and you would not need to judge me. Give me time—for eternal mercy's sake which God himself shows to sinners—for Christ's blood sake which was shed in love for us—give me time."

"It is God that has spoken the sentence, not I—the execution of it is in your power, I have nothing farther to say," and Correntian rose. "Now leave me, for it is unlawful for us to remain any longer in secret conference—this is not the confessional."

The youth stood yet a moment before him, hesitating.

"Correntian—you despise me for not doing what the scripture commands?"

"What do you care whether I esteem you or not?"

"Everything—from this hour everything!" cried the youth passionately.

"You are made of other stuff than I am," said Correntian, with a strong gesture of repulsion. "My whole nature rejects you. If you were a brave warrior, or a wandering Minnesänger, I might esteem you, for you would be what you seem. But as a monk I despise you; for under the mask of self-denial you cloke worldliness and vanity, and the sacred robe you wear smells of the burning of wild and fevered desires. This is the true hell-fire, and fearful is the ravage it may commit if it is not trampled out in time."

"I will trample it out—before God I will!" cried the tortured boy. "Oh! cannot a drop of holy water mixed with the tears of true repentance extinguish the very fires of hell? Repentance and grace—what can the devil do against them?"

"There is but one moisture that can surely and for ever extinguish the flames in which you are burning, and that is the limpid crystal in which all the world is mirrored; and it must be spilt by your own hand, poured over your own cheeks. It is indeed a precious dew, more precious than tears or blood, and because there is no man who would not keep it at the cost even of his life, it is so precious that only the highest crown of martyrdom can requite it! You may win this crown—you may rise out of the pool of sin of which the flames are already licking you, to be a saint before whom everyone shall kneel—I the first, I who have so long despised you; and earth and heaven shall rejoice over you—! And all this bliss you may obtain by one stroke of a knife, guided by a steady hand! Now go and choose."

The door closed on the victim. "Now go—and choose." The young man leaned against the outer door-post unable to go any farther. His heart quaked and a deadly chill ran through his veins like cold lead at the thought of such a choice. The highest crown of martyrdom! What! could he win this with one stroke, without any inward vocation or natural ripeness for it? And even if he were to succeed in snatching this super-sensual extasy in one moment by one hasty stroke, could he bear it and support it worthily? And he must not do the deed for the sake of the crown—what we do for a reward has no value. It must be an act of deliverance, of deliverance from the utmost danger—but was it indeed so with him—was he so weak, so wanting in self-control that he needs must shut himself up in a dungeon of eternal night like a thief to keep himself from stealing forbidden fruit?

And oh! what a dungeon it will be! Will he not be crushed in the narrow confines of such impenetrable darkness—when his eye can see no space before it—neither before it nor around it? Will not all the torments of being buried alive come upon him and stop his breath so that his heart will burst under the pressure of the stagnant blood?

Drop after drop of cold sweat ran down from his forehead. What had he done to deserve a punishment so unspeakably horrible? Was he indeed a thief —had he stolen the forbidden fruit? No, he had not done it, he had only longed for it, and as soon as he was conscious of the temptation he had prayed and scourged himself till it was conquered. Was temptation in itself a sin? Nay else there would have been no Saints, for there was not one of them that had not had to pass through some struggles. Else Father Onofrius of saintly memory would not have needed to burn off during a night of visitation all the fingers of his hands, nor need the holy Founder of the Order, Saint Benedict, have accustomed himself to sleep on nettles! And must he do more than they all had done, to win the crown of the Saints? No, no; this could not be the will of God; it was Correntian's stern severity that lay such fearful penance upon him; and outraged nature, revolting against it, tore him from the spot—in wild flight from the lashing of this superhuman asceticism—away—away—over all the barriers of his tortured conscience. His body, numbed as it were into unconsciousness, bereft of all power of resistance and urged by ungovernable terror, obeyed the impulse—he fled from the door of the terrible monk, as if he might open it again and by one commanding word stay the flight of these trembling vital impulses and compel them to a hideous, suicidal, annihilating struggle—Away—he must away. He fled down the steps with the swiftness of the whirlwind, pushed back the rusty bolt of the court-yard door and flew out into the fresh air, across the yard to the porter's little gate-house. Without pausing to consider, he seized the key of the outer gate from the table, unseen by the sleeping warder—opened the gate and went out into the moonlit night, without stopping to take breath; on and away to the heath—to the harsh mother that bore him—as though he there might find counsel and consolation. Never before had his feet borne him on such an expedition, and yet some unconscious urging guided him on the way that his eyes had so often longingly traced from the turret-window. Up he went, higher and higher, his feet winged by terror—higher and higher as he ascended, rose the guiding light of the broad, bright moon in the pure sky.

His face was streaming with the sweat of exhaustion—fully two hours had gone by when at last he reached the height, and before him lay the wide, level heath, a boundless lake of light. The white mists that floated and broke over it were bathed—soaked—in moonlight, like silvery billows—now rising, now falling—now floating formless, and anon swirling together into fearful wreathing pillars as if they would overwhelm the lonely wanderer in their silent ghostly tide. Light—light, of which the eye might take its fill—across to the invisible distance and to where the great Ortler peak seemed wrapped in sleep and dreams. Light and peace—chaste and divine solitude! the hapless tortured child of man stood still in intoxicating contemplation, and spread out his arms to the splendour now first revealed to him, "Almighty Lord—Thou that art great!" he prayed aloud, "Thou that art merciful! Thou hast shed upon the world this inexhaustible ocean of light, and wouldst Thou rejoice if a miserable worm of earth should bury himself in the night of the grave?" And the words of the Psalmist sprang from his soul to his lips, "O Lord my God! Thou art become exceeding glorious, Thou art clothed with majesty and honour, Thou deckest Thyself with light as it were with a garment, Thou spreadest out the heavens like a curtain, Thou makest the clouds Thy chariot and walkest upon the wings of the wind." And then he hastened on again, farther and farther. Psalteries and harps seemed to sound in his ears while his feet were cleaving the illusory intangible flood that closed over him without wetting him. Thus might Christ have walked dry foot over the waters—for the foundation he stood on was God, and all earthly things seemed to have vanished like the mist.

And yet the Son of God perished on the cross in the anguish of death like a torn up flower, and endured in patience and bore the woes of the whole earth —He who could command the elements, who had need only to spread his wings in order to soar away into the fields of eternal bliss! God, the All-merciful, the Omnipotent, suffered this to happen to his own Son!

Again he stood still, as if face to face with a problem that must be solved before he could go any farther; and he bowed his head, saying, "It must be so, for suffering is our portion; that which we call the hand of fate and which crushes us to the earth, is in fact the hand of God laid in love upon our shoulders—and what we call the anguish of death is but His fatherly kiss that drinks our soul! For so great is He and so small are we that we are destroyed if He do but touch us. And in like manner he gave his only Son, raising him up that we might see and acknowledge what His love is. Woe to him who resists his sufferings—he resists God! O! Father, I will bless Thy hand even if it grind me to powder—I will die in Thy kiss and the agony of death shall be bliss to me."

Suddenly—it seemed to him that the fearful Correntian was standing behind him, saying with freezing scorn, "Thus you swore just now and yet you refuse to make the first sacrifice that the Lord requires of you! Look, He holds out a craving hand that you may lay your eyes in it, and He says graciously, 'Give them to Me that I may keep them for thee till I give them back to thee one day to see more gloriously in Heaven above'—just as a father might take from the hand of a child some dangerous instrument with which it might hurt itself; and you, like the wilful child, cling to the dangerous possession and push away the hand that asks when it might strike."

"Woe is me! Correntian! dark, avenging angel! must you follow me wherever I go?" groaned the tormented soul. "Whither may I fly from you; and where can I save you, my poor eyes, from the two-edged sword that he has planted in my heart there to gnaw in fury against myself."

Then again he heard the threatening voice, "Coward, what do you fear? And what is it after all? You destroy a mirror in which hell focuses its rays— you destroy a transparent vessel, and empty out once for all the fount of those tears which you then need never again shed. One stroke—and it is done; a stroke so slight that a child might drive it home, a hail-stone, a thorn—and you tremble at that?"

Nay, nay, it was not the stroke of the knife, not the flow of blood that he quaked at. In losing his eyes, he must extinguish the sun, moon, and stars, put out all light with this lovely world that is as the very presentment of God— plunge himself into nothingness, an outcast in the midst of the joys of all creation.

The sweat poured down his face, his knees failed him; he sank down in the tall, reedy grass, sobbing as he cooled his burning face in the moist, dewy earth.

END OF VOL. I.

VOL. II.

BOOK II.

MARTYRDOM.

(CONTINUED.)

CHAPTER IV.

The heath lay silent and still, as a mother might refrain from disturbing her weeping son; thus the night wore on; dew fell on the victim's head—he heeded it not; the bright moon paled and the young day painted the first streaks on the rim of the eastern horizon—he saw it not. The icy morning-breeze swept keenly down from the glaciers—he did not stir.

Presently a silvery tinkle sounded across the heath through the morning air; it was the bell ringing for matins at St. Valentine's. This roused the penitent from his torpor, and so strong are the ties of obedience that at the first stroke the simple sound of the bell recalled the whole scattered troop of his vital faculties to their duty. His rebellious defiance, the first impulse of disobedience he had ever known, and which had driven him to his nocturnal flight, vanished like a wild dream. As the bell was ringing up here for matins, he would just have time to get down to mass; for prayers were an hour earlier here than at Marienberg. If the brethren met together for common prayer in the familiar chapel—and he—he were missing!—An unspeakable sorrow came over him—a home-sick longing for the Abbot, for his companions, for the place where he was so tenderly brought up; and without further delay he started up and hastened back to the convent. As day grew broader reflection and composure returned to him, and he was ashamed of his weakness. Without once looking behind him, he left the heath—his mother earth—the earth that had drunk his despairing tears—and walked stoutly on, down to Marienberg again; but in his too great haste he missed his way and suddenly found himself on a thickly wooded hill at one side of the monastery. An extensive ruin stood up among the dark umbrageous branches; he knew where he was now—on the hill of Castellatz, where stood the remains of an ancient Roman castle that had served at a later period as a stronghold of the Trasp family. Huge walls lay fallen one upon the other; walls that had once been inhabited by a defiant race who had borne themselves manfully in many a bloody fight. The labouring peasants still dug out bones of extraordinary size —broad angular skulls of Huns and high narrow skulls of Goths—they had all fought round these old walls and none of them had yielded, only faith had conquered them. When Ulrich, the pious scion of the race, had built the convent at Marienberg because he thought that a House of God was the surest fortress that he could take refuge in, he razed the castle to its foundation so that no enemy of the Church should henceforth make use of it as a bulwark against the people of God.

Thus fell the proud walls that had defied the power of man. The youth trod the soil that had a thousand times been drenched in blood, with a reverent step; peace now reigned over the spot, and silence—a Sabbath stillness. High above his head the shadowy tree-tops rustled as though they were murmuring some long forgotten heroic legend, or a battle-song of which the echoes had long since died away. And he, the peaceful son of that stern mother, the Church—he stood there as one ashamed of his own feebleness, and humbly folding his hands he prayed—"I am no warrior, no hero—I need not fight with the sword or measure the strength of my young limbs, man for man with others—my heroism must lie in obedience. Strengthen me therein, my Lord and God, that I may never fear to fulfil Thy will."

And he went forward again, renewed in strength; here—on this old scene of many struggles, where every blade of grass had sprung from blood that heroes had spilt—here, in this bitter hour, he had grown to be a man and his courage had ripened within him; courage for that hardest fight of all, for the heroism of suffering. His resolve was formed—not in mad terror and haste as before in Correntian's cell, but quietly, clearly, aye joyfully—his resolve to purchase his salvation. He will await the Lord's will, and if the Lord give him the strength to close his eyes against all temptation, he will accept it as a gift of mercy saving him from the worst. If he fall into one single fault more—if he turn one single longing look more on a woman's form—then he will carry out the sentence as it has this night been passed upon him—for then he will know that it is God's will.

A broad sunbeam broke through the bushes which grew on all sides, their tough roots forcing their way between the grey stones; close by his side a bird twittered in a juniper bush which grew out of a ruined window arch. The little creature had its nest there and it looked at him with its keen eyes to see if it had any cause to fear for its brood; and there in the shrub sat the little birds with gaping, yellow beaks clinging in helpless fright to the swaying branches and screaming for their mother. A pretty picture!—How many a mother might have sat, long ago, under this arch, anxiously watching the foe that threatened her nest while the father was far away—at the chase or fighting in bloody feud in some enemy's country for all that was dear to him.

"Oh! sweet and wonderful bonds of love, and faith, and closest ties of blood! can it be that ye are not of God!" The question came involuntarily from the depth of the young man's heart.

And there!—as if ghosts walked in the ruins—there was a sudden movement among the shrubs; a tall girlish figure broke hastily through the boughs and behind her came a boy—a sturdy lad, the wood-cutter to the monastery. He threw his arm round the girl's buxom form and whispered, "And if I ask you where you went so early, what will you say then?"

"To gather berries," she cried laughing and swinging her basket.

"Just wait and I will kiss your lips till they are so red that folks will think you tumbled down among the berries," said the lad. "Come, we will find a quiet place to rest in." And he disappeared again amongst the bushes dragging the girl with him without much trouble.

Donatus hastily turned to go, but suddenly they both gave a little cry of alarm, "O Lord! a wild woman of the woods!" and they fled crossing themselves. Donatus stood still; "What was there? what had frightened the pair so much?" He went towards the spot where they had been sitting; the briars hid a ruined arch-way through which he could look into the desolate castle-yard all overgrown with weeds, and there—wonder of wonders—lay a woman, asleep on a bank of turf artificially constructed and screened by a projection of the wall, that might at some former time have formed a niche where the poor and wretched sat on a stone bench to eat the meal they had begged. But the woman who was sleeping there was neither poor nor wretched; there she lay wrapped in a rich cloak of costly furs and dressed in a green robe embroidered with gold—like a forest-fairy! The playing beams of the morning sun that fell upon her through the whispering boughs, threw a bright light on her cheeks that were rosy with sleep, and the morning breeze blew her soft, silky hair across her dreaming brow, like a film of golden vapour.

Donatus stood as if spell-bound, incapable of going either forwards or backwards—he gazed and gazed and the whole world around him was forgotten. Was it a real living woman—or a trick from hell—it seemed to him that it was the same woman—yes, it was she—! She opened her eyes and a flash of delight, brighter than the morning sunshine sparkled in those eyes.

"Is it you! you?" she exclaimed, springing up. And as Donatus looked into her blue eyes he knew that it was she—she, who, dressed in a peasant's garb, had yesterday so bewildered his senses—she, who so lately had stood before him as the maid-of-honour. And to-day she was here—up here, sleeping on the grass, with no roof over her head—like a wood-fairy—Could she be indeed a real woman and yet capable of such sudden changes? He had never believed in fairies, but could there be such beings? and were they good or evil spirits? And while he thought over all this he stood as if rooted to the spot, regarding the wonderful apparition with astonishment. He saw her sign to him, he heard her call him, and he made no reply—It was not real, it was only a vision, a dream.

"Are you turned to stone? Wait a minute, I will go to you as you will not come to me." The voice was close to his ear and the brilliant figure lightly climbed up the ruined stone-work and in a moment was standing close to him under the arch and bending over towards him.

Those azure lakes, in which, only yesterday, his whole consciousness had been lost, were again close to his intoxicated gaze and pouring their flood of blueness into his soul. It stopped his breath—it ran through all his veins—he leaned against the mullion of the window like one stunned, and gazed and gazed—he could not take his eyes off her—Heaven and earth had faded from his ken—She was too lovely!

"How come you here? What has troubled you so? You are pale and your hair is wet with night dews?" she asked him, softly stroking his tangled curls with her slender white hand.

He staggered as if a flash of lightning had struck him without destroying him; a strange shiver ran through his limbs, a gentle tremor as when the morning breeze shakes the dews of night from the topmost branches of a tree; and nearer, nearer comes the sweet face, and warm breath floats round him— Still he stirs not.

"Do not fix your eyes on me so—as if I were not a creature of flesh and blood," she whispered in his ear. "Put away your sternness; I deserve it of you. For your sake I have passed the night here with my people; here in this uncanny ruin, under the open sky, only to find some way of seeing you again. You have done for me, once for all, with your dreamy face and your severity, and deny it as you will—that which drove you at night out of your narrow cell was my image which pursued you, and while you fled from me you went in truth to seek me! Have I guessed rightly?" And she laid her arm softly round his neck and her lips were close to his ear, while she spoke so that every word was like the breathing of a kiss. He let his head drop and lean against her bosom—he felt dizzy, as if in that instant he had fallen from some towering height. She took him caressingly by the chin, raising his head and looking longingly into his eyes.

"Oh, those eyes! those maddening eyes. Who looks into them is lost! A man who has such eyes as yours can never be a monk!" she exclaimed in a tone of tender jest. "Those eyes give the lie to all your severity—they look fire and kindle fire."

"And that fire shall be extinguished for ever!" cried Donatus suddenly, tearing himself from her arms as if roused from a dream. "It is well for me that you have warned me. With such eyes a man can never be a monk!—it is God himself who has spoken by your lips."

And he fled away as from the City of Destruction, leaving the temptress startled and astonished. She called after him to stay—she implored, she conjured him—in vain. The matins bell was ringing in the valley below, and he heard that above all her tempting; that was a mightier call. Like a hunted deer that can find no shelter, the unhappy man fled back to the sacred cloister walls where only rest and peace were to be found.

The gatekeeper on awaking had sought everywhere for the key in the utmost terror, but he had said nothing for fear of being punished, and as Donatus came in he started up angrily—"Who dared have done it?" But he was pacified as soon as he recognized him.

"You!" he said smiling. "Oh! you may be forgiven, for you are to be trusted."

"Aye, you are indeed to be trusted," said a voice suddenly behind him, and Correntian stood in the doorway of the little gate-house.

"Oh, Correntian!" cried the youth, making a movement as though to throw himself on his breast; but Correntian drew back a step.

"That will do," he said. "You know the rules of our order forbid such caresses. But I repeat it—you are to be trusted—for as you have come back to-day you now will never flee!"

CHAPTER V.

The day was drawing to its close. It was a sultry evening; lead coloured clouds swept across the sky; the swallows flew uneasily round and round the convent towers, their wings widely spread as if the heavy storm rack weighed upon them and hindered their flight. The veiled sunlight threw but a faint shadow on the sundial, pointing to the Roman *VII.*

Vespers were ended, the brethren were walking in the garden, silent for the most part and oppressed by the stormy atmosphere; not a leaf was stirring, even the bees hummed but lazily as they went from flower to flower, inconstant to each and seeking no plunder.

The Abbot detained Donatus as he was going into the house.

"Where are you going all alone, Donatus?" he called out. The youth stood still, but was silent, and the Abbot beckoned him to come back to his side.

"What ails you, my son?" he asked. "You seem to be ill. Your temples are throbbing and your eyes have a feverish wandering glitter; you have refused every kind of nourishment since yesterday—Tell me what ails you?"

"Nothing, father; I am quite well."

"Then some new temptation assails you, my son; for it is of no avail to tell me that all is well with you as usual," said the Abbot, and he drew him aside into a retired vine-alley. "You cannot deceive me, for I have brought you up from the time when you were four years old. My watchful eye has been upon you night and day, in joy and in grief, in health and in sickness. I know every line of your face and mark every shade that passes over it, and you have become so completely one with me that every throb of your heart is felt in mine, and every burden that weighs on your soul oppresses mine. You cannot deceive me, and I am filled with a cruel forboding, as if some fearful evil were lowering over your darkened brow."

Donatus breathed painfully under the Abbot's searching gaze; he was like a sick man who conceals his sufferings the longest from those that love him most. His eyes fell; an unutterable and tender sorrow came over him for the faithful guardian whom he purposed to betray in so frightful a manner as soon as sleep should have closed his watchful eyes.

"You are silent! You are concealing some evil from me?" continued the Abbot. "For I never before saw you thus. I am not satisfied at your having had so much private talk with Correntian since yesterday—and indeed one of the brethren declared that he had seen you steal at night to Correntian's cell!

What can you two have to say to each other?—Why, he has been your mortal enemy ever since you were old enough to think! How is this! when such an unnatural alliance is formed there must be some terrible trouble or dividing of heart at the bottom of it. You are young and generous, you indeed may forget and honestly forgive—but not Correntian—never. He is a rock on which many a poor heart has struck and bled to death when only a loving hand was needed to rescue it. It is this hard nature of his that alienates him from us all, and it is with the greatest anxiety that I see you falling into his power."

Donatus walked on in silence and reserve by the side of the Abbot, who waited in vain for his answer.

Presently the Abbot stood still, as if he would force the young man to look at him. "My son," he said, "Do you remember the evening when that sinister man tore you from your nurse's lap, and how you struggled and screamed till I came and took you in my arms? Do you remember how you threw your arms round my neck and clung to me, and how I myself put you into your little bed, and you would not leave go of my hand till you had sobbed yourself to sleep? This heart of mine is still the same as when you found refuge in it, these arms are the same as those to which you then ran for protection; throw yourself into them again, my son, and shake off the burden that torments you, so that I may once more protect you against the powers of darkness that threaten you."

Donatus could bear it no longer; tears rushed to his eyes, and crying out, "My father, my dearest father!" he threw himself into the Abbot's arms. The two men stood clasped in a mute embrace, but at this instant of sacred silence Correntian came hurrying up.

"For God's sake," he cried, "go in! The storm is just over our heads, and it will be a fearful one," and he dragged them apart as if in dutiful anxiety for their safety.

They went into the house in silence. It was now bed-time; the younger brethren went to the dormitories, the elders each to his own cell.

"Good night, my son," said the Abbot, and his eye once more rested on Donatus with a mournful and searching glance. "Remember my words! And one thing more: Go up to brother Eusebius, and see if he needs anything. I am sorry that he should have felt too feeble to-day to come to table. Besides a talk with the wise old man will do you as much good, as a cooling draught." Then he called to the other brethren, "See, all of you, to the fires and lights, it will be a dreadful night. At midnight we perform the mass for the soul of the Lady Uta; see that you none of you oversleep yourselves!"

Up in Eusebius' cell, as the Abbot had desired him, sat Donatus, opposite to his old friend in the dim light from the little window; the lurid clouds swept on in endless succession, grey on darker grey.

Eusebius was weaker than usual, but he was sitting up half-buried in books, parchments and instruments, writing-materials, rulers, compasses, and what not. For of all the fields over which the human mind had roamed there was not one which father Eusebius, in his quiet cell, had not explored and investigated. While he talked Donatus' fingers were unconsciously playing in their fevered restlessness with the thousand objects that were lying about, and thus his hand fell on a large pair of compasses; they were half open, and the two sharp points were parted. He took them up as if absorbed in reflection, he closed his eyes and laid the two points on his eye-lids.

"I could easily put my eyes out with these," said he thoughtfully. "Both at once with one blow. With a knife or dagger I should have to strike twice, and even if I had the courage for the first—for the second never—no never!"

Eusebius took the compasses out of his hand, and laid them on the table. "What mad words are you saying! What has put such hideous ideas into your head?"

Donatus looked wildly at him; his eyes glared strangely in the gloom that had gradually spread itself in the little room.

"I have often thought lately that a man who would fain avoid all love must put his eyes out," he said in a low and strangely tremulous voice, like a broken lute jarred by the wind.

Eusebius shook his head slowly and disapprovingly.

"Of what use would that be?" he said. "It would come all the same. However sadly a man may picture it to himself, and fancy he has hedged himself in from it—man's wit and man's presumption always succumb to it; nay, even if he tore out his eyes and stopped his ears, it would be of no avail. Who would dare suppose he could prevent a tree from budding and sprouting in February? He can pull off the leaves, and cut off the branches, but he can not stop the rising sap that is working within. And it is not the devil that stirs the sap in the tree, and the blood in man—no, it is all wonderfully ordered by God the Lord who has made us thus. And though one of us may have succeeded in resisting the law of nature, it is only by some special grace of God who has stood by him, and helped him with particular favour; but that which he has vanquished in the fight is not the devil, but his own weakness which hindered him from freeing himself from the universal law to which all creatures are subject."

Donatus started up in horror. "Woe is me," he cried, "I may not listen to you! What spirit possesses you, your very words are a crime, God help you!" And snatching up the compasses with which he had been playing, the boy fled from the room.

"Donatus!" called the old man, rising hastily to follow him. But a strange dizziness came over him, and he sank back in his chair; his hands and feet alike refused their service. The door of the cell had fallen shut, the old man was alone with his books and manuscripts. He looked up in silent resignation at the wide and stormy heavens. The winds were rushing and roaring round the tower, nearer and nearer came the storm—but to the old man it seemed as if all that surrounded him were passing into the far, far distance. Farther and farther away sounded the rolling thunder, and the outlines of the narrow walls that enclosed him grew fainter and fainter. They were parting asunder, vanishing away, these earthly walls and bonds, and infinity lay before him.

The hour-glass on the table had run down; it was the hour at which he was wont to turn it, and as the last grain of sand ran through, the old habit made him try to put out his hand; but the hand fell helpless by his side—the sand had ceased to run. The thunders paused, the winds held their breath, the light was extinguished. "And yet it will come!" he whispered with his last sigh, and the liberated soul soared away into the empyrean without pain or struggle. There he sat silent and peaceful—the lonely dreamer, his head sunk on his breast, his hands folded—sleeping the eternal sleep.

A thunder-clap came crashing down on the convent, such a clap as shook the old building to the foundations, and all that were living crossed themselves in terror; only the still sleeper up in his solitary tower will wake and tremble no more. The brethren had all shrunk away to their beds; Correntian only remained without, calmly defying the uproar of the elements. Suddenly there was a repeated hasty and terrified knocking at the convent-gate; the porter did not hear it for the roaring of the storm, but at last it caught Correntian's ever watchful ear. He went in and opened the door; outside there stood a strange child clothed in rags; her beseeching eyes shone with a weird brightness in the darkness, the storm and rain tossed her waving hair and it shone with a reddish gleam in the fitful flashes of the lightning.

"Where is Donatus?" asked the trembling child.

"Donatus!" exclaimed Correntian in horror. "Are the messengers of Hell sent for him already? Away with you—your eyes shine in the darkness like an owl's—your feet shall not cross this sacred threshold!" and he made the sign of the cross over her; but she folded her hands over her innocent bosom and threw herself at the priest's feet.

"My lord! my lord! my mother is dying, she was Donatus' nurse—she asks to see him; just once more grant her this last comfort."

Correntian pushed her wildly from him, "His nurse—is she there in spite of our prohibition? And has that snake engendered another snake that the race may not die out? Away with you, leave clasping my knees, or I will crush you like an adder."

"My lord! my lord!" cried the child wildly. "My mother is dying down there in the wood—without shelter—in the storm and rain. Pity, oh, pity—Donatus, where is he? Oh Donatus!" The storm carried away her words, the door closed with a loud clatter; no one could hear her cry of anguish, for it could not reach the monks in the dormitory, above the rushing and roaring of the rain in the dragon-headed gargoyles.

"Alas! and woe!" rang through the night. "Woe!" howled the storm from the forest as though with a human voice—"Woe!" groaned the whole terror-stricken earth under the crashing thunderbolts which fell clap upon clap in inextinguishable fury, rending the trees to their roots.

Dumbly and silently the old stronghold of faith stood on the giddy height, facing the unchained elements with its stony brow; and the uproarious strife raged round about it, as if it were bent on tearing it from its rocky foundations and hurl it into the roaring abyss. What is the meaning of all this fury and tumult, why have the whole rage and might of the elements concentrated themselves on this spot, why does the hand of Terror knock so fearfully at these silent gates, of all others, to-night?

They are the agonised cries of Nature, the eternal mother, over one of her children who this night is outraging her and himself; who is struggling in solitude with the very madness of self-annihilation, with none by to pity him. She rouses the brethren from their sleep, she thunders in their ears, she shouts to them in the wailing of the storm and in torrents of tears, "Rise up—save your brother!" They hear the warning indeed, but they understand it not; they start in horror from their beds and cross themselves, "Help, oh Lord! What is Thy purpose with us?" They pray in impotent terror and are full of some unspeakable fear, but they know not whence it came nor how it will end.

Now long drawn groans came up from the forest, each deeper than the last, striking as it were at the very roots of the building, collecting their forces for one mighty blow, one overwhelming shock. The house stood firm, but the beams groaned and the boards cracked under the pressure; the lime fell from the walls with a dull crack and the lead and tiles torn from the roof were flung with a rattle like hail on the stones of the court-yard and on the garden-beds, crushing and devastating everything. The fiery tongues from the clouds licked the spires with unsated greediness, discharging their electric tension with a deafening roar; and as if the waters of the abyss would fain extinguish the fires of heaven, they rushed in wild and foaming torrents from the mountains into the valleys, dragging the uprooted trees with them in their fall and dashing against the rampart-like wall as if they were Nature's battering-rams.

"Forgive us our trespasses as we forgive them that trespass against us!" prayed the brethren who had gathered together; a little trembling flock in the middle of the dormitory. Suddenly one of the brethren grasped his neighbour's arm, "Look," he exclaimed, "up there in the eastern turret-window—do you see a light?" The monks could hardly look up, for at every instant the sky was all aflame and they hid their faces in fear. But it was true, they all saw it now—up in the window of the Lady Uta's room there was in fact a dim light. Was it a fire? had the lightning struck it? No, for it remained always the same. The brethren were seized with superstitious horror; was Lady Uta's ghost watching over her bequests—or was it Stiero the strong, now long since dead, and of whom it was said that he always walked when all the elements of nature were in revolt? The monks stood gazing helplessly, hardly daring to breathe, and half-blinded by the flashes. Should they call the Abbot? should they let him know? At this instant there was a blast so mighty that it seemed as if every joint and seam must part—as if the very earth must be blown out of its course, and they heard a crash on the pavement of the court-yard, while the windows flew open and the vessels and utensils danced on the shelves. It was the copper roof of the eastern tower that had fallen; the light in the turret window was extinguished. The monks fell on their knees, mechanically stammering out Paternosters. But what was that? Was it not a cry of pain from the tower? The brethren held their breath to listen, they convulsively clasped their rosaries in their cold hands and pressed them to their trembling hearts. There it was again—their blood ran cold, a long drawn cry of anguish was audible above the howling of the storm and the roaring of the waters.

At this moment the door was flung open and the Abbot rushed in, his lamp in his hand.

"Did you not hear—" he asked. "Was not that a cry from the eastern tower?"

"Did you hear it too?" whispered the monks, their voices choked with terror.

"Who can it be? There is no one there, the tower is locked up?"

"What a night!—hark—there, again!"

"But now it sounds from the forest."

"We cannot distinguish in this uproar of noise."

"Very likely it is some wild animal hurt by a falling tree."

"No, no, it is the spirits wailing in the air—a bad omen!"

"Heaven help us—what evil can it bode?"

"Lord, have mercy upon us!"

The Abbot meanwhile had glanced round the room.

"Where is Donatus?" he said, "his bed is empty."

Donatus—in the general panic no one had missed him.

"Donatus—my son, my child!" cried the Abbot, struck by a horrible suspicion. "Look above, below, every one search the whole house for him."

And foremost of them all, driven by some inexplicable dread, the Abbot rushed out into the storm, bareheaded, heedless of the pelting of stones and tiles, past the lofts that were threatening to fall, across to the eastern tower—the door was locked.

"The key! see for the key of the eastern tower," he ordered across the dark court-yard; no one had followed him but Correntian; the rest stood scared in the door-way—their lamps blown out.

Correntian hurried out to the gate-house. The key was gone! beyond a doubt Donatus had locked himself up in the tower.

"Hapless, struggling child!" cried the Abbot. "What demon is tormenting you that you must fly up there and tell your woes to the winds." And for the first time in his life he turned upon one of the brethren in anger; in the glare of the lightning that relieved the darkness and revealed them to each other, he fixed his eye piercingly on Correntian.

"I fear, I fear,"—he said, "that you must have a heavy burden on your conscience and that the cry of anguish of that poor tortured soul is gone up to God against you."

Correntian stood before him, dogged and invincible, "I only did my duty."

"Donatus!" cried the Abbot again. "Donatus, come down, open the door to me, your father—Donatus—my son."

No answer, all was still; it seemed as though the very storm had paused to listen; but in vain—nothing was moving.

"He cannot hear us call," said Correntian. "The storm roars too wildly round the detached tower; leave him, it is midnight and time for the service for the dead. The bell will soon ring and he will hear that. When the bell calls him he will come—I know him well." And he went back into the house.

The Abbot followed him with a deep sigh.

"My poor child! God help him to be victorious."

The storm had exhausted its fury and had swept away towards the heath at Mals. The pauses between the lightning and thunder were longer, the rain did not lash the windows so furiously, and the bell for the mass in memory of the Lady Uta tolled solemnly above the now distant tumult.

The monks assembled in the chapel in grave silence, for they were not yet free from the spell of the night's alarms, and went down into the crypt or founders' hall.

All were there but Eusebius and Donatus.

Eusebius was now often absent, excused by reason of his advanced age—but Donatus had never before been missing. The Abbot delayed beginning the solemnity, his anxiety increasing with every minute; the bell had long ceased to toll, still Donatus came not.

The brethren looked at each other in silence; none dared to increase the Abbot's trouble by uttering a word—but it was a mystery to every one. In vain did they strive to collect their thoughts for devotion. Each one secretly felt his heart beating wildly, he himself knew not why. Hark—what was that? A rustle—a sound of doubtful shuffling steps; slowly and hesitatingly they came down the stairs—slow, dragging steps like those of Fate—some one was feeling the way painfully along the wall—feeling for the latch of the door. Full of an unaccountable horror all the monks fixed their eyes on the door; it opened and a figure entered—pale and stark as death, like a walking corpse— there was a scream of horror, for it was Donatus, his face streaming with sweat and blood—eyeless.

CHAPTER VI.

A lonely rider was at this same hour of the night traversing the storm-beaten forest that lay below Marienberg. His cloak clung dripping round him; his horse's hoofs were inaudible on the soaking moss and he rode noiselessly forward towards a red, glowing spot in the distance, which looked to him like a little heap of burning charcoal shining dimly through the damp night air. He was not deceived, and a woman close by it lay with a child who vainly endeavoured to keep up the smouldering fire. The woman was lying on the bare earth, the child knelt close by, and the rider was startled as he caught sight of her face lighted up by the ruddy glow, and her large eyes which reflected the flame she strove to fan with her breath.

At this instant the midnight toll sounded out from the tower on the mountain, the woman raised her arm and shrieked in a piercing voice, "Aye! ring away! If there is a God in Heaven that is your knell. On the heath, in the wilderness, in the wood—thus may you all die as I am dying; may your house fall as my hovel fell. May despair rend your hearts, and remorse scorch your brains as they have mine."

"Mother, mother, do not curse, it is a sin, you yourself said so," implored the little girl, clasping the woman's outstretched hand with a soothing gesture.

"It is only what they have done," complained the woman. "Oh, I was pious and good like you once; I would have been content if only they would have let me see Donatus for one hour."

The rider pulled up his horse behind the bushes, and dismounted to listen.

"Only one hour," she went on, "in return for a whole ruined life-time! But even that they would not grant me—not even that. No, let me be, I have nothing but curses that I can fling at their heads; give me an arm to strike with, and I will spare my words."

"Woman," cried a voice suddenly behind her, "here is the arm you need to carry out your curse, I am just in the mood for such a task!"

The child started up in alarm at seeing the grim looking man, and fled to the other side of her mother.

The woman gazed thoughtfully at the stranger; something in his face struck her, but she could not tell what. The rider tied up his horse, and flung himself down on his cloak by the woman's side.

"Your rage is against the monks of Marienberg; what have they done to you?"

And the woman told him at full length all that had happened from the beginning, how she had lost her child and her husband for the sake of the strange infant, and how she had loved him so much all the same, that she would willingly have sacrificed everything if only she might have clasped him once to her heart, and have made her last confession to him. But not even that would they grant her, a dying woman. They had driven the little girl from the door, and called her an adder. Ah! and there was a great weight on her mind about the girl too, and now the child must perish miserably; for when she was dead there would be no one to care for her in all the wide world.

The stranger looked absently at the child; he paused for a moment as if the large, tawny-brown eyes with their dark, meeting brows had struck him; but another idea possessed him wholly.

"And you do not know who the boy was that you nursed?" he asked almost breathlessly.

"No, they did not tell me."

"Do not you know either where he was brought from?"

"Yes," said the nurse, "a lay-brother of Saint Valentine's was there when I went, who had brought him to Marienberg."

The man vehemently grasped the woman's wasted arm.

"Do you not remember his name?"

"I do not know it, my lord, no one told me. But he was very old, and must be dead long since."

"Saint Valentine's," repeated the stranger between his teeth. "Indeed, Saint Valentine's—there perhaps I might find a trace," and he started up in haste to remount his horse; but the woman clutched him by the sleeve,

"My lord, my lord," she cried, "for God's sake! you will not leave us in our misery—and my child, the poor orphan—My hour is near—Have pity on the child or she must starve."

The knight flung a gold-piece into the sick woman's lap. "Here, that is all I carry with me in case of emergency; now, keep me no longer."

But she clung to him in her dying agony, "Gold is of no use to us, what does the child know of gold; wicked men may take it from her, and then she will be as helpless as ever. Shelter, my lord, and protection for the innocent! Oh, my lord, she is not my child, she is a child of sin; but the child is pure, my lord, as pure as the dew, as innocent as the fawn in the forest. I have brought her up in decency and the fear of God. Take charge of her, she is of noble blood; her mother was a lady, and the knight, her husband, was so long away in the field that she thought he was dead; then she fell into trouble. And the child's father—God save his soul—was a minnesänger at Count Albert's court, and the child has come by many gifts through him; she can sing and is full of pretty tunes, and hidden things are revealed to her. You would find her a joy to you, my lord."

The dark-looking man struck his hand against his forehead with a loud and scornful laugh.

"It serves me right! I cast out my own flesh and blood, and in exchange I get a bastard; now I am searching again for my own outcast child, and again, oh! mocking Fate, you fling the bastard scornfully into my lap. Ay, Thou art just, Thou severe God, and Thy ways are past finding out."

The woman and the girl looked in alarm at the powerful man; but after a pause he spoke more calmly,

"I am the Count of Reichenberg," he said, "whose guilty wife gave this child into your charge."

"Great God!" cried the nurse, crossing herself. "Do not harm her, my lord, she could not help it."

The count's gaze gradually softened as he looked at the girl's childish beauty.

"No, you cannot help it. You have your mother's eyes, but they are not false like hers. I forgave her on her death-bed, and how could I be cruel to you? By Heaven, the child bewitches me as her mother did before her. Be off with your sick nurse there to Reichenberg; you shall no longer wander about homeless. Give this ring to the warder as a token that I have sent you, and that he is to take you in to the castle, and take care of you. I shall come after you later, but first I have important work to do in this neighbourhood."

"Thank you, my lord, and may God reward you," cried the nurse, who was almost bewildered by such unexpected good fortune; "I cannot get so far, for I feel my end is near, but the child—I will send her to you at once."

But the little girl shook her head, and threw the ring from her.

"No," she said, "I will not go with the strange man, I will stay with you, mother."

"Child, do not be foolish; when I am dead, what then?"

"Then I will stay with the angel, he will take care of me."

"Oh, you silly child!" wailed the woman. "He cannot help you, for he is only a man, and is himself shut up a prisoner among the monks there."

"Then I will go to the blessed maidens that they may set him free," said the child confidently.

The Count had not been listening to the last words; he had thrown himself on horseback and set off again—away through wind and weather, straight across country, over roots and broken branches in fevered haste, to the heath of Mals, and he raised his fist threateningly at the convent on the height where the gleaming windows shone far out over the dark scene around.

Up in the convent all were astir. The monks were assembled for a solemn and fearful task; they were sitting in judgment on a breach of their holy rule—the crime of self-mutilation—of which Donatus was guilty.

This was *culpa gravis*, punishable by the heaviest penance that could be inflicted.

One word could absolve the criminal; he had only to say that one of the priests had ordered the deed, that he had done it in obedience to a superior command; but this word he did not speak, for his guilt would then fall on that other one, and he would have none but himself bear his cross.

And he, that other who could save him, he spoke not. The lips of both remained sealed. If Donatus had still had eyes, the cruel instigator of the crime might well have blenched before the silent appeal with which his victim turned to him; but those eyes were gone which might have spoken, and the bloodstained bandage concealed even the unspoken anguish stamped on the pale brow.

The enquiry was ended, the sentence only was wanting; the monks stood in a half-circle round the Abbot who supported himself on the arms of his chair; his hands trembled, his face was as pale as death. The younger brethren covered their faces and wept; Donatus waited in humble resignation for the sentence to be pronounced.

Three times the Abbot rose, three times his voice failed him—at last he spoke.

"Seeing that the holy rule of Saint Benedict strictly forbids any follower of his to lay violent hands upon himself, in that he is no longer his own but belongs to the holy Church, and, as such, may not injure himself any more than any sacred vessel, garment, altar, temple or whatever else is the Church's property—

"Seeing that you, unhappy child, have been instructed and indoctrinated in that holy rule and have wittingly sinned against it out of your own pride of judgment as to what is best, and have thus rendered yourself unfit to do the Church that service for which God had especially chosen you—

"Seeing that by the commission of this deed, you have rebelled against the will of your spiritual and temporal superiors and so are guilty of the gravest disobedience—

"We declare and pronounce that, as a terrible example to the votaries of all Orders and at all times you—" here again his voice failed and he had to draw a long breath, "that you shall be imprisoned to all perpetuity in the Convent dungeon."

Donatus bowed his head in silence—the Abbot sank back in his chair and clasped his hands over his face which was bathed in tears. One single inarticulate sob broke from all the conclave; only Correntian stood unmoved and his eyes were fixed upon the prisoner. A long silence followed; over their heads stared the fixed stony face of Duty—that pitiless divinity—suppressing every outward expression of the sorrow that filled their shrinking hearts.

At last the Abbot rose and turning to Correntian with an awful and reproachful look,

"You, Correntian," he said, "may fill the office of executioner and lead him away—for not one of us could bear it."

And, just as he had long ago snatched him from his nurse's arms, ruthlessly and without delay Correntian grasped the blind man's arm—to tear him from the last hearth of humanity that was open to him—from the midst of the brotherhood. Donatus obediently turned to follow him.

"Forgive us!" cried the sobbing group of monks, "We only do our duty."

The blind man spread out his arms as though he would clasp them all in one embrace, "If I had eyes to weep, my brethren, it should be for you all and not for myself."

The Abbot could contain himself no longer; with a cry of anguish he flung himself upon Donatus; "My son, my son—why have you done this to me?"

The youth sank into his arms with unutterable affection and they stood in close embrace through a long silence.

But even these loving arms, which had once rescued him from Correntian's iron grip, could not save him now; that iron hand tore him from them and led him away—an unresisting prey. Correntian remained the victor.

"Let us mourn and fast for forty days, my brethren, as for one that is dead," said the Abbot to the conclave. "And send for brother Eusebius—why is he not here?—He must bind up that poor boy's eyes to the best of his skill—the law does not forbid that," and as he spoke he tottered and put out his hand to cling to the man nearest to him—the strong man's powers were spent and the brethren had to support him, or he would have fallen.

Correntian led his victim down the slippery dungeon stair; two of the convent servants followed him with hand-cuffs. They reached the damp vault in silence. Correntian led his prisoner to a bed made of a heap of straw in a corner, close to which, riveted to the wall, were the rings to which he was to be fastened.

"Chains too?" said Donatus; and in the tone in which he spoke these two words there was something which penetrated even Correntian's hard heart to that secret human core, which up to this minute no lament, no dying sigh of any mortal had ever touched; but he strangled the emotion before it found birth, and said calmly, "So it must be."

"If it is possible," said Donatus humbly, "spare me that—Yet, not my will but thine be done."

"So it must be," repeated Correntian, and the lad was silent. Only once he pressed his hand on the bandage which covered his burning sockets, then he submissively held out his trembling hands for the chains; it was quickly done, the irons were riveted and the servants went away. The two monks were alone.

"Now you have indeed preserved yourself from temptation!" cried Correntian, as Donatus dropped his fettered hands without a sound of lamentation passing his lips. "Martyr! open the eyes of your soul, the crown is hanging above your head!"

Donatus fell on his knees before the terrible monk and folding his weary, iron-bound hands as if in prayer, he exclaimed, "Now, now, I understand you."

"Donatus!" cried Correntian, as if his lifelong torpor was suddenly unpent in a lava-flood of extasy—his eye flashed, his pulses throbbed, his breast heaved—"At one word from me you would have been exempt from this fearful punishment—and I was silent. Donatus, tell me, have I been your salvation or your ruin?"

"My salvation and I thank you!" groaned Donatus, and a terrible smile of bliss passed over his drawn lips; he feebly grasped Correntian's hands; the damp walls, like an open grave, echoed back his words: "I thank you."

Correntian hastily threw his arms round the unconscious boy as he sank to the ground; for the first time in his life a human form rested on his breast, and with the first rays of morning, which fell on him through the slit in the wall, high above him, the first ray of love sparkled in the stern master's eyes and was merged in the martyr's crown that shone on the disciple's head.

BOOK III.

GRACE.

CHAPTER I.

Morning dawned slowly over the heath of Mals and the dismal tolling of the bell of Saint Valentine's proclaimed far and wide that one of the brethren lay at the point of death. It was brother Florentinus, the grey-haired watchman, who for more than half a century had lived in constant warfare with the deadly and inhospitable powers of the moor, and whose tender and protecting hand had snatched from them their storm-beaten victims. How old he was no man knew—but it must be near on a century; yet Death found it no easy task to crush the life that had defied a thousand snowstorms. He lay close to the chimney, breathing painfully, his dim eyes fixed on the dingy painting of Saint Valentine. His withered body was like a dried up mummy, his hands and feet were already stiff and cold, but his hardly-drawn breath still fanned the trembling flame. It seemed as though he were waiting for something; and yet what should he be waiting for? He had closed his account with the world.

The lonely rider was scouring across the moor from Burgeis at the maddest pace to which he could urge his horse. He too heard the knell, and without accounting to himself for the impulse, he struck his spurs into the horse that started forward with great leaps—he felt that he *must* reach the Hospice before the tolling ceased; before the unknown life was extinct that was in that hour wrestling with death.

The dying man listened to the beating of the hoofs and turned his eyes to the door.

"He is come," he said in a faint, hollow voice.

"Who?" asked the brethren who knelt round him in prayer.

At this instant there was a violent knocking at the door; the old man raised himself with a wonderful exertion of strength.

"Open quickly," he said. The astonished brethren obeyed him, and in walked the rider clanking and clattering, straight up to the dying man; it was in vain that the brethren signed to him to be silent and not to disturb the dying man's rest.

"You are old enough—maybe you are he!" cried the Count roughly, and he threw himself on a stool by the old man's couch. "You must not die—you must speak with me."

The old man bowed his trembling head. "It is well, it is well," he muttered feebly, "I have thought of him a great deal—and it was a sin. We meant it well —but we all must err."

"Do you know me?" asked the knight in astonishment.

"Aye, aye—you will find him again—I know, I know." The Count began to be frightened at the old man.

"How do you know?" he asked.

"She has appeared to me twice—again this very night and announced to me that you would come to fetch him."

"She—who?" asked the Count with increasing emotion.

"She, the Countess—the angel of Ramüss."

"Do not make him talk," said one of the brethren, coming up to the Count. "What good can the wanderings of a dying man do you?"

"Silence!" thundered the Count so loud that the sick man started, "Let him speak or I will make you all dumb for the rest of your days."

The brethren stood helpless and consulting each other in whispers.

"Did you know the Lady of Reichenberg?" asked the Count, bending over Florentinus.

"Did I know her—Why she lay here, where I am lying—she and the baby-boy."

"The boy?" repeated the knight, and his heart laboured sorely; but he controlled himself to listen to the sick man, whose breathing grew weaker and weaker, that he might hear the words he might speak before it had altogether ceased. "The boy—where have you put him?"

"Up there—at Marienberg—they kept him—but the mother has given me no peace—three times has she come to me and said, 'Give him his son again'—"

The last words grew fainter—the Count felt as if his head would burst with its throbbing. He bowed his ear over the dying lips, they still moved mechanically—

"Do not die—do not die," he implored him in anxious expectation—"Only say his name—the name they gave the boy in the convent—"

The dying man's lips moved and muttered as though to say "Do—" but he could no more, his breath failed him. The Count took him in his arms and raised his head—he would not let him die—he must pronounce that name on which all depended.

"Don—Don—" he stammered, and his very pulses stood still while listened.

"—nat—" murmured Florentinus with a last effort.

"Donatus!" cried the Count, no longer master of himself.

The dying man bowed assent—a peaceful smile overspread his face and his head fell back—no more now than a noble marble image.

The Count's blood boiled as he looked at the peaceful corpse; it mounted to his forehead and hands till his veins stood out like cords, and his eyes were ominously blood-shot.

The brethren were in the utmost terror. "He was talking nonsense, my Lord, do not believe what he said, he had long been childish." But it was of no use. The Count, without vouchsafing them a glance, walked straight out of the house, flung himself on horseback and rode madly off, the blood trickling from the flanks of his tired beast—towards Marienberg.

"Oh! luckless day!" cried the Abbot, when the brethren who had gone to seek Eusebius brought down his dead body from the western tower.

"Oh! luckless day!" was echoed by the brethren, who from the upper hall had seen a rider spring from a horse which fell down dead at the door. It was Count Reichenberg. Grim rage sat on his brow, grim rage had ridden the noble horse to death, grim rage flapped her angry wings above his head as he knocked at the door with the hilt of his sword.

"Open, in the name of God!" said the Abbot; he divined what it was that hung over him and that nothing now could avert.

He stood in the middle of the still convent-yard, immovable as a statue, and the brethren gathered round him as round the pillar which upheld them all.

The Count walked silently up to him, his white lips trembling with such violent agitation that he had to control himself before he could speak. The Abbot quietly awaited what he might say, while the Count included him and the whole circle of monks in one glance of hatred, for which his tongue could find no adequate expression. At last he muttered between his teeth,

"And dare you actually look me in the face—can you bear that I should look at you? You liars and hypocrites—do you not tremble before me?"

"We tremble before no just man," said the Abbot, "for our consciences are pure. As to the unjust—them the Lord will punish."

"Spare your words!" cried the Count. "Every breath of your throat is a falsehood."

"My Lord Count," said the Abbot, "do you believe that we—"

"Believe!" interrupted the Count, "I believe nothing—I know.—Do you understand? Since my visit with the Duke I have lurked round your convent. The nurse whom you maltreated betrayed the track; the old man at Saint Valentine's has confessed. He is dead and he made his last confession to *me*."

At those words, which fell upon them like a thunderbolt, the brethren turned pale and were dumb. Now was God's judgment come upon them. But with a comprehension of the danger came resignation; if they had sinned, God might punish them—if they had done right, He would surely help them.

"Where is my son?" cried the Count impatiently, glancing round at the whole circle of monks.

"My Lord, at this moment he is doing penance for a heavy sin," said the Abbot in an uncertain voice.

"What sin?" asked the Count.

"A breach of obedience to the rules of our Order," explained the Abbot.

"Obedience! that is at an end! A Count of Reichenberg owes obedience to no man!"

"He is not a Count of Reichenberg—he is a brother of our Order; he has taken the vows and he cannot be absolved from them."

"It was a forced vow, against all law and justice—he was cheated into it!" shouted the Count. "I was lately with the Bishop of Chur and informed myself on the subject. If you refuse to give the boy up to me, I will accuse you before the Pope himself, and you will be laid under an interdict. For, as the Bishop told me, that is the law; Pope Celestin III. decreed that the decisions of the Church in Council at Toledo and Aix-la-Chapelle should come into force again, and that no Order might receive a child before he was of age without the consent of his parents. And will you hold him to a vow thus surreptitiously extorted from him—will you assert your claim to stolen goods? Am I not his father and did I ever give my consent to his becoming a monk? Answer!"

The brethren had come to a rapid understanding among themselves in Latin.

"Well and good, my Lord," replied the Abbot, "you speak truly, and according to the letter of the law you are in your rights when you require at our hands that which is your own. The only question is this: is that still yours which you threw away of your own free will and abandoned to destruction? I know very well that such an incredible instance of a perverted nature is not provided for by any law, and if you appeal against us the judgment will be in your favour; but, my Lord Count, you were no doubt also informed that the same Canon law permits young people when they come to full years of discretion to enter an order without their parents' consent. Are you or are you not aware of that?"

"Yes," said the Count, biting his lip.

"Well then, my Lord," continued the Abbot, "you may punish us according to the letter of the law, for that wherein we have sinned against the letter of the law—but you cannot break the vows your son has taken, for he is now of age and if he now renews them, he is answerable to the law."

"But he will not renew them now that his father is here to fetch him home to splendour and dominion," said the Count confidently. "Only bring him here and let me speak to him myself, and put my patience to no farther proof. A Reichenberg can never learn to wait."

Again a few Latin words passed from mouth to mouth in a low whisper.

"If it please you to follow us into the refectory and refresh yourself with a cool draught, my Lord," said the Abbot. "You are exhausted and everything, whatever it may be, is better done when men have rested and strengthened themselves with a cup of wine."

"Very good—let us go in; and send me the young Count that he may empty the first bowl with his father," said the Count, somewhat pacified, for he thought the monks' opposition was broken, and his newly awakened fatherly feeling made his heart beat impatiently for the son to whom he must now make up for the neglect of twenty-one long years. So they went into the refectory where bread and wine had been set ready; still the Count would touch nothing,

"My son," said he; "first fetch my son."

The monks looked at each other in their difficulty; God had forsaken them —no farther escape was possible. After another short consultation father Correntian went "to fetch him." The Abbot stood like a condemned criminal at the foot of the cross on which he is to be crucified; "God help us! have mercy on our wrong-doing! Thou who canst read the heart, Thou knowest we meant it rightly!" Thus he prayed silently.

The brethren were one and all incapable of speech. "When the father sees the state of his son—what will happen?" That was the thought that filled every mind.

But Correntian came back alone.

"Your son refuses to appear," he said. "He has this very hour renewed his oath never to quit the cloister—and he will not see you."

Reichenberg laughed loud and wildly.

"You silly fellow! you crazy fool! Do you suppose that I—the Count of Reichenberg—can be sent home like a blockhead, with such an answer as that? Aye, you may glare at me with your wolfish eyes—they cannot pierce my mailed breast. Fetch the boy, on the spot—or I will search the building for him through and through."

"He must come, there is no help for it;" the Abbot whispered to Correntian. "You are not afraid that we cannot rely upon him now, when this severe punishment—"

Correntian smiled. "Be easy," he said; then turning to Reichenberg, "I will bring him to you, that he may tell you himself—then you will believe me."

The Count paced the room with long strides; was it near at last—this consummation—did he at last see the term set to half a life-time of remorse and goading despair? Oh! when he held his son in his arms, in those strong arms, nothing should tear him from them—he would make up for everything.

Minute after minute passed, louder and faster beat the father's heart—more and more shrank the terrified souls of the monks—"How will it end?"

Now—now close to the door—the footsteps of two men—but slow, much too slow for the father's eager impatience. Reichenberg rushed to the door to meet him—the monks turned away not to witness the terrible scene. There stood the longed for son, pale and wasted, and his face covered with a blood-stained bandage. The father tottered back—his eyes fixed, petrified with horror at this vision of suffering. But no! this is not he, he is deceived; this is not Donatus. "Donatus!" he cried, with a choked utterance, "Donatus, my son —where is he?"

"I am here," answered the youth. The father, to convince himself, snatched away the bandage from his face—his son was before him—eyeless!

A cry broke from the strong man that made the monks' blood run cold; "Blind—blinded—my son—blinded. Who has done it?"

"I myself," said the young monk, in a firm voice. "You—

yourself? and why?" groaned the miserable father.

"Because it was God's will."

There was a moment of silence; not one of the monks dared utter a word of consolation. But the torrent of blood that for a moment had been checked in its flow in the heart of the betrayed father, rushed wildly on again, and he turned on the monks in terrible fury,

"This then—this is what you have made of my son! Executioners—murderers! A father's pride mutilated and disfigured—the last scion of an illustrious race! Woe to you! God shall requite you sorely for this service."

"Count Reichenberg," said the Abbot, "we are innocent of this blood, nor are your son's eyes upon our conscience, for indeed they were the sunshine of our gloomy walls and everyone of us would willingly have given his own in lieu of his."

"Spare your speeches, Abbot, I do not believe them. Even if you have not yourselves been the executioners your accursed teaching has done it. Put out your eyes to serve God! Aye, that is your priestly notion of a hero. If you had given the boy a well-tempered sword in his hand that, for my part, he could have used against your enemies, he would never have committed such an outrage on himself! Oh God! great God, here I stand before Thy face; Thou knowest all my iniquity, Thou knowest wherein I have sinned—but the sorrow that is now rending my heart was of no purpose of Thine—no God can be so cruel—but only man." And he beat his brow in a frenzy of rage as if he would strike himself dead with his own hand.

Meanwhile the blind man stood by in silence, his hands folded, his head sunk on his breast; a picture so touching that even the strong man's heart was melted to pity. "What shall I do?" he went on. "I am a lonely, childless man and you are a poor, maimed creature, a dishonour to the chivalrous house of Reichenberg—still you are my own blood and I feel that I can love you with all your infirmities. I will take you with me—Come, and like a beggar who picks up pot-sherds, I will gather up the remnants of my ruined race and carry them home under my roof—to weep over them. Come, my son." His voice broke as he spoke. "Your father will lay aside shield and spear and turn sick-nurse to tend the last of his race till we are carried out of the decaying house to which we two belong." And he took hold of his son's arm to lead him away with him; but the blind man stood as if rooted to the spot, not a foot did he stir to follow his father.

The Count looked at him as if he could not believe it.

"My son!" he shouted in his ear, and he shook his arm as if to rouse him from a stupor, "my son—it is your father who calls you."

"Forgive me," said Donatus wearily, for fever induced by the wounds was beginning to exhaust his strength, "but that is not my father's voice."

"In God's name do not you hear me? It is I—your father—Reichenberg," urged the Count.

The blind youth shook his head. "I have no father but the Abbot."

"Donatus!" shrieked the Count, "are you in your senses?" He turned to the Abbot, "If any earthly bond is still sacred in your eyes—tell him what a son owes to his father."

"Donatus," said the Abbot, "you are this man's son—it is to him that you owe your existence in the world! According to all human rights and duties you belong to him—according to the rights and duties of our Order you belong to us.—You are of age and free to choose—Choose."

All eyes were fixed on Donatus. He felt for the Abbot's hand, "My father," he said, "I can have but one choice; to live or die with you."

"Son, son!" cried Reichenberg. "Is all your nature subverted? Can you repel your real father for the sake of a stranger who did not beget you?"

"My Lord," said Donatus, "how can you say you are my father, when you have never dealt with me as a father? while these have treated me as you ought to have done. How can you talk to me and chide me for loving them and calling them father, when I have never known any other father?"

Reichenberg's eyes fell; "You speak the truth," he replied. "I have erred and sinned grievously towards you; an evil spirit possessed my senses—but of that God is the judge and not you. The children may not be their parents' judges, for the ties of blood are sacred and no law can tear them asunder."

"My lord, I am dedicated to Heaven—I recognise no ties of blood—"

"And is this the doctrine in which you have brought up my child?
Almighty God! it would have been better for him if the wild beasts had devoured him! The son renounces his father who comes remorsefully to atone for his past crime. Oh! it is hideous, and I turn from you in horror! You are not men, you are stones—stones of that proud edifice under which the whole earth groans, and all wholesome life must perish.—And you, blind shade, out of which they have wrung the very blood and marrow, can you reconcile it to your creed of mercy to plunge a dagger in cold blood into the heart of a father who opens his arms to you with eager longing, and cries for atonement as a hart for the water-brooks,—to renounce him when he would fain lead you home under the roof of your ancestors?"

Donatus drew himself up; his father quailed before him.

"My lord," said he, "the winter-night sky was my parental roof; the bare earth was my cradle; the snow-storm sweeping down from the heights gave me the first fatherly kiss. Hunger and cold, exhaustion and death were the nurses that tended your wife in her need. Pitying love came in monk's garb through the night, and snow, and storm, and snatched the deserted woman and child from the cruel earth, and carried them home, and warmed them, and laid them on a soft bed. And when my mother succumbed to her miseries, again they were monks—these whom you see here—that made me a cradle in the name of Him who is Love. They have carried me in their arms, they have sheltered and tended me, and watched over me all my life; and shall I leave them and follow a stranger only because an accidental tie of blind nature binds me to him? My lord, sooner could I tear all love out of my heart, as I have torn out my eyes, than do such a thing!"

The Count had listened to the words of the son he had lost with apparent composure, but he now said to the Abbot in a sullen tone, and with lips that were white with anger,

"That will do; command him to follow me without resistance, or mischief will come of all this."

The Abbot drew back a step. "I cannot," he said; "I desired him to choose, I cannot compel him."

The Count grew paler and colder.

"Then I will compel him," he answered. "Send down to the village for a strong horse that may carry me and the boy."

"My lord," urged the Abbot, "you surely will not against his will—"

"Do you think I will entreat him any longer? He must obey, willingly or not; he is my son, and he belongs to me," and with a rapid movement he snatched the enfeebled boy from the midst of the brethren, and threw his mailed arm round his slight form. "Sooner would I throw you to the wolves, unnatural child, than leave you here with these monks, and come what may, I will carry you away."

"Oh, God, help me!" cried the blind man, and in an instant the brethren had flung themselves on the father, and freed the son; the solitary man was forced to yield to numbers. Donatus clung to the Abbot and Correntian who supported him. The Count drew his sword.

"You will have it!" he cried. "Then take it," and he flew like an infuriated wild boar on the unarmed group, so that the foremost recoiled in terror.

"A sword, a sword!" Donatus heard them shout, and he understood what was happening. In an instant he drew a blood-stained weapon from under his robe—the compasses that he had taken from Eusebius—and he turned the two sharp points against his breast.

"Father!" he shouted above the tumult, "if indeed you are my father, will you kill your own son? See this steel which has already pierced my eyes; I will this instant plunge it into my heart if you touch a hair of one of my brethren!"

Reichenberg dropped his sword, and for an instant struggled for breath; then he raised his arm again, and the words poured from his lips like a fiery torrent. "You have conquered! Your strength is so great, so unfathomable that it is vain for man to fight against it. But still you are of flesh and blood, and still you can die! Then hear my solemn oath. In seven days, when the moon changes, I will return with a force, strong enough to destroy you and the whole body of your lansquenets, to rase your convent even with the earth. So bethink yourselves: if by that time you have not turned the heart of the son to his father, if you do not give him up willingly, I will mutilate you as you have mutilated my son; I will rend every tie of humanity as you have rent them by dividing the son from his father; I will trample on your sacred rights as you have trampled on the holy rights of nature. Blood for blood, and struggle for struggle! I will require at your hands the heart and the eyes of my son, and you shall answer to me for them."

"Count Reichenberg, we do not tremble at your threats," said the Abbot proudly. "You may indeed destroy a poor and helpless monastery, and murder a handful of unarmed monks, but you know very well that a whole world would rise up to avenge us, and, even if you conquered that, our holy Father can hurl an anathema at you which will overwhelm you to all eternity, and which you cannot escape from in this world or the next."

"And do you believe," cried the Count with a wild laugh, "do you believe that I quail before curse and ban?—Do you believe that I can fear hell when such wrath as mine is boiling in my veins?—Do you believe that I care for Heaven—for Heaven whose revolting indifference has let every earthly evil fall upon me?—for Heaven that did not annihilate you all rather than leave this poor young son of a noble house to blind himself for your doctrines? Woe upon you! But there is still a power that you know not of—because you have never felt as men feel, and that is a father's vengeance; neither death nor damnation can terrify that!"

He turned towards the door. "So I say again, bethink yourselves; in seven days I shall return and perform my oath—You yourselves have taught me that an oath must be kept."

The door closed with a slam—while the brethren, pale with fear, were still looking after their grim enemy.

"My brethren," said the Abbot, clasping Donatus in his arms, "this our brother has proved himself such as never a man before him. He might have escaped the severest penance by following his father, and we gave him his choice. He has chosen perpetual imprisonment and chains, and has refused freedom and happiness. My brethren, when we consider this our disciple's greatness of soul, we must say that we have done right. And they to whom the Lord vouchsafes such fruition will not be abandoned in their time of need—for this youth's sake. He will stand by us."

"By the help of this youth—aye, truly—but not if you put him in prison," said a voice behind the door. It was brother Wyso who had slipped in from the infirmary, somewhat paler and leaner than of yore, but in as good spirits as ever.

"I wonder you were not smothered long since in your own fat!" muttered Correntian between his teeth.

"Have you heard what threatens us?" asked the Abbot.

"I was standing behind the door. I kept myself discreetly hidden, for when he slashed about him with his sword it struck me that my whole head might be of more service to you than the half."

"What do you mean?" asked the Abbot.

"We are lost—lost even if we had reared a whole garden-full of such holy fruit for the Lord. Why! did you ever see a tree escape the lightning because its fruit was good? Has not the Almighty let many a cloister perish for all that it seemed a pity? Think of our convent at Schuls that was burnt to the ground, and yet it was no man's fault! But this time you yourselves are in fault! You should have listened to me when I warned you; now it has come upon you. The Count of Reichenberg neither can nor will forgive you. Either you must give the boy up to him—" a cry of horror interrupted him, but he proceeded with his speech undisturbed—"or he will hack you in pieces with your protectors and your handful of people, so that at the last day there will be no knowing the bones of priest and peasant apart. There is one, only one, who can save us—Donatus!"

"And how is that?" asked the Abbot.

"Do you not remember how he bewitched the Duchess, and how she said, 'Send this lad to me and whatsoever you desire shall be granted.'"

"Aye, aye!" murmured the brethren, beginning to understand him. "But she will turn from him in horror, now."

"Nonsense! if he pleased her then when he had his pious eyes, he will please her twice as much now because he has put them out for piety's sake. Such a thing melts a woman's heart with pity. The Duchess is now staying at Münster—Count Reichenberg is ruled by the Duke and he is ruled by the Duchess—send the boy to her and she will help us."

"It seems to me brethren, that brother Wyso's counsel is good," said the Abbot.

"Listen to me," cried Correntian; but the excited monks would listen to him no longer.

"No, no; Wyso is right; none but Donatus can help us, Donatus shall go to the Duchess at Münster."

"My son—you can save us, will you venture on this journey?" asked the Abbot.

Donatus kissed his hand. "My father may dispose of me as he will and whatever he does is well."

"Well then, my son—there is indeed no other way—set forth. You do it for us—your brethren—and for God. You will get there and back again in two days; but then, my son, your punishment shall be remitted, for you have this day ransomed yourself by an act of fidelity which outweighs a whole life-time of penance."

"Donatus," said Correntian in a low voice, "once again the Evil One sends you forth. Are you strong enough?"

"Strong!" Donatus smiled—a strange and bitter smile.

"What can the world do to me now! I am blind."

CHAPTER II.

When a brother of the Order went out on a mission he received a pair of new shoes made out of one piece of goat-skin, and a willow-staff sprinkled with holy water. The Abbot gave him his blessing and the brethren said the prayer "*cum fratribus nostris absentibus*" for him. For his sustentation and comfort he carried on his back a scrip with some bread in it, and a wooden flagon of wine. Thus cared for, body and soul, the wanderer could set forth cheerfully on his way. Not so brother Donatus.

He was indeed provided with bread and wine, with willow-staff and shoes, with blessings and with prayers; but that was lacking to him which the traveller chiefly needs—he had not eyes. With a hesitating step, sick and fever-stricken, he crossed the threshold of the convent for the first time in his life, excepting that short wild night-excursion. He was dazed with the thought that he must thus wander on from night to night, ever onwards without support, without any power of measuring far from near, without any dividing of the infinite darkness. Would his next step even fall on the firm earth; might he not lose his footing in space or fall over some obstacle? Would he not run up against something, find himself unexpectedly in front of a wall or be caught in the thick brushwood that he heard rustling round him and that often touched him as he passed? And he stopped again and again in involuntary terror before this or that imaginary danger. Nor could he put full confidence in his guide, for brother Porphyrius had no idea of what blindness was and led him on his way so heedlessly that the poor youth often stumbled and fell.

It was indeed a weary journey; sweat stood on his brow, his temples throbbed and many a blood-streaked tear fell from the unhealed wounds of his eyes. But he was patient; he thought of the procession to Golgatha and when his foot stumbled—was he not treading in the Redeemer's foot-steps! A number of young trees were lying about felled by the recent whirlwind and his guide dragged him across them, suddenly he picked one up in his strong arms and laid it across his shoulder.

"What are you doing with that tree?" asked his companion.

"I bear it instead of a cross, as Simon of Cyrene bore the cross after the Saviour."

"That is not right," said his guide. "You must not overburthen yourself, lest your strength should fail you before you have fulfilled your task. And this is not the Saviour's cross and it will profit you little to bear a mere profane log of wood."

"Oh, shortsighted man!" cried Donatus, with a glow in his cheeks. "If the bread which we ourselves have baked can be turned into the Lord's body, may not a tree be turned into the Lord's cross if it be borne in the name of the Lord? Truly I say unto you who doubt of such miracles, that you know not the power of faith."

"But how can it avail the Redeemer when you do such things to serve him; he is enthroned on the right hand of God and no longer bears his cross."

"But he still bears the burthen of the cross, and heavy enough it is; a burthen that each one of us must strive to lighten: the burthen of our sins that He took upon Himself in the sight of His Father, and that every act of true penance serves to diminish. Do you believe that He who died for us threw from Him at His death all that he had suffered and bled for, and that He now for ever rejoices in celestial bliss, and says, 'Let them do as they will, I have done my part. If they will not follow they may be damned, what do I care?' Do you think He would be indeed Christ if He thought this? I tell you that when He sees that He has died in vain, and that His holy teaching has no power over our sinful natures, He mourns over us, and His loving heart is oppressed with woe. And when one bears his cross in His name that he may follow Him into the kingdom of Heaven, he serves Him as Simon of Cyrene did."

"Donatus, you are indeed a Saint," cried the monk. "We truly are the blind and you it is that see."

And they went on, each lost in his own thoughts.

A light step seemed to be following them, close to them but yet invisible; Porphyrius looked round several times, but he could see nothing in the thick bush of the upland forest. It was not like a human foot-fall, but could not be the fleeting step of some forest animal, for it kept up evenly with theirs, now near and now distant; a devotional shudder ran over brother Porphyrius: it must certainly be an angel sent by the Lord to be an invisible support to the penitent, to help him to bear his burthen; and he dared to look round no more, lest he should drop down dead if he caught a glimpse of that Heavenly face. Thus they proceeded for about an hour through the damp wood; the dripping boughs flung a cooling dew on the penitent's head, the wet brambles brushed against his robe, and his parched lips inhaled the reviving freshness. But the consuming fever which was burning in the two seats of pain which he himself had made, seemed to dry up every kindly drop of dew like a red hot iron; at every pulse his arteries drove the blood more furiously to his temples, his breath grew shorter and shorter, his steps slower and slower, his tall figure was bent and panting under his heavy load. When at last they reached the hem of the forest, and stepped out on to the high road, he began to totter and fail.

"I can go no farther," he gasped, and fell to the ground under his burthen.

"I knew it would be so!" cried the monk, looking helplessly round for some succour.

Far and wide there was no living creature to be seen. By the wayside stood an old picture of a saint under a weather-beaten shrine, overgrown with wild roses; the storm had half overthrown it, and no one had set it up again; not a soul could have passed that way. A few birds were perched on the roof bickering over their food. It was in vain that brother Porphyrius listened for the steps that had accompanied them through the wood, they had ceased since the monks had come out of it. The protecting angel appeared to have forsaken Donatus, and that was why his strength had failed. Porphyrius relieved him of his burden, and laid him in the scanty shade of the shrine, for the sun had risen again, and pierced very sensibly through the mists which rose from the deserted and flooded road; it could no longer dazzle the eyeless man, but it scorched his shaven head which he grasped in his hands with faint groans. There was no spring in sight whence to fetch water for the unhappy man. Should he go back to the wood? Could he leave the blind man alone for so long?

"Is there no one near," he shouted to the empty distance. "Hi, hallo, help! —help." Then again he listened to the silence, holding his hand over his eyes.

Something moved at the edge of the wood, a young girl came out of it. In one hand she held a rush basket, and in the other a hazel-rod; on her shoulders she carried a small bundle and a round wooden water-jar, such as pilgrims used. Her hair shone in the sun like flaming gold, her little bare feet showed below her short petticoat like white flowers. Her gait was as light, and she ran forward as quickly as if she were moved by some mysterious power. That must be the light step that has accompanied them so far.

Brother Porphyrius stared fixedly at the marvel as it came forth from the dim shade of the wood, so brilliant and yet so modest, simple, and maidenly —half a child and half a maiden—so sweet and yet so grave. Had the blind man's guardian angel indeed assumed a human form, so as not to reveal itself in all its glory to the unworthy eyes of the brother who could see?

Before he had time to think of all this, the little girl was by his side.

"Did he fall down, has he hurt himself?" she asked, and her large golden-brown eyes were filled with tears of unutterable anxiety; brother Porphyrius did not answer, he gazed at her, speechless; she did not wait for the answer, but knelt down by the sick man. "My angel," she said softly, "my lord and my angel, do not die and leave me." And she gently raised his head, and poured water on his brow from her flask; Donatus began to breathe again, and raising himself he asked,

"Who is that?"

"A child that has been following us," said Porphyrius. "She does not belong to our neighbourhood. I never saw her before."

"I thank you, my child," said Donatus. "You refresh the weary; blessed are the merciful."

"Let me wet your handkerchief, to cool you," said the girl, carefully taking the bandage from his eyes. He instinctively covered the wounds with his hand, but she did not heed it, for she was wholly absorbed in her helpful zeal. She wetted the linen with the water in her bottle. "It is all bloody," she said. "Have you hurt yourself?"

"Yes," he replied hardly audibly. She folded it into a square pad and laid it on his head; but he still kept his eyes covered that the child might not be frightened.

"That will do you good," said she, and then she took some of her wood-strawberries and put them into his mouth. "There, eat them; I picked them for you, and you—the other one, have some too—but the best are for Donatus."

"Do you know me then?" asked Donatus in surprise.

"Certainly I know you. You are the angel I saw that day."

"Are you in your right senses, child? When was I ever an angel?"

"Yes—don't you remember—that day when they made you a priest?"

"Oh! I never was farther from being an angel than in that hour," murmured Donatus, and he let his hand fall from his face.

"But you had wings then; why have you lost them?" continued the girl.

"Child, you are dreaming, I never had wings."

"I thought I saw you with wings. But there is something different in you now—" she studied him attentively; suddenly she started up, "Oh—now I know—you have not got any eyes?"

Donatus clasped his hands over his face; the child stood by pale and trembling, and tear after tear forced its way through her long lashes and fell on her little clasped hands. "Poor, poor man!" she sighed from the depths of her child's heart. Brother Porphyrius had to turn away his head, he was so deeply moved.

Donatus started up. "Let us go on," he said hastily.

"I will go with you," said the little girl.

"Why, where are you going?" asked Porphyrius.

"Wherever you go."

"Do you know then whither we are going?" asked Donatus.

"No."

"Then how can you know that our roads are the same?"

"Your road is my road, where you are I will be—and when you stop I will stop."

"Ruth!" exclaimed Porphyrius involuntarily.

"Child, what has come over you!" said Donatus. "What do you want with me?"

"Nothing," said the child, for in truth she herself did not know.

"But you cannot wander about the world alone in this fashion," said Donatus.

"Alone! I shall be with you," answered the girl.

"But think, what will your mother say?"

The child's eyes filled with tears. "My mother is dead," said she.

"And your father?"

"He is dead too."

"Then you are an orphan?"

"Yes."

"That makes a good pair, an orphan and a blind man. Where is your home?"

"Nowhere."

"You must have been born somewhere."

"I do not know."

"But how came you here, what were you seeking in this neighbourhood?"

"I was looking for you."

"Leave her alone," Porphyrius whispered in Donatus' ear. "Do you not perceive that she is no mortal being?"

Donatus drew back a step. "What do you mean?"

"It is a spirit that has taken a maiden's form—your guardian spirit sent to you by God—believe me. Do not press her any more with questions or you will drive her away."

Donatus pondered on the marvel for a while, "Suppose it were a demon?" he said.

"You say that only because you are blind; if you could see you could not doubt," Porphyrius persisted. But Donatus made the sign of the cross over her and drew his missal from his breast.

"If thou art born of woman or sent by God, kiss this book; but if thou art come from the nethermost pit to lead us astray, depart—in the name of the Father, and of the Son, and of the Holy Ghost," and he held up the open book before her to exorcise her. She seized his hand and drew it towards her with the book to kiss it. It was still warm from the fevered heart on which it had been lying, and she pressed her lips to it long and fervently. It seemed to Donatus that the book was part of his very self, and he felt the kiss as she impressed it on the book.

"She is pure," he said, and concealed the breviary again in his bosom. "If then you will accompany me, come on. I will ask you no more questions. If you will tell me whence you come, do so unquestioned."

The girl was silent, she knew not what to say; she took up the sick man's scrip and slung it over her shoulder with her own.

"What are you doing?" asked Donatus, feeling himself suddenly relieved of the weight.

"I will carry it for you."

"Nay indeed you shall not; you are yourself but a tender child."

"Yes, let me, let me, I will do it willingly, it is for you," said the child and they set forward. But Donatus still paused for a moment. "The log that I was carrying for a cross, can I leave that?"

"Yes, let it lie, you have cross enough in your blindness."

"Do you hear?" Porphyrius said in a low awe-stricken tone. "It is God that speaks by her."

"Then break off a twig from it and give it me that I may keep it, it will bring me a blessing."

The little girl ran back and broke off a twig which she brought to him.

"If you will only wait a few minutes longer I will make you a wreath of leaves from the little tree so that the sun may not burn your head."

The two men were quite content to do everything the child wished, was not her will God's will? And with nimble fingers that moved as if by magic, the little one twined a broad wreath to give a cool shade to the wounded man's burning head; then they went on again.

"Let me lead you, I shall do it better," said the child, and she took the blind man's hand from that of the other monk. This too they agreed to, and Donatus felt as if the child's touch infused new strength into him.

"There is a blessing in your hand, it leads me softly," he said gratefully.

The little girl was silent, only her eyes told of unutterable happiness as she looked speechlessly up at him. And on went the three, now over slippery morasses, now over green hills and fields, and after taking the little girl's hand the blind man's foot stumbled no more, and the thorns no longer tore him; she carefully cleared every stone out of his path; where it was uneven she warned him by word or sign and guided his steps slowly and cautiously. No mother could guide her child, no sister tend her infant brother, no angel lead a soul to Heaven, as she watched over the blind man in his helplessness. The girl's pure breath fanned him like forest-airs when her bosom rose and fell quickly from some steep ascent or the fatigue of guiding him. He neither saw nor heard her; for her little bare feet went on by his side as softly as those of a fairy, he only felt her. He felt as if an angel of pity was walking by his side to cool his deadly pain with the waving of tender wings. They spoke no word and yet they understood each other as spirits do without any earthly speech. What they could say to each other was but little and very simple, but what they told in that dumb discourse was higher than human wit and worldly wisdom and echoed in their soul like angelic hymns.

It was by this time noon; the sun brooded hotly on the gorgeous landscape. The wanderers took their first rest outside the village of Glurns in the shade of the churchyard wall and eat their meagre meal, while far and near the solemn noontide peal was rung. The glaciers looked down kind and radiant from above the high cliffs of micaceous schist, which, turning here towards the south-east, form the opening of the gorge of the Münster-thal. Far and wide, spread a picture of blooming life and sturdy strength; villages and towns lay scattered all round while, veiled in the misty noon-tide blue, the haughty walls of the fortresses of Reichenberg and Rotund stared down from their rocky eminence like border watchers over the Münsterthal overlooking the smiling plain.

Porphyrius looked across at them with grave consideration. "I would we were only safely past Reichenberg," he exclaimed. "They can overlook the whole valley from thence and it seems to me that it is dangerous to take the road by day; our dress will betray us and we might be carried prisoners to the castle."

"Does any danger threaten you from thence?" asked the girl.

"Yes," said Porphyrius anxiously.

"Then let us rest in the wood till nightfall," the little one counselled, "and take the road at dusk."

"That will not do, we might lose our way in the dark," said Porphyrius.

"Not if I lead you; oh no! I am used to find my way in the dark," and a shadow of deep pain passed across her face as she spoke. Porphyrius looked at her much disappointed. "Do you not come from higher realms than we do?"

"Oh God knows!" sighed the child, folding her little hands across her bosom. "My foot has carried me as a fugitive about the world all the days of my life, and my eyes shun the light like a nightbird's, for the sun has rarely shone on me. I have hidden myself by day in the darkness of the wood and walked about at night."

"God preserve us!" cried Porphyrius, signing himself with a cross.

"That is a hard lot," said Donatus.

"Oh, it was well that it should be so, for thus I am able to guide you wherever you must go in the dark."

"But, you poor child, you were not born merely to be my guide," said Donatus compassionately.

"What for then?" asked the child.

"That I do not know," replied Donatus. "But you must have some purpose and some end. What will become of you when our journey is ended and we must part?"

"Oh! no," said the child, "we shall never part."

"Child, you are talking foolishly, we must part, I shall return in two days to the convent, and unless you have the art of making yourself invisible, you cannot follow me there."

"Then I shall go to the blessed maidens up on the heath and ask them to set you free—or I will ask them to let me find the blind worm that makes folks invisible. Then I will go into the convent and stay with you."

"What folly are you talking, child, in the name of all the Saints! The blessed maidens and the blind worm! who put them into your head?"

"Did you never hear of the blessed maidens?"

"No—of such blessed maidens as those—certainly not."

"Don't you know that—not even that? Oh, the folks that brought you up can have very little sense if they did not tell you that. Up there on the heath—going towards Nauders—there is a cave which is called the way to the blessed —that is the entrance to their country. You must have a wishing-rod made of a white hazel stick which has grown where cross ways meet and that was cut with a pure heart at the new-moon; then the door will fly open. Take hold—here is one," and she gave him the hazel wand she held in her hand that he might feel it; but he fell into a fit of righteous rage and broke the rod into pieces and flung it away.

"Oh, folly, folly! Woe to you if you carry on such night-magic and witches arts—we can never go on together, for these are not the ways that lead to the Light."

The girl had cried out with alarm when she saw him break the hazel-rod that she had been searching for all her life and had never found till the last new-moon; with that wand all she had ever hoped for had fallen into ruins— all the splendour of the kingdom of the blessed that it was to have opened to her—the help of the beneficent phantoms—all, all was gone. But worse even than the loss of her joys was her "Angel's" wrath and the words he had spoken; their ways could never lie together. The child threw herself at his feet crushed with despair, and wept bitterly. "Forgive me—I only meant to do it that they might release you from the convent and so I might always stay with you. Only tell me what I am to do so that you may never be angry with me again. I will do anything in the world that you tell me. If you wish that I should hunger and fast, I will do it, and if you wish that I should die, I will die —only be kind to me again, I beseech you."

The blind man laid his hand lovingly on the child's innocent head, and a strange emotion came over him as he felt her trembling beneath his touch. "Do not tremble, young soul! You have had pity on me and I will have pity on you. I will save you from the ways of error and darkness; I will show you a path to the blessed—but to the truly blessed. It opens not to wishing rods nor spring-herbs—only by penance and prayer may it be found."

"Aye, my lord, teach me to act according to your will, as I guide your blindness do you guide me where you see while I am blind."

"Amen!" said Donatus, and he felt as though the tears which he could no longer shed fell back like heavenly dew on the drought of his lonely heart. God had sent him this soul to be saved by him for Heaven. For the first time in his life he had found something he could call his own, and he felt that she was wholly his, absolutely given up to him, and that her salvation was in his hand. Thus must a father feel when a child is born to him.

He clasped the girl's head as if he wished to grasp this new-born joy, and said only one word; "My child!" but in a tone like the soft melodious ripple of the newly melted snow as it trickles down from the cliff under the beams of the first spring-sunshine; and the girl bowed under the touch of her "Angel's" hand, speechless and motionless, as though she feared to disturb the miracle even by drawing breath.

The soft breath of noon bore the perfume of lilies and roses from the graves in the churchyard, and the little screech-owl[3] shouted from the wood his cry of "Come here, come here." The girl listened to the call knowing what it betokened, but she only smiled at it; for her life had but just begun—a life in which there is no death. And as soon as Donatus released her she sprang up, and her shout of joy went up to Heaven like the song of the lark, and she ran through the little gate in the wall into the church-yard and flung herself down by the first grave to pray in front of its wooden cross. But she could not pray—could not think; she flung her arms round the cross and pressed her cheek against it as against her mother's breast. Brother Porphyrius meanwhile, sitting under the wall, shook his head.

"We have been deceived in her, Donatus, she is not a spirit, but a child of man like us, and God only knows whence she came, for her paths lie through the darkness as she herself told us—"

"But I shall lead her to the Light!" interrupted Donatus.

"Be not presumptuous—to me there is something uncanny about her since I have learnt that she is of this world; she is too fair for an earthly maiden and I am uneasy about you." Donatus smiled in melancholy but proud calmness as in the morning.

"What is there to fear?" he said. "Am I not blind!"

CHAPTER III.

It was now night, but not dark; the moon illuminated the valley with a light almost as bright as day, and displaying every object, even in the remotest distance, in trenchant outlines of light and shade. The pinnacles of Reichenberg, of Rotund, and of the tower of "Helf mir Gott" were bathed in a mysterious splendour. Once upon a time a maiden who was wooed by a wicked knight threw herself from this last-named tower down into the valley, but fell unhurt, for the saints spread out their mantles to bear her up. This was the story that the little girl told the monks; but in a low voice, as if her prattle could wake the sleepers upon the heights, and her soft voice mingled with the murmur of the Ram which danced along in the moon-light close to their path.

"Do you know this neighbourhood?" asked Porphyrius.

"Certainly. I was here as a child when the pretty lady used to come and see me at night, and the handsome man whom I used to call father; and then mother had to fly with me to the Trafoy Thal where the Three Holy Springs are, and then, as we were never safe there, across the heath to the forests by Finstermünz. I know every road and turning far and near."

"Why had you to hide so constantly?" asked Porphyrius. "Had your mother committed some crime?"

"Oh! no, my mother never did anything wrong. But she was always afraid they would try to kill me."

"Very strange! What then did she live upon?"

"The pretty lady gave my mother money, and with that we bought food and clothing. It lasted till I was a big girl, but now it is all gone; and we wanted to work by the day, but they drove us away everywhere, and at last we were obliged to beg. Begged bread is hard bread—my mother died of it." The child wiped her eyes with her sleeve, and was silent.

"Here is some dark secret," said Porphyrius softly to Donatus.

"Poor child, when did your mother die?" asked Donatus.

"Last night, in the forest."

"Why, then she is not buried?"

"I laid her in a hole where the storm had uprooted a tree, and I covered her with branches, and I rolled some stones down on her too, as many as I could; and a little wooden cross that she always wore—I stuck that in and prayed by

140

it."

"What was your mother's name?" asked Donatus thoughtfully.

"Berntrudis, my lord, you know her well, for she was your nurse."

"Berntrudis," exclaimed Donatus sorrowfully; "was she your mother?"

"No, she was not really, but she brought me up and I called her so."

"Alas, poor woman, and was this your end—like the beasts of the field, on the wet earth, in storm and whirlwind, and now to lie unburied like them. Could not the Church even give you Christian burial, you who reared a son for her, and why, child, did you not fetch one of us this morning, so that we might have given her a grave in consecrated ground?"

"Whom then should I have fetched? I dared not go up to your people any more since the cruel man drove me away in the night. Ah! if you had only come to her you would certainly have made her well again, and she would not have died."

"I? How could I guess it! If only you had come to fetch me."

"But I did go to fetch you, but the dark man kicked me away from the door."

"Who?"

"The pale dark man, with black eyes—"

"Correntian!" cried Donatus. "Did you tell him that it was Berntrudis that was ill?"

"Indeed I did, and I entreated him to send you to comfort her at the last. But he threatened to tread me to death like an adder."

"You!" groaned Donatus, and as if it were his part to protect her, he threw his arm round the child's shoulder, and pressed her closely to him. "Correntian!" he repeated, "may God recompense him!"

Porphyrius laid a warning hand on his companion's arm. "Donatus!" he said.

But Donatus heeded not.

"To cast out this child in the night and storm when she had come to ask for the last consolation for a dying woman! Woe to Correntian! That is not the spirit that ought to inspire us," and he held the child clasped to him as a father might. "Poor, forsaken orphan! here, here you have a home, I will make up for what the hard man did to you; I will repay to you, her nursling, all that my faithful nurse did for me, all she suffered for me! Yea! I will, as true as the spirit of Love lives in me which Correntian so outraged."

"Oh, my dear, dear master," said the child, her voice husky with blissful joy.

But Porphyrius shook his head. "What are you doing, Donatus? I am only a humble lay-brother, but it seems to me that it can be no duty of yours to pick up girls by the wayside, and offer them a home in your affections."

"The brethren picked me up by the wayside, and shall I not pity the forsaken? Rather is it well for me that I may at last know the joys of compassion."

"But you lack moderation in it, as in everything," warned Porphyrius.

"Moderation! Who shall set the limits to loving kindness? This is the first creature to whom I have ever been able to do any good; do you know what that is?"

"A vagabond girl who herself confesses that she has been driven out wherever she went; is she worthy of your kindness?" grumbled the more deliberate monk. "Child," he shouted at her, "confess, why have you not earned your bread honestly by the labour of your hands, why were you hunted from place to place, if no evil report attached to you?"

The girl turned pale and trembled, "I—I cannot tell you."

"What, you hesitate!" cried Porphyrius. "Why do you tremble so if your conscience is clear?"

"Oh, my lord, you will abominate me and drive me away from you."

"Is it so? God preserve us! we have indeed been deceived in you," roared Porphyrius. "Confess at once, confess, are you a witch or a sorceress?"

"Indeed, my lord, I do not know. Folks say so because my brows grow together and I have little feet. I have never done a harm wittingly to any one, really and truly never, and yet the boys run after me wherever I go and scold at me because they say I oppress them in their sleep and am a witch; and the women throw the three white gifts after me, and the children throw stones, and laugh at me and hang wisps of straw about me. And so I fly from place to place, but it pursues me everywhere, and nowhere can I find peace, and the child burst into heartrending sobs.

"Now we have it!" cried Porphyrius clasping his hands in horror. But the child in her anguish clung to Donatus.

"Oh! my lord! Oh master! do not cast me out, have pity upon me. I will confess everything. Yes, indeed, it is true I have many signs about me that I myself am almost obliged to believe in. I have always been glad to creep into a hollow tree and sit and dream that I really was a night-bird and shunned the light, for by day they were always tormenting and hunting me—so how should I love the daylight? And often, often I have felt as if I must squeeze my mother to death for love; and when I have had some pet animal, a lamb or a little dog, I have hugged it till its breath was almost spent, but I never did squeeze one to death, and I was always sorry when I had hurt it at all. And often when I had no living thing I have run into the wood and bent down the little young trees till they split, and then I felt better again. Nay, my lord, I will confess to you, that even with you, who are to me so high and sacred, I have felt tempted. When I held your hand, and led you along, a feeling came over me as if I must press your hand, till I almost dropped down dead. Tell me, is that sorcery? But you know even witches can be made good, and if I am one, help me that I may fight with my nature—I am to be saved, do not let me fall away, my lord!"

Donatus felt her sink at his feet—felt her whole frame trembling with deadly anguish, and he raised her with his strong arm. "Be you what and who you may," he said, "I believe in you."

Then he suddenly felt that the slight form was flung violently to the ground, and he heard a low cry from the girl; then a strong arm gripped his and tried to force him from the spot.

"What is that?" he cried.

"Away with you!" whispered Porphyrius. "Do you think I will let you league yourself with such a being? Get thee gone, accursed witch!" and again Donatus heard a blow fall as it were on some soft body. Something was all at once roused in him, as if only in this moment he had suddenly grown to manhood. With one hand he pulled up the ill-used child from where she was lying at his feet, the other he raised against the monk.

"If you touch her again it is at the peril of your life."

"Donatus," screamed the horrified monk, "are things gone so far with you?"

"So far?" cried Donatus. "Do you dare, you miserable man, to doubt me, me the votary of death? Is the impenetrable darkness that shrouds me not too sacred for your suspicions to spot it? This child is my child; I have put myself in her father's place, and I will protect her with my heart's blood."

The poor little head had sunk wearily on his breast like a scared bird, he felt her painful breathing, and rage and grief gave him a giant's strength; still the imprudent monk ventured once more to try to part them, but the fist of his aggravated companion, though blindly aimed, hit his temple so that he fell tottering on to a stone and lay there unconscious.

"Woe is me!" cried Donatus who heard the heavy fall. "Is he dead?"

The child knelt down by the fallen foe and rubbed his brow and temples. "No, he is alive, but he has hit himself against a stone and is bleeding."

"Great God, what have I done? Raised my hand against a brother; what evil spirit possesses me? God have mercy upon me!"

The girl meanwhile had sprinkled water on the unconscious man and he opened his eyes; Donatus stood by wringing his hands and helpless. The monk pointed up in the direction of Reichenberg. "Look there!" he exclaimed.

The little girl looked up—lights were glancing in the castle, and just above a low copse they could see the heads of men on horseback who were riding quickly down the road.

"Those are the Count's men—we are lost!" groaned the wounded monk, "If you are not wholly a child of hell, save him, in God's name."

"And you? can you not come with us?" she asked.

"No, my strength fails me, I cannot stand; leave me, it matters little; but everything depends on him, save him and God will show you mercy for his sake."

The riders were already turning the corner of the copse. "Away, away!"

The child seized the blind man with supernatural strength and dragged him, half springing half tumbling, down the bank into the thick willow-scrub that at this spot bordered the deeply excavated bed of the river. "Lie still and do not stir," she commanded him in a whisper, and she hid him as much as possible among the bushes; she herself crouched down beside him, and the tepid waves washed round the couple, softly and soothingly, like the downy cushions of a cool, freshly made couch.

"Here lies a priest!" cried one of the horsemen, pulling up his horse. "That is a good find, for the Count has promised us a gold piece for every monk of Marienberg that we take him."

And they dismounted to examine the wounded monk.

"You have had a blow. Who has been beforehand with us?" asked one with a laugh.

"No one," said Porphyrius. "I fell over a stone."

"Were there not a couple more with you? I thought I saw something of the kind as we came round the corner."

"Yes, yes, it was like a shadow that slipped down into the water," cried another.

"You saw rightly," said Porphyrius quietly. "It was my cloak; I lost it when I fell down." The horsemen leaned over the edge of the road-way, but could perceive nothing. "It is washed down the stream long ago. Wait a bit, friend monk, we will take you to a place where you will be hot enough even without your cloak! Your time is come, you fat monks; in seven days we are to have a jolly butchery up at Marienberg. Now you may ride with us to bid the guests to the feast." And they lifted him on to one of their horses and rode off with shouting and laughter.

Their hoofs sounded for a long time in the distance; at last they died away and deep silence reigned on the lonely road. Donatus and his companion still listened for some time in their hiding-place; at last the lights were extinguished in the castle and they were safe once more.

The girl helped the blind man up the steep bank with much difficulty— again and again he slipped back on the sandy declivity in his wet robe. But she was as clever and resolute as she was slight and supple, and she succeeded in getting him to the top. There they stood, the two of them alone, a blind man and a defenceless child; but they feared nothing, they had each other and they asked for nothing more.

"Child, what am I to call you? My soul would fain utter your name to the Lord in praise and thanksgiving. My heart is full of you, let it know your name that it may overflow in praise of you."

"My name is Beata."

"Beata! you have saved me—God is with you. Now lead me on that I may rescue my brethren. We must not lose an instant, for the danger is pressing."

"Come my lord—my Angel! Here below I will lead you, you shall lead me above! But in order to guide you I must know where you are going? I should never have dared to ask while that stern brother was by, but now you must tell me everything, for now you have no one else to take care of you."

"I am sent to St. Gertrude's, the convent of nuns, with a message to the Duchess; lead me thither by the nearest way."

"Good—you shall soon be there. Ah! do not be sad; it is so delightful now I have you all to myself." And she pressed the hand by which she led him so tightly in the extremity of her joy that he started involuntarily; but she released it as if in alarm. "No, no, I will not squeeze you—no, I will not indeed!" she said, controlling herself.

"Poor child, I know just how you feel—there was a time when I too used to clasp the wooden cross to my breast, and kiss the cold earth in my impetuous and unspeakable longing; when I could have exhaled my very soul in one single embrace, in my thirst for love."

"Yes, yes—that is it," whispered the child, quivering with excitement.

"But I have found what will quench that thirst and that longing; the water of which Jesus spoke: 'Whosoever shall drink the water that I give him shall never thirst.' I will teach you to draw that water and peace will be with you."

The girl walked by his side in silence, her eyes fixed on the ground so that no stone might hurt the blind man's foot, for the road was rough and ill-constructed. So they went on together without speaking.

"Your hand is as hot as fire," said the girl at last, "and it throbs and beats as if there were a little hammer inside; and your step is uncertain. Do your wet clothes hinder you, or are you ill?"

"Oh! child—ask me no questions."

"But you frighten me. Trust me and let me know about your troubles."

The blind man stood still for a moment and pressed his hand over his eyes.

"They burn and ache like live coals! My God, my God! grant that I may not be discouraged."

The little girl was overcome with grief at seeing him stand thus wringing his hands in a convulsion of pain, as he pressed them to the aching sockets.

"Oh! poor, poor man—and I cannot help you. If I could cure you by tearing out my heart, oh! how gladly would I do it."

"Your words are balm, they have a wondrous healing power. Come, now I can go on again."

"Wait a little while—I will fetch some water and bind you up afresh," said the child, and she would have gone to the river, but he held her firmly.

"No—not an instant more. Let us hasten onwards—every moment is of importance. Think of my poor brethren."

"I can think of nothing but you and your suffering!" cried the child—but she had to obey and to lead the blind monk forward. He pulled her on without farther delay.

They were now passing by the foot of the fortress of Reichenburg, and the little girl looked anxiously up at the blank and towering walls.

"God be thanked!" she sighed, when they were past, "Reichenburg is behind us! now we have nothing more to fear."

"How long will it be before we reach Saint Gertrude's?" asked Donatus.

"Before sun-down we shall be there. What shall we do then?"

"There I shall beseech the Duchess to grant me an escort and an efficient force to protect my brethren at Marienberg, and I shall hasten back with them. I shall give you into the noble Lady's charge that she may obtain your reception among the brides-of-heaven who dwell in the cloister of Saint Gertrude, for that is the path-way of the blessed in which I promised to lead you, and there flows the well of living water of which you must drink."

"Jesu Maria!" shrieked the child. "You will shut me up in a cloister!"

"What else could I do with you that would be pleasing to the Lord?"

"Oh!—no, never, never!—" the child groaned under her breath.

"Beata—is this your obedience?"

"I will follow you, as faithful as a dog, for that is my destiny—but free—of my own free will. I will not be imprisoned, I will not be shut up, if you mean to rob me of my freedom, I will fly from you—and no one will ever be able to find me again."

"Woe to you, Beata! will you spurn the salvation that I offer you? Unhappy child. To-morrow I must go home to my convent and then you will see me no more. What then will be your lot? You will wander about homeless as before, and hunger and freeze, while there you would find food and nurture for soul and body."

"Do you think I am afraid of hunger and cold? I—the homeless, the vagabond? Offer a wild dove the handsomest cage under a roof, the Host for food and holy water to drink—it will sooner creep into a hollow tree in the hardest winter, and starve rather than be captive. And the Lord will have pity on the wild bird and will forgive it, for it is He himself that has made it so that it cannot live except in freedom."

Donatus stood still in astonishment and drew his hand out of hers.

"Child! what spirit is this that speaks in you? What power possesses you? You fear not that which man fears—that which tempts others does not tempt you; nothing earthly has any influence over you and you are sacred in your innocence. The beasts of the forest spare you, and sin cannot touch you. Yes, your simplicity has vanquished me, and I bow before your childish wisdom. I will lead you on, wild dove, according to your destiny. Perhaps, indeed, God has called you to bear the olive leaf to some lonely and erring soul that it may be reconciled to humanity." He took her hand again and walked on. "Now lead the blind traveller to his goal and then spread your wings and fly away—my soul will know where to find you, flee where you will. And when storms rave round our towers and a feeble wing beats against my window, when the snow covers the land and the starving birds crave their crumbs of us—then I will think of my wild dove out in the wood—God preserve her!"

He was suddenly silent; a strange and unfamiliar pain overcame him, and the words died on his lips. The child looked up at the stars with moistened eyes and an expression of immutable faith on her innocent brow. Those stars above could never purpose that they should part—it could not be—nay, it would never happen.

They neither of them spoke again till the towers of Saint Gertrude's were visible through the darkness. The little girl's heart beat faster for all her confidence, and she involuntarily slackened her pace as they neared the spot. But at last they had reached it, they stood at the gate—the moment of parting was come.

CHAPTER IV.

"The Duchess is gone," was the terrible news which the porter announced to Donatus. "There is no one here now of all the court but Count Reichenberg, whom the Duchess came here to seek. Will you speak with him?"

"God have mercy! Let me go—quickly—away at once!" cried Donatus, "he must not see me, not for worlds. Tell me which way the Duchess went, and can I overtake her?"

"She set out for Saint Mary's; if you do not linger you might yet meet with her. But will you not first take a morsel to eat? The convent lets no one pass the threshold without some hospitable entertainment, and least of all a holy brother."

"No—no—nothing; if the Count of Reichenberg sees me it will be the ruin of my cloister. Let me go without any delay, and do not betray me if you have any reverence for the sacred will of the Abbot of Marienberg. Farewell, and the Lord protect your holy house."

"And good luck to you on your way," the gatekeeper called after him. The door closed, and the two wanderers again stood alone on the road.

"Beata," said Donatus gravely, "it is God's will; he has delivered me into your hand as helpless as a child; will you guide me farther still?"

"God be thanked, God be thanked!" cried the girl with a fluttering heart, and her cheeks crimson with delight. "You will stay with me and I with you, for ever—for ever."

"Child, your thoughts are as busy and erratic as wild bees. The most impossible things seem sure to you, and what we count by hours to you seems eternal. You are but a child, but the Lord has said, 'Suffer little children to come unto me, for of such is the kingdom of Heaven.' And so I think that your simplicity must be pleasing in his sight. But let us walk faster. I tremble at the thought of Reichenberg."

"I am walking as fast as I can, but if I go too fast you will fall, and then we shall be lost indeed."

"I shall not fall while you guide me. Oh! make haste, you know not what the stake is."

"But here there is no need, it is woody here, and my mother taught me how to hide from the sight of men. And I learned it so well that she often said, it was as if I had the art of making myself invisible, I could creep away so

149

quickly, and keep so very still."

"Why was your mother always afraid of losing you?"

"Because they had taken you away from her, and she was in terror lest they should take me too. She often said how foolish she had been not to fly away with you into the woods, as she did with me. It would have been a very different thing no doubt, for they would have hunted for you, but no one ever wanted me.

"Did your mother often speak of me?"

"Oh, very often, constantly; not a day passed that she did not tell me something about you; but her recollections were always of a little boy, so I could only fancy you one, just as we always picture the Lord Jesus Christ as a baby in a manger. And oh! I loved you so dearly. At first, to be sure, when I was very little I was often jealous of you when my mother cried for you, but as I grew older she taught me to love you as she herself loved you, and taught me to pray for you."

"Oh wondrous Providence! There lived on earth, though far from me and unknown, a soul that had thoughts of love for me while I, alone and a stranger to the world, prayed within convent-walls. Was it you who were present to me in the spirit when I flung myself with fevered longing down in the grass, or on a grave, and believed that some response must come to my soul's cry, either from above, or from the abyss below! Was it you?"

"Indeed it must have been, for I often shouted your name to the distance, and thought you would hear it and come. We waited for you, day after day, but at last my mother could wait no longer and she took me to Burgeis, to be nearer to you. Yes, and when I saw a pretty little boy, with dark curls and brown eyes, I asked my mother if you had not looked like that, and if she said 'yes,' I would take him up and nurse him and kiss him and call him Donatus. And when I saw you in the procession, I did not know you, because you were no longer a boy, but tall and dignified. I took you for an angel; but mother knew you again. Still, now I have you with me and you are so poor and helpless I can quite make you out to be the same with the little boy I used to picture. Oh! I wish you were still so little."

"And why?"

"Because then I could carry you in my arms and shelter you in my bosom from wind and weather and every danger."

"Oh merciful Providence—what wonders dost Thou create. Yes, you are a wonder, you pure and holy child-spirit. It is such as you that God in his mercy sends to lonely pilgrims on the way to Heaven to fare forth with them and strew the path of death with flowers. All my wild longing was but a vague seeking for you—pure and holy child—for you too are not of this world; you, like me, are not of the earth, earthly; you, like me, have no hope but in the other world."

The girl leaned her face on his arm and wept softly, but she was weeping for happiness; for had he not himself said that God had created them for each other, and whether for life or for death, it was all the same to her. They were two stricken souls flung together into a dark sea; for an instant they might cling to each other, and then, clasped in that embrace, must sink in the hopeless depths—but that one moment was worth a whole lifetime.

Thus they went on to the little village of Saint Mary—the namesake of Marienberg. It was only three quarters of an hour from Münster, but he had to gather up all his strength to drag himself along; Beata felt with increasing anxiety how he gradually leaned more and more heavily on her shoulder, and how his power was failing. If only they could reach their destination, thought she with an anxious sigh, then he could rest. But no such good fortune was in store for them.

They had reached St. Mary's, here was the same terrible news. "The Duchess is gone."

"Whither?"

"On a pilgrimage to Trafoy, to the three Holy Wells."

"All-merciful God!"

Trafoy was eight miles away—a day's journey; and his feet would hardly carry him. They must return all the way to Glurns, almost three miles, for there was no path which a blind man could climb across the mountains that divide the three valleys. Past the convent at Münster and the towers of Reichenberg, where they might meet the dreaded Count, once more under the burning sun, over the shadeless fields of Galfa, which they had traversed last night in the cool moonlight, and all this with strength impaired by fever and pain.

"Almighty God, Thy hand is heavy upon me!" sighed Donatus. But he did not pause to consider, he did not hesitate.

"Forwards," he exclaimed seizing the child's hand, "God will help us; Beata, we must go on!"

A short rest, for Beata's sake and not for his own, at the farm in the village he did however allow; once more she dressed his wounds. Then they set out on the whole weary way back to Glurns, and from thence to the wild valley of

Trafoy and the three Holy Wells.

"Oh, my brethren, how anxiously you will be waiting," lamented Donatus. "Woe is me, for a useless worm that can only crawl when wings are needed. Woe is me—I have done you an injury by injuring myself, and you were very right to punish me; my eyes belonged to you, I had no right to rob you of them."

"Do not be disheartened, dear master. When we reach Trafoy you can moisten your eyes at the Holy Wells; perhaps that may make you see again."

Donatus shook his head with a bitter smile.

"Everything else on earth may heal and grow again—a withered stick may blossom again as a sign of grace; the body of the Lord may grow for us in the dryest bread, but eyes cannot grow again—never, never."

He was forced to stand still, a dull groan broke from his lips. He felt something light and soft laid upon his breast; it was the child's hand, she dared not speak, but she longed to comfort him, and a stream of sweet peace seemed to flow from that little hand; the tumult of his despairing heart subsided under that innocent touch. He stood for some time struggling for breath and holding the consoling hand tightly to his breast.

"You heal every pain," he said. "You are one of those of whom the Lord said, 'Behold, in thy hands I have signed thee'—!"

"They belong to you, so you may make use of them; my hands, my eyes—all that I have is yours," said the child, and a solemn thrill ran through the blind man.

The sun shone with pitiless heat down in the valley, the naked cliffs of gneiss and micaceous schist that shut it in reflected the burning rays with double fervour, and out of the sea of glowing vapour uprose the frowning towers of Reichenberg on their rocky height. The girl shaded her eyes with her hand and looked up—a line of armed men at that moment were riding up the mountain-side, at their head a leader on a black horse—the child thought she recognised the Count; she clung to Donatus in terror.

"There they are," she whispered, "they can see us as well as we can see them—your black robe betrays you."

"What can we do?" said Donatus.

"All around is bare—but there is a shepherd's cart and close by it the man himself minding his flock. I will ask him to hide you in it till night-fall—we cannot go on by daylight. I will mind his sheep for him till evening, in return."

"Great God! must another day be wasted without our being any nearer to the goal?" said Donatus.

"There is no other way. If Count Reichenberg finds us you will never reach it at all, for he is of a bad sort and is plotting evil against you."

"What, do you know him?"

"Of course I do, he was with my mother just lately and they talked of all sorts of things that I did not understand; they stormed and threatened at the convent up there, and I could plainly see it was no good that they were promising."

"And your mother was in league with him? Oh Berntrudis!"

"She was furious with the fathers of Marienberg on your account."

"Oh! woe is me that I must say it—we deserve it, for they made her a bad return for all her love and fidelity. But I bring misfortune and fatality on all that come near me."

"Not on me—you have not brought them on me," said the child, and Donatus felt as if he could see the smile of rapture with which she spoke the words.

They had reached the shepherd's hut, Beata stood still in front of it. "Now hide yourself in here while I speak to the shepherd."

"Beata—devise some plan for God's sake—I dare not wait till evening, for if we miss the Duchess all hope is lost."

"I know of no plan—unless you will change dresses with the shepherd. He must give you his smock and you must give him your clothes instead."

"What! lay aside the dress of my order?" cried Donatus horrified. "I can never do that—the rules forbid it."

"Then you must stop here till night-fall—one or the other is the only possible course."

Donatus wrung his hands, "What can I do? disobedience and infraction of the rule are my fate wherever I turn. And yet if I must infringe one law it had better be the lesser. More depends on my saving the brethren than on the outward observance. Call the man here for God's sake; I will change clothes with him that I may go on unrecognised."

"But—one thing more," said Beata reflecting. "If afterwards the Count were to see the man in your monk's cowl—that might betray you. I would rather burn it and give the shepherd something more valuable for his smock frock."

"Have you any valuables then?" asked Donatus in surprise.

"Yes—here, feel; I have a ring that Count Reichenberg gave me. At first I flung it away, but my mother put it on me again, and said, 'who knows of what use it may be yet!'"

"The Count gave you a ring?"

"Aye—and a gold piece. That I have kept—we can buy bread with that when we have none left. He gave them both to me that night. The ring I was to show to the warder of the castle that he might admit me. He wanted to adopt me as his child."

"And you did not go?"

The child smiled.

"Why, how should I? I went with you."

"But by-and-bye—consider—the ring will be the key to a new life of pleasure and splendour."

"And even if it were the key to the cavern of the blessed—what do I want with it—I have you."

Donatus stood overpowered by this simple fidelity; at this moment the shepherd came forward, curious to see the strangers.

"Blessed be the name of the Lord!" he exclaimed in astonishment. "How comes a cloister-brother here?"

"Here, you man," said Beata quickly, "have you another smock frock?"

"Aye—my Sunday clothes and my cape; what does the girl want with them?"

"Give them here, coat, cape, and hat, this blind Brother has enemies—they are plotting against his life and that of his brethren—and if he cannot disguise himself in your clothes danger threatens him."

The man shook his head. "I want my clothes myself," he said, "particularly the cape and hat; I cannot do without them."

"Consider—you have a house to shelter you from wind and weather, and he has nothing if you refuse to give him the cape and hat. Look here, I will give you this ring for them, it is of pure gold—you may believe me, only don't consider any longer. I will mind your sheep—help him to put them on, and then we will burn the monk's dress."

"The girl is no fool!" said the shepherd, laughing and turning the ring about as it sparkled in the sun, "for such a jewel as this you might strip me of my skin as well as my shirt." He glanced at the girl as she ran lightly off to keep the sheep together. "A smart girl she is! and it all slipped off her tongue as easily as a Pater noster."

And he fetched the things out of the hut, and began to help the blind man to put them on. In a few minutes Donatus appeared from behind the hut, another man. His breast and arms were bare, for the scanty garment scarcely met round his shoulders and loins, and he had modestly wrapped the ragged cape round his slim white knees.

"How handsome you are!" said the girl, gazing up in innocent astonishment at the manly young form that had hitherto been so completely concealed by the monk's black frock and cowl. Donatus blushed involuntarily, the simple words disconcerted him; to this moment he had never thought whether he were handsome or hideous, and he was full of regret at having to exhibit himself in such a guise before the eyes of men. Already he was considering whether it might not be possible to face all the danger of proceeding in his monk's dress. He was overwhelmed with shame, shame at his undignified disguise—when he suddenly perceived the unpleasant odour of burning wool; the girl with quick decision had flung the monkish garb on to the fire by which the shepherd was cooking his midday meal; it gave Donatus a shock of horror, it was as if he himself were being burnt.

"The sacred garb that you wear smells of the scorching of your too-easily inflamed desires," Correntian had said to him in that last night. Now the flames had indeed taken possession of it and consumed it. He stood by in brooding silence, and with deep sighs he made the sign of the cross over the fire and himself. Then he pressed his breviary and the cross of his rosary to his lips and hid them carefully in the scanty robe that covered his breast.

"Beata, where are you?" at last he asked, putting out his hand.

"Here," said the child, going quickly up to him.

"Let us go."

"Here is the hat," said the little girl with prudent forethought, and she put the hat of coarse straw plait on his head. "Now we can go on. Farewell shepherd, and as you hope for salvation do not betray us, promise me that, by the Holy Virgin."

The shepherd laid his right hand in hers which she held out to him. "The Holy Virgin need not trouble herself when you forbid it. I think no one could refuse you anything. Go in peace, I would rather you should stay with me and help me to mind my sheep, but it is better so, for if I had you to look at I should forget the sheep! It is well that the pious brother there is blind, for if he had eyes to see you it would go hard with him."

"Farewell," said the child, interrupting him and hurrying Donatus away.

"You are trembling, Beata. Do not let his idle prating annoy you. The world is full of these baser souls, but they cannot come near us; they vanish before us like the dust clouds that whirl up beneath our feet."

"Ah! but you see, my lord, this is what happens to me wherever I go, first they torment me with friendly advances, and then when I fly from them they curse me and call me a witch."

"Poor little witch!" and an expression played upon his lips, a faintly sweet and merry smile.

"Oh! you are smiling, you are smiling," cried the child joyfully. "I can see you smile for the first time!" and again she would have said, "How handsome you are!" But for the first time in her life she coloured consciously, and the words died on her lips.

Donatus laid his hand on the child's head. "Let me feel how tall you are?" said he, "are you quite grown up?"

"I should think so," said the child, leaning her head on his breast. "See I reach up to there." Donatus felt the height with his hand.

"Only so far! Oh! then you will certainly grow taller yet. How many summers old are you then?"

"That I do not know."

"What, child, do you not even know how old you are?"

"Wait, not by summers, but I can count by trees."

"By trees?"

"Yes, wait a little. Every year since I could run alone my mother made me cut a cross in a young tree when the birds were building their nests. Now here in Münsterthal there was one tree," she reckoned on her fingers, "on the road to Marienberg there was one; two at Nauders, and five in Finstermünz, and in the Ober-Innthal three, that makes twelve, then there are three in Lechthal, and one on the way down, in Vintschgau; that makes sixteen little trees. So that since I came into the world there must have been seventeen springs, for when I cut the first cross I was so tiny that my mother had to guide my hand with the knife; so she told me, for I cannot remember it."

"Then you are already seventeen summers old? I thought you were still quite a child," said Donatus thoughtfully.

"And what colour are your eyes?" he went on presently. "Brown or blue?"

"Brown I fancy, but I cannot be certain, for I have no mirror but the water, but mother used to say they shone at night like owl's eyes."

"And your hair?"

"Reddish-brown. The children used to call me Hairy-owl when they saw me combing it, because I could cover myself all over with it like a cloak; here, feel my plaits, they are as long as I am tall. I have to fasten them up." And she laughingly drew the thick, half unplaced locks through his hand while he wondered at their length and weight.

"And your eyebrows grow together, the true sign of a witch?"

"Alas, yes."

"And a little rosy baby mouth?"

"Yes, may-be—I do not know."

"Beata! oh, would I could see you!" he said for the first time since they had been together. It thrilled her with delight as he said it, she herself knew not wherefore.

CHAPTER V.

It was now noon-day; Beata and Donatus took a short rest to eat their bread. The forest waved high above their heads, and close to them the noisy Wildbach tumbled down the cliff, and the girl fetched some of the cool water for their frugal meal.

"I cannot hear you, Beata, are you there?" asked the blind man.

"Certainly, my good master, quite close to you!"

"Why are you so quiet?" he asked.

"I have been thinking of a little song that says in rhyme just what you asked me to-day. Would you like to hear it?"

"Of course; are you skilled in such things?"

"A little," and in a low voice she sang as follows.

"The blind man to the maiden said:
  'O thou of hearts the truest,
Thy countenance is hid from me;
Let not my questions anger thee!
  Speak, though in words the fewest!

"'Tell me what kind of eyes are thine?
  Dark eyes, or light ones rather?'
'My eyes are a decided brown
So much, at least—by looking down—
  From the brook's glass I gather.'

"'And is it red—thy little mouth?
  That too the blind must care for!'
'Ah, I would tell that soon to thee,
Only—none yet has told it me.
  I cannot answer, therefore!'

"'But dost thou ask what heart I have
  There hesitate I never!
In thine own breast 'tis borne, and so
'Tis thine in weal and thine in woe,
  For life, for death,—thine ever!'"[4]

"Beata, who taught you that song?" cried Donatus, starting up from the soft moss. The tender words had gone to his head and heart like sweet wine. He passed his hand across his brow as if to wipe away the spell which had been lightly woven over him.

"Who taught you that song?" he asked again.

"No one, who should? No one could have heard what we were talking of to-day."

"But who taught you to say what you felt in that sweet fashion?"

"My father," said the child, and a deep melancholy rang through the words.

"You have never told me about him, Beata, how is that?

"Because I never can help crying when I speak of him, and that will not make you happy."

"Beata," said Donatus gravely, "you share my sorrows, and shall I not share yours? Tell me who was the wonderful man that taught a wild wood-bird to sing with such sweet art?"

"He was a troubadour; it was his profession to turn thoughts into artistic verse, and so he taught me. Poor father! The song of his lips was most sweet, and whoever heard him and his beautiful lute-playing, was made thankful and merry of heart. And yet he had to wander from place to place like me, and hide his handsome face under hideous disguises. For he was an exile and an outcast, and every man's hand was against him."

"And what crime had he committed?" asked Donatus.

"I never knew—my mother said I was guilty of it all. It was because I had come into the world that things went so hardly with him—oh!—and how could I help it!" she hid her head in her hands and wept bitterly.

Donatus drew her hands away and took them consolingly in his own. "My child, my dear child!"

"That is just what my father always used to say when he came to see us and took me in his arms. You know he never could stay with us; he was obliged to go into the towns and sing to people for his daily bread. And when he did come it was by stealth, and only when we were at Finstermünz, or the valleys of the Inn or the Lech, where no one from these parts was likely to see him. He used to bring us as much food and money as he could spare, and would stay a few weeks with us in the forest. There he taught me a number of little proverbs and sayings and pretty tunes, and the arts of rhyming as far as I could learn them, but I was still quite young when he died—I could not count more than twelve trees that I had marked."

"How did he die?" asked her companion.

The child's hand trembled as she answered.

"They fell upon him like a wild deer—some people out hunting who recognised him—and he dragged himself to us almost bleeding to death. We nursed him as best we could, but it was too late to be of any use. Oh! and he was so patient and gentle even when he was dying; he laid his hand upon my head and blessed me, and said, 'May God never visit the guilt of your parents on your head—expiate in faithfulness their sin against faithfulness.'"

Donatus took her hand solemnly in his. "Yes, you will be faithful and expiate the guilt of your parents whatever their sin was—a strange divination tells me this, and my soul is possessed with a deep sadness for your sake. What dark secret hangs over your birth, poor child—Who may you be? Did you never ask your mother Berntrudis?"

"No—why should I? What good could it do me? I am a poor, useless creature, I come and pass away like a wild heath-flower, no one asking whence came you or why do you bloom?"

"Poor heath-flower—lonely and sweet, how sacred you are to me. The perfume refreshes the weary pilgrim, and the dreaming spirit, like the dainty bee, gathers golden honey from the blossom of your lips. You grow firmly rooted in the dry rock, and humbly bend your head to the wind as it sweeps over the desert spot—and yet you stand firm and live on through sunshine and rain, through the fury of wind and weather! Oh! heath-flower—I will not ask whence you came—I only rest my weary head in your shade and bless you!" And he threw himself on his knees before her, and bent his brow on her hands. Thus he rested for some time in silence; not a breath, not a sound roused him from his dreams.

In such a moment of exquisite rapture the girl almost held her breath—feeling herself like a holy vessel into whom the Lord was pouring out his mercies.

But suddenly he started up. "Great God!" exclaimed he, "time is flying and I am delaying and dreaming. Come, Beata, 'of hearts the truest,' lead me onward."

And on they went again, on and on, these two who might not rest; but was it the intoxicating perfume of the heath-flower, or his rising fever that made his steps uncertain? He knew not which; but he felt that his strength was failing.

"Hold Thou me up, O Lord!—for this day only hold Thou me up, till I have brought succour to my brethren!" so he prayed fervently, as he put his arm round the girl's shoulders for a firmer support.

"Am I too heavy for you?"

"Oh no—never!" cried the child, though she could hardly hold herself up under the beloved burden, for her long walk through the night had by degrees crippled even her young limbs and made them feel like lead. But she would rather have died than he should know it.

"Poor little one, how much rather would I carry you!" he said, and he involuntarily dropped his head on to hers which reached just to his shoulder. He felt her silky hair like a soft pillow under his cheek, and the breath of her lips came up to him like incense. Then he whispered softly—and the words sounded like a sad caress—

"Is it your heart that I have to carry in my breast that is so heavy that my feet totter under the weight of it?"

"If love and truth can be weighed in an earthly scale, then, indeed, dear master, you could hardly carry it."

"I could almost believe that you are a witch, and that your little heart was an incubus that weighed on mine!"

"What you too! you say so?" cried Beata pitifully. "Then it must be true."

Suddenly they heard a distant rush through the wood on each side of them, like the tramp of hoofs, and the startled creatures of the wood scampered through the brushwood, or whirled across their path in hasty flight.

"God help us! it is the mounted soldiers!" exclaimed Beata. "But collect yourself—your dress disguises you perfectly. Do not betray yourself." And she hastily snatched the bandage from his eyes and hid it in her bosom; then she pulled the hat low over his brow so that his eyes might not be seen under its broad brim.

"Do not say that you are blind," she whispered.

By this time the riders broke through the bushes; they were the followers of Count Reichenberg and the lord of Ramüss. They were heated and angry.

"Have you met a Benedictine?" said one of them, in a tone of authority.

"A Benedictine! what was he like?" asked Beata.

"We had taken him prisoner and he has vanished—his name is Porphyrius, he was tall and stout, and had blue eyes," said the man.

"That does not matter," interrupted his companion. "We will take every Benedictine we find, whether his eyes are blue or green. Our master Reichenberg gives a ducat for every cowl."

Beata turned pale, but she preserved her presence of mind.

"This morning I saw one at Saint Mary's in Münsterthal; he was resting there, and meant to go on again at noon," she said with prudent forethought.

"Where to?"

"To the Engadine, I believe. If you make haste, you may easily overtake him."

"Good, forward then to Saint Mary's," cried the first speaker.

"You had better come with us," cried his companion to the two wayfarers. "So stout a lad can surely fight, and so pretty a wench can surely kiss. We will take you on horseback, and when we have caught the shaveling we will make merry together out of the ducat. Come, little one, I will lift you into the saddle."

"Get away with you, we are not for the like of you; my brother is ill, I must get him home."

"Your brother is it? Then all the more you belong to me!" said the rider with a laugh.

"Do not come near me, I am a witch!" screamed Beata.

The man spurred his horse forward, and tried to snatch at her from his saddle. But she had quickly drawn a knife from the folds of her dress, and she plunged it into the horse's flank, so that he started aside with a leap.

"Good God, she really is a witch!" cried the others. "Let us be off or she will bewitch our horses."

And thereupon the whole troop rode off; the danger was past.

"All praise to your cunning, Beata, you are as soft as a dove, and as wise as a serpent."

Beata supported herself, breathless, against his shoulder. "Oh, my lord— oh, my angel! If they had carried you off from me, and perhaps killed you—" she burst into convulsive sobs, and threw her arms round him as if even now he might be torn from her.

Donatus stood trembling in her embrace; then he felt that her knees failed her, and that she sank speechless before him.

"Beata, my child!" he said, kneeling down beside her. "What is the matter, what has bereft you of your strength for the first time since we have been together?"

"It is only the fright—it will soon pass off—in a moment—" but her voice died away, and she lost consciousness.

He felt for her drooping head, and laid it on his bosom; he rubbed her forehead and temples; a stream of unutterable feeling ran through him, a sweet compassion, a rapture of anxiety.

"Beata!" he cried, "poor stricken deer, wake up, listen to the voice of your friend. I cannot go to the stream to fetch you water as you did for me. I am blind and unable to return you even the smallest service for all you have done for me. Listen to my voice, sweet soul! wake up."

And she opened her eyes, and found her head resting on the breast of the man who to her was so sacred and dear, and she would fain have closed her eyes again, and have slept on into eternity; but obedient to his call, she collected her strength and answered, "My good master!"

"How are you?" he asked softly.

"I am quite well, I can go on now," she said, though her voice was weak.

He felt, however, that she was still exhausted, and required rest.

"No, my child," said he, "I have already made the most unreasonable demands on your strength. I should have a heart of stone if I could drive my poor lamb any farther. The rest that I would not give myself, I must grant to you," and he took off his cape, and laid it under her head for a pillow.

"There, rest for an hour, and repair the mischief that my negligence has occasioned."

"But you, my lord, what will you do if I go to sleep? For since I have lain down sleep weighs upon my eyelids like lead."

"I will watch over you, and though indeed my eyes are closed, my ear is sharp and will warn me if danger threatens."

"Give me your hand," she said, and as he gave it her she laid her head upon it, and fell asleep. The blind man sat by the sleeping child without moving.

"Now, Angels of Heaven, spread your wings over us," he prayed.

She slept soundly and calmly; exhausted nature drew refreshment from the dark fount of sleep.

He waited patiently for her awaking; he knew not how long a time had passed, he could not see the sun's place in the sky and his mind was so full of wandering thoughts, so steeped in the charm that the breath of the sleeping child cast round him, that he lost all estimate of time. Suddenly he felt a burning ray of sunshine fall on his cheek, as sharp as a bee's sting; a single ray that had pierced between the boughs from the westward. By this he knew that the sun was sinking; the sultriness of noon too had much diminished, and there was more life stirring in the brush-wood and in the air than during the midday heat. He perceived at once, by many vague and yet unmistakeable signs, that evening was drawing on, and he lightly touched the girl's eyelids to feel if they still were closed. "Beata," he whispered, leaning over her, but the call had only a magical attraction; she turned towards him in her sleep, as a flower turns to the light. He felt her lips close to his and a thought flashed through his brain, a thought at once intoxicating and terrible. And yet, no, not a thought, only an involuntary impulse of his lips, as when a draught of water is withheld from a thirsty man. He shrunk in horror of himself; was he still capable of such emotion—he, the blind man, the ascetic, cut off from life and its joys? He drew back far from the tempting lips so that their breath could reach him no more. Why did his heart throb so violently? Was it from anxiety at the long time the child was sleeping? He was sparing the girl, and neglecting to rescue his brethren. Should he awake her? No, she must awake soon of her own accord, and then they will make up for lost time all the quicker. By evening they will reach Trafoy, then he can speak with the Duchess at once and by night ride home again with the armed escort. But Beata! oh God what will become of her? Can he ever find it in his heart to turn her out, a wanderer on the earth?

"Sleep, poor child, that heavy hour will come soon enough," cried his tortured soul.

Far and wide all was as still as death. A sharp ear could hear the squirrels' little claws scratching against the branches, and the birds twittering in the tree-tops, while on the ground there was not a sound but the light foot of some wild animal or the rustle of a beetle in the grass. Donatus felt the dancing sunbeams that fell here and there between the trunks, he felt the cool breeze that came down from the nearer glaciers. Perhaps they were looking down through some cleared opening in the thicket, those royal, shining forms, and bathing the sleeping child in their broad reflected splendour! "How beautiful it must all be," was his involuntary thought, and he hid his aching brow in his hand. He felt again and again as if, like another Samson, he must break through the dark vault that imprisoned him, for every power and muscle and nerve in his body was in a state of tension; and in the next instant he sank back overwhelmed by the mere thought of the ineffectual effort. For those walls, intangible and incorporate, would yield to no earthly force; no earthly ray might pierce them even if the blind man stood in the very eye of the sun— that was over for ever. Now at this hour, when he was alone for the first time since meeting Beata, now he is conscious that it is the child's presence that has this day kept him upright. For so soon as he is left to himself, despair lifts its dragon head and threatens to darken his soul with madness.

And he had to summon all his self-command to keep himself from crying out aloud, "Beata, wake and save me from myself!" At this moment the girl awoke and opened her eyes, as if she had heard the dumb cry for help that came from his struggling soul. Donatus was sitting motionless, his hands convulsively clasped and his head leaning against the trunk of a tree. She thought that he slept, overcome by fatigue, and she propped her head on her hand and silently contemplated the pale suffering face with the sunken closed eyelids, a still and sublime martyr's face, while her heart overflowed in tears that coursed each other down her cheeks. She folded her hands in worship of him. What were earth and heaven to her, what was God even? All were contained in this one man. He was love, he was patience, he was goodness. In earth and Heaven there was none but he; and she rose to her knees softly, not to wake him as she thought, and prayed to him, the martyr, the blind man who could see no light but from whom all the light of her life proceeded. She gazed at his sunken eyes and unutterable pity came over her; he was fast asleep, he could not know—gradually—irresistibly—it took possession of her. She did not know what she was doing, nor even that she was doing it— her lips breathed a kiss on those closed lids; a soft, deep, tender kiss. He started up and pressed his hands to his eyes. "What has happened, what was that? Beata, you kissed me—on my eyes. Holy Father, what have you done?"

"Forgive me!" cried Beata, sinking into his arms almost distracted. "Or kill me, kill me, my lord, my angel, my deliverer?"

"Oh wonder of wonders! I see again! it is fire, red fire that I am gazing into. Woe is me!—you have opened my eyes, and I see that which I ought not to see. I see you Beata, just as you are, your tawny shining eyes that gaze at me so imploringly, your rosy mouth that kissed me so sweetly. I see your waving hair, I see your whole sweet figure down to your little feet that have followed me so faithfully, I see it all, and I would fain sink in those fathomless eyes, and bury my face in that soft hair and drink death from those sweet lips. What is this feeling that shakes me to the very stronghold and foundation of my being? All-powerful God, this is love—it has come, it has come! I have suffered in vain." And he clasped the tree-trunk against which he was leaning as if to chain himself to it by his own arms, so that he might not snatch the girl to his breast and sink with her in the overwhelming torrent of fire.

The child stood by trembling like a young sapling in a whirlwind; Donatus pressed his face against the bark of the tree and a few blood-stained tears ran down his cheeks. St. Benedict slept on stinging nettles when temptation approached him, and he, what should he do? "Quench, oh quench the fire!" he groaned. "Let it rain, let the brooks overflow, oh God! to cool my fever. Water, Beata, for pity's sake; lead me to the spring or I shall perish." The terrified girl took his robe, as if she dared not touch him again, and led him to the torrent which fell with a sudden leap over the rocks, foaming till it was as white as the glacier snow from whence it came. It had worn a deep channel in the earth into which it fell, and the spray leaped up again in a fountain. The blind man flung himself into the icy glacier water, as if he were pursued by the fire-brands of hell, and the cataract came splashing on to him, throwing him down; the cold waves of the pure and purifying element rushed over him with a deafening roar; the burning pulses of his blood turned to ice under it, his limbs grew rigid, and it penetrated to his very heart like the icy touch of death.

CHAPTER VI.

It was night; the white heads of the glaciers looked down like pale watchers into the silent and sleeping Trafoy Thal. There it lay, deep in the shadows of the sheltering mountain walls, the lonely little valley. Fragments and boulders of fallen rocks strewed the earth—a sea of stones—and only here and there a red glow shone in the darkness, the light of the smelting furnaces of which several were scattered about; not a living creature was to be seen far and near.

Tired to death and with bruised feet the lonely couple toiled through the stony chaos towards the still invisible green nook, where the miraculous waters of the three Holy Wells take their rise.

"Do you see anything?" asked Donatus in a weary tone, "all is so still—"

"I see nothing far and wide," answered the child.

"Beata," said Donatus, "if she is not here either!—" he broke off, the terrible thought choked his utterance.

And on they went again. He listened for the least sound that might betray the presence of a travelling encampment and she strained her keen sight for his sake; but sharp as were her eyes, quick as was his ear, there was nothing to be seen, nothing stirring. They had traversed the whole valley.

"I can hear the rush of water, are we not near the Holy Wells?" asked Donatus.

"Yes, here we are," said Beata, trembling as if she feared to tell him.

"And there is no one to be seen?"

"No one," she said hardly audibly.

"All merciful God!—and I can go no farther." Donatus sank to the ground on the spot where he was standing, and hid his face in his clasped hands.

"Oh, good God! what misery!" lamented the girl. "Lie here a while, I will go back to the smelting houses, and get some news of the Duchess."

"Beata, you can walk no farther," sighed Donatus.

"For you I can do anything," she said boldly and steadily, and soon the blind man lost the sound of her steps in the distance. An endless term of waiting in motionless patience ensued, and the agonised watcher felt the dull silence around like the influence of a petrifying basilisk, slowly tormenting its

167

victim to death. He listened and listened, and yet could hear nothing but the singing of the blood in his ears, the ceaseless trickle of the three streams close at hand, and the distant thunder of the waterfalls that fling themselves from the precipices of the Königspitze. From time to time his thoughts became confused; he heard the noisy travelling-train of the Duchess approaching, he called to her what his errand was, but she did not hear, he could not make himself intelligible and he tried to scream but he could not. The horses went over him, he felt their trampling feet, then he started up and felt all round him; the hard stones on which he was lying had bruised him all over, and the tramp of horses that he had fancied he heard was no more than the roar of the water. All was silent, and all remained silent. Then again a dread came over him lest Beata should never return, some harm might have befallen the child among the smelters—a half wild crew—and he, a miserable mere shade of a man, he could not save her, he must depend for succour on a weak and helpless woman. He loathed himself; could God take delight in such a miserable cripple? "Wretch, blind feeble wretch—die!" he groaned, and his limbs shook with fever. "Son of all misfortune, what are you alive for? That you may scatter abroad the seeds of misery which you bear in your bosom—" and then again fear for the child overcame him, and he shouted to the night, "Beata, Beata, where are you?" till once more his consciousness was clouded.

At last she bent over him, and softly called his name.

"Is it you, Beata?" he cried, starting up, and his trembling arms clasped her slender form as though he thought she might be a dream and would melt away. His hair clung to his brow, his breath came quickly, his face was flushed with incipient fever. Beata saw in a moment that he was ill, very ill.

"My dear master—I have brought a boy, the smelter's son from the hut out yonder, and he will help me to carry you under his father's roof, so that you may get some rest."

Donatus staggered to his feet. "No—no—I cannot rest—the Duchess, where is the Duchess?" he cried.

"We shall never catch her up, my poor master," said Beata hesitatingly. "She set out at night on account of the heat—she has been gone an hour, and no one can tell me where."

"An hour!" shrieked Donatus. "That was the hour of my temptation—that was the hour that I wasted dreaming in the wood—the hour I let you sleep because as you slept your breath kept me spell-bound, and I forgot everything —everything depended on that one hour, and now it is lost—all lost—by my fault." He stood tottering and tried to take a few steps. "After her—I must go after her—"

"How can you, my dear master—consider, they are on horseback and have an hour's start of us. Besides you are ill and cannot stir from the spot."

"Oh Lord God! work a miracle—Thou hast done so many for others—do one for us! Help me, bear me up—we shall overtake them—only go on, go on!" he panted; and he sank into the arms of Beata and the boy. "The clouds, the clouds, they are strong enough, they will bear me—no, stop, I am going too fast—Heaven and earth! I am giddy—do not let me fall."

"Oh, dear master—!" Beata burst into tears and sank on her knees under her heavy burden, resting his head in her lap. The boy, a smutty fellow with dull, staring eyes, stood by stupidly looking on.

"Go and fetch your father to help us," said Beata.

The boy shook his head. "Father cannot leave the ore till the furnace is tapped," he said.

"Well, go and beg him to come as soon as he can," and the boy slowly strolled away.

The towering peaked walls of the Ortler—Madatsch, and the glaciers of Trafoy—stared pitilessly down on the forsaken pair—there was not a projecting rock, not a cave that could offer shelter to the sick man. They stood up appallingly bare and steep and almost perpendicular, like giant walls built up to protect the world's Holy of Holies. And there it was too—that Holy of Holies. The three Holy Wells poured out in the moon-shine like rivulets of light, from the hearts of the wooden images of the Virgin mother, the Redeemer and the Baptist, which were protected by a little wooden structure which might well afford shelter to the sick man also. There—if she could only get him there; and she whispered in his ear, imploring and urging him till at last he heard her and began to move.

"Dear master—if you could only go a few steps farther—there flows the holy water—that will make you well—"

The sick man caught her words. "Where—where?" he said.

"Come—only come, I will help you up—there, now one step—one more —we are there now." With a tremendous effort she had got him there, and she let him softly slide down on to the soft ground under the shrine in front of the Madonna.

"You are kneeling before our Mother Mary," she whispered reverently, and she bathed his brow and eyes with the miraculous water.

"Oh, Holy Virgin! have mercy upon us," she prayed, and she held up the folded hands of the blind man who no longer had strength enough to raise them in prayer.

"Have mercy upon us!" he stammered, after her *"Rosa mystica, maris stella, stella matutina"*; his feeble lips went through the thousand-times repeated rosary, and then his head sank back in the girl's lap, and he lost consciousness.

CHAPTER VII.

Nine times had the sun risen and set without the sick man's darkened spirit being conscious of it. It is true that his blinded eyes would not have told him even if he had been conscious, but the measure of time of which men have an instinctive idea would have served him even in his darkness, and have driven the tortured man home to his imperilled brethren. From time to time indeed he had roused a little, and had asked the time, but the girl—God will forgive her —had deceived him; had taken advantage of his blindness, and had made him believe he had slept but an hour, while a whole day or a whole night had gone by. She meant it well, that he might be content to rest, and not get so ill as to die. So each time he had laid his head down again, and let himself be persuaded—"till it was day"—to go no farther. And thus it had nine times been day, and nine times night. To-day for the first time the rage of his fever was subdued, and his reawakened consciousness began to light up his pale face.

"Beata, are you there?" he asked.

"Yes, master."

"I believe you have not slept the whole night through—whenever I have called you you have been awake. Is it not yet day?"

"Yes, dear master, very soon; but rest a little longer."

Donatus felt around him; he was surprised to find a soft straw-bed under him, and by his side a wall.

"Where am I?"

"In the smelter's hut; we carried you in that you might be sheltered from wind and weather."

"Then we are among men?"

"Yes, they are poor folks, but compassionate and helpful."

"How many are they?"

"A man and his son."

"Do you think the boy could conduct me to Marienberg?"

"To Marienberg?" said Beata, turning pale.

He did not answer for some time, then he said,

"It is so sultry and heavy in here; if you would do me a last service, help

171

me up and lead me out into God's open air that I may collect my senses."

"You are still too weak to stand; have a little patience," she begged.

"Not a minute longer must I delay; I must go home to my brethren to share the danger which I could not avert." He rose from the bed, and the girl led him silent and tottering out into the air. The sky bent in ethereal blue over the mighty glaciers, an icy morning-wind blew down from them and waved the sick man's hair across his face, for it had grown long. He inhaled the pure air of the heights in long deep breaths like a man risen from the grave. Heaven sent him a greeting from the cloud-capped peaks, it invited him up there; he felt it, the flames of hell thirsted for him in vain; the child seated him on a stone bench by the door of the hut.

"Beata," he said in a hollow voice, "we must part." The child uttered a cry of pain that pierced him to the very heart. He went on, "Beata, I have erred and gone astray. I believed that I might escape love if I blinded myself, and I lulled my soul in that security, till temptation was upon me before I suspected it. It was so fair a dream, Beata, when we wandered on together in innocence, as in Paradise, but original sin has driven us out of it! From the first hour when your sweet charm stirred my soul with earthly longings, from that hour our Paradise was lost. Beata, hell would fain have power over the immortal part of us, let us snatch it from its power. It is yet time; I have as yet withstood that hellish temptation, but now let us part lest the darker deed should follow hard on the dark thought. I gave up my eyes that I might keep myself pure, now I will give you up too. Be strong, Beata, prove yourself worthy of the suffering I endure for your sake, and obey in silence."

"No, no! Require what you will of me but not that," shrieked the child. "Plant a knife in my heart and I will not shrink, but do not require me to part from you without crying out like some wild creature that is only half killed, and can neither live nor die."

Donatus clasped his hands, and a cold sweat stood on his brow; Beata flung herself before him.

"My lord and master, do not drive me away; you cannot be so cruel, you only fancy that you can, and you will rue it when you are gone a few hundred yards, and you will call your child to come back to you; but it will be too late. I have been with you in the hour of anguish, my eyes are dim with watching by your bed, my bleeding feet have stained the stones on the paths along which I have led you, and you will drive me away? Oh, dear good master! you would not drive away a lost dog that humbly licked your hand, and have you no pity on my suffering and my tears?" And she laid her tear-bathed face on his hands and tremblingly clasped his knees.

The tortured man cried out from the depths of his soul, "Oh God, my God! is it not enough? Beata, have pity, have pity, no devil could torture me as you are doing. Beata, if you are not indeed of the powers of hell, if you are not an emissary of the devil sent to torment me, go from me. Oh holy Spirit! enlighten her, purify her, deliver her, as Thou hast delivered me."

He rose and solemnly lifted his hand, "Beata would you win everlasting bliss?"

"I ask for no bliss without you," said the girl.

"Beata, do you wish me to lose it too?"

The child shuddered but did not speak.

"Beata if you renounce me I may yet be saved. But if you will not quit me, if you make me faithless to my vows, I must be eternally damned. Now choose, which is it to be?"

The girl answered in a tremulous and hardly audible voice, "I will—go."

All was silent, as when the last life struggle is past, and the bystanders whisper, "All is over!"

For a few minutes longer the wretched man listened, his face bathed in a sweat of anguish; then he threw up his arms to heaven as if to ask, "What can be left to me to suffer more?" then he felt his way back into the hut.

"Spare me your boy," he said to the smelter, "that he may guide me to Marienberg."

"Do you want to go on again?" asked the man. "Where is the girl that was leading you?"

"She—she must stay here, take care of her; you are a good man. Take care of the child as the apple of your eye; oh! Angels of Heaven will guard your hut so long as she is in it." He hid his face in his hands and burst into loud sobs.

"If it troubles you so why do you leave her?" asked the man.

"Do not ask, do not talk, give me your son and let me go. When I have got back to the Abbey, I will send you a rich reward by your son." The boy sprang forward when he heard of a reward; Donatus took his rough hand, his heart tightened as he took it; it was not Beata's soft and loving touch.

"Farewell!" he called out to the man, and the rocks dismally echoed, "Farewell."

His foot had crossed the threshold, and he set forth without delay towards

Marienberg.

For the ninth time since he first had set out the sun was setting behind the cliffs of Mals and Burgeis when the weary wanderer returned from his dreary and fruitless pilgrimage. Poor and wretched as if the wind and waves had tossed him on shore after a shipwreck; scorched and desolate in spirit as if in some pilgrimage in the Holy Land the burning sun of the Desert had consumed him heart and brain, and he had fled without earning his title to Salvation.

He laboriously climbed the mountain, led by his clumsy guide; the boy had heedlessly brought him by the lonely and little used 'Goats'-steps,' so called because only goats and goat-herds could climb it without turning giddy; at every step the blind man was in danger of falling into the yawning depth below.

The dank mists of evening fell thickly on the mountain, the vesper bell must presently ring, Donatus had been listening for it all the way.

"Boy, do you see no lights in the convent."

"No," said the lad, "all is dark."

"And yet it must be late," said Donatus, panting but hurrying still more up the steep ascent.

"Aye, it is late," said the boy.

At this moment the vesper bell rang out and up from Burgeis; now they will ring here too—

He listened, his heart throbbed once, twice, thrice, all was still.

What had happened? A shudder ran through him, the cold night wind blew down from the peaks and chilled his very marrow. The vesper bells rang out, each in a separate note, from the valleys far and near; only up here was it dumb.

"Can you see the convent yet?" asked the blind man.

"Yes, there it is," said the lad indifferently.

"Take me to the door."

The boy obeyed; Donatus put out his hand for the knocker, his hand grasped the air.

"The door is open," said the lad.

"Wait out here," said Donatus, and he went in. He easily found his way across the familiar court-yard; it was incomprehensible that the door should be open and no one in the way. He felt his way by the wall to the inner entrance—this too was open. He felt to right and left of him—the door-posts were there, but no door! Perhaps he had mistaken his way in the open space, and was in a quite different direction to what he believed. But how could there be a gap in the walled quadrangle that formed the court-yard if it were not the doorway? He will call out—does no one hear him? he listens—no answer! There is something gruesome in this silence; an unaccountable alarm takes possession of him. He can feel the stone of the threshold quite plainly with his foot—he is standing in the very doorway; then if he feels to the right the wall must be there, and the holy-water vessel of stone—yes, there it is, and the vessel too, so he has come the right way, he dips his hand in the piscina to take the holy-water—it is empty. It is strange, who can have emptied it?

He comes to the door of the refectory—there at last the brethren must certainly be. Here are the carved and iron-bound door-posts, he feels for the massive handle—again he grasps the empty air, and his foot is on the vacant threshold.

Is he delirious? or does his blindness cheat him with false ideas of space? His sense of touch perhaps betrays him—or some demon is tricking him, and juggling with his senses to torment him? Perhaps he is still out in the sheds, and only fancies he has made his way to the refectory?

A searching draught blew in his face through the open halls and corridors; a sickening wind bringing a horrible reek of smoke as if it blew across the dead embers of a burnt city, and a cloud of dusty ashes was wafted into his face.

"Is no one there?" He called aloud—all was still.

Then he walked on again—aimlessly, taking no particular direction in the darkness; suddenly his foot struck some unwonted object. He stooped—the refectory table lay in pieces at his feet—again he perceived the same strange smell of burning, and his hand fell on some charred fragments—the table was half burnt. Donatus walked all round it; wherever he trod there were ruins; he started back, finding himself suddenly at the opposite wall. Then he felt for a window—his feet trampled on crashing splinters of glass—the opening was empty, the wood work all charred.

Invasion had been here, and the fearful traces that it leaves wherever it enters—terror and desolation—depicted themselves vividly on the blind man's fancy.

"My brethren—my Abbot—where are you?" he shouted in despair to the darkness and chaos.

"My father—my brothers!" he cried out—but the words rang in the deserted rooms—and he wandered on without aim or purpose among the ruins and timbers—now straight forward, now round and round, without knowing why or whither.

"To the chapel—to the sacristy!" an inward voice suddenly suggested. "Perhaps they are there, praying—" and with infinite trouble he felt his way on through the chaos of destruction. He could no longer find his way, for everything he was familiar with, and that could serve him as a starting point had been torn from its place or destroyed, and he toiled in vain through the darkness to reach the spot which he always missed though so close to it.

"Help—light!" he shrieked as if demented—as though he could see the light even if there were one. He forgot his blindness—he forgot everything, he was half crazed with terror.

Then again he stood still and listened—nothing was stirring but the storm which sang unceasingly its wild lament through the ruined windows.

He wandered on again towards the chapel. At last the smell of burning was mingled with the odour of stale incense, and a wild confusion of broken choir-seats, images, and candelabra impeded his steps.

"Are you here, my brethren? Is no one here?" He shouted again and listened. He heard something—this time it was not the wind, it was a low groan from some human being.

"Who is there? answer me!" he cried, trembling.

"Who are you?" A well-known but broken voice fell upon his ear.

"Correntian!" cried Donatus, between fear and joy.

"Donatus!" answered the voice, and a strange shudder ran through him—as if he were called to the last judgment, and a voice from the clouds had read his name on the list of the damned.

"Donatus," repeated Correntian, "miserable son, why are you come so late? You have been our ruin."

"Correntian, my brother, I will tell you all; give me your hand and help me over these ruins."

"I am lying with crushed limbs under the overturned altar, I cannot help you," groaned Correntian.

"All-merciful God! How has this happened?"

"I wanted to rescue the charter of the convent from the enemy, and to hide it under the altar, but they surprised me, and in the struggle the altar was overturned upon me," groaned Correntian.

"And the brethren, where are they?"

"They have fled, driven away stripped and bare, the whole party. Our herds are driven off, the convent destroyed and plundered. Your father, who had leagued himself with your mother's kindred, committed the crime."

Trembling as he went, and with infinite effort, the youth had made his way through the medley of fragments and ruins towards the spot whence the voice proceeded; a hand now arrested his lifted foot.

"Stop, you will tread upon me." He stooped down, there lay Correntian on the bare stone half buried under the enormous mass of the stone altar.

"Oh! misery and horror!" screamed the blind man. "Crushed like a worm, a great, strong man! and no one to help you, no one!"

"The brethren could scarcely save their own lives, the people of the neighbourhood fled from the fearful scene; for three days I have lain here, abandoned, and not a hand to give me a draught of water."

"I will fetch you some water, I will find the spring," cried Donatus, but Correntian held him back.

"No, never mind, the well is choked, and it would not serve me now. My torture is near its end, I feel—"

"Oh poor soul, and must you end so miserably?" lamented the younger man. "Crushed by the altar you so faithfully served!"

"Do not grieve for me, I die as I have lived—for the Church. It is the highest mercy that God should grant me to die such a death. There is one who is yet more to be pitied than I." Donatus staggered.

"God help me, not the Abbot?"

"Yes, unhappy boy, the Abbot, who loved you with a love which was a sin against the rules of our holy Order—he expiated his sin fearfully."

"Speak, for pity's sake, torture me no longer," implored Donatus. "What happened to him?"

"Count Reichenberg demanded that he should give you up, for he thought you were hidden in the convent, and when he refused—was obliged to refuse—he had him bound and dragged into the court-yard and then—" Correntian paused for breath.

"And then, what then?"

"Then they made him give his eyes for yours, as the Count had sworn."

A scream rang through the chapel, and its quivering echoes shook the broken panes; then there was a silence as if the youth's heart had cracked in that one cry, and he had fallen lifeless.

Correntian breathed slowly and painfully; angels of death spread their dark wings and hovered round that ruined altar. Presently the stupor that had followed the first blow was broken.

"Oh! eternal Justice, where art Thou that this should happen?" sobbed Donatus. "God of grace, God of mercy! where wert Thou that such things could be done? That pure, innocent and saintly man, punished for my guilt— God of pity, how could'st Thou allow this?" And he sank down by the broken altar, and wept as though he could shed all at once all the tears that flood the world.

"Those eyes, those kind eyes, that so often looked at me with affection, that watched over me so faithfully. Oh God! give me mine again that I may weep for those far dearer ones!" But his lamentations grew less loud and violent as though he were kneeling at the Abbot's feet, and were listening tenderly to his soothing words as of yore.

"Oh! Lamb of God, patient and long suffering victim. You, in your gentle soul, forgave me, for you were too lofty a spirit to remember evil, but I, I can not forgive myself; my father, give me once—only once, your beloved hand, that I may press a kiss of remorse upon it—only once, only once, and then will I sink into damnation and expiate for ever that which I can never make amends for." And then again he was silent, all his strength of soul, which is needed even for suffering, was spent; he was forced to pause and draw breath for a fresh outburst.

"And the brethren," he groaned at length, "could they not protect him?"

"They were out numbered, there was a whole host of marauders," said Correntian. Donatus stood up, "Oh if I had been there I would have protected him. I would have covered him with my own body against a whole world of them."

"Aye, if you had come at the right time, then it would all have been different. Why did you not come, where were you waiting so long?"

"I followed the Duchess in vain for two whole days."

"And then?"

"And then I hastened home."

"And did that take nine days and nights!" cried Correntian.

"Brother! what are you saying? I left you only three days since."

"Woe upon you, son of the evil one!" screamed Correntian. "Where were you? What cheated your senses as to the time? Did you linger in the nether world that the days hastened by uncounted? Were you bewitched that you did not observe that since you left more than a week is past?"

"Merciful Heaven! a week?" said Donatus, "and she told me that I had slept but a night. Oh Beata! Beata! could you so deceive me?"

"Beata!" repeated Correntian. "Then it was a woman who stole all consciousness of time from you! And you ruined all for a woman's sake. This is how you kept your word to us, this is what came of your vows? Woe, woe, all is come to pass that I foretold at your birth; you were the changeling laid by the devil in our peaceful home to work our ruin, and yet you deceived even me into recalling my own prediction and trusting you. Nay more, Hear, oh Lord! and punish me for my sin. You were the first human being I ever loved. And at the very moment when I thought to set the crown of martyrdom on your head you relapse into the base element whence you rose and drag us all down with you in your fall!"

"Correntian, hear me. Yes, it is true, I have sinned; yes I have led you all into ruin for a girl's sake, and I will expiate it through all eternity. Not even my blindness could save me, Eusebius was right, the devil is more cunning than man, and yet I am innocent and pure!"

"Pure," shouted Correntian. "How dare you call yourself so, criminal," and with all the added horror of his suffering he raised the upper part of his body and stretched out his arm towards Donatus. "The curse that was upon you even in your mother's womb, I take it up and pour it, a double curse upon your head. Only your father's curse has weighed upon you hitherto, I add to it your mother's curse; for your mother is the Church you have brought to shame. An outcast shall you be, perjured wretch, an outcast from the Church, an outcast from humanity—an outcast from the flock of penitents who yet may hope. The grass shall wither under your feet; the hand be palsied that offers you the sacred Host; death and pestilence shall visit him who takes pity on your hunger. Your bones shall fall to dust, and that their pestilential reek may not poison the earth that yields food for other mortals, I bid you flee away to the ends of the earth, up to the realm of death, to the ice of the glaciers, as far as your feet can bear you, where not a blade can grow that can imbibe the poison of your corpse. All that is mortal of you shall be blotted out from creation to the very last jot, and what is immortal shall suffer to all eternity such torment as has racked my very marrow for these three days—" His voice failed, the rigor of death had fallen upon him, he fell back on the stone floor. Once more he raised himself, his clenched fists clutched at the fissures in the ground in his last agony.

"Oh, Lord God! have mercy on my sins!" he groaned, seized with sudden horror at the thought that he must depart without the last sacraments and with a curse on his lips. He felt that death had laid its icy hand on his heart; it was too late, his lips tried to stammer some words, but his jaws were clenched in a convulsion. Thus he gave up his cold and stubborn spirit, without consolation, without atonement, hoping for no mercy, for he had shown none; yet he had been true to himself and the Church, true even unto death.

But Donatus, crushed and banned, knelt by the corpse and prayed for mercy on the hapless erring soul. Would God hearken still to the prayer of the accursed? Could it reach the Throne of God? He bowed his forehead to the dust, and gave the cold stones a farewell kiss. Then he rose, and made his way back to the door where the boy was to wait.

"Boy, where are you?" he called out. No answer, the boy was gone. He had heard Correntian's curse, and had fled; the blind man was abandoned wholly.

Where should he go? The Church had disowned him, the earth cast him out. "Lord, hast Thou not a drop of mercy left for me out of Thine inexhaustible fount of grace? Did I not obey Thy will in so far as I understood it? I gave the light of my eyes to escape love; the staff that was the prop of my darkened life I broke and cast from me, and all my sacrifices have turned to curses and my obedience to fatal ends. I may well say with Job, 'My face is foul with weeping, and on my eyelids is the shadow of death. Not for any injustice in mine hands, also my prayer is pure.' Oh, Lord my God! if Thou didst see me in the hour when I drove away the girl, that pure and faithful child, Thou must know whether I then did not expiate my sins, and deserve Thy mercy or not. Yea, I will flee from all the ties of life, I will die alone like the chamois that hides itself in the glacier when its end is nigh; I will efface the trace of my steps on earth that fatality may no longer pursue me. Oh, God, my God! will the measure of my sorrows never be full?"

So he stood, his arms uplifted, a dumb image of suffering—like a tree stricken by a storm.

A few stars peeped out from time to time between the driving clouds; the abyss lay in slumberous silence at his feet, and the night-breeze snatched pitilessly at the ragged garments that scarcely sufficed to cover him. The empty windows of the ruined stronghold of faith stared at him like hollow eye-sockets, in dumb reproach. No cry from Heaven above or the earth beneath responded to his lament, no pitying hand clasped his to lead him to his last bourne; he sank down on a stone, and hid his head in his hands. "O! God, my God, why hast Thou forsaken me?"

CHAPTER VIII.

High, high up where no blade of corn can grow, in the glacier desert of the Ortler chain, the solitary penitent lived on the extremest verge where it was possible for flesh and blood to live and breathe—fulfilling literally Correntian's curse. Below lay the unfathomable depth of the valley of Trafoy between its deeply cleft walls, like an open grave. The glacier torrents roared down through fissures and crevices, feeding the three Holy Wells in the gorge below; the rock crumbled away beneath the volume of the mighty waters, and wide floods devastated the land.

A strange herd-boy had led him up whom he had met with that night at Marienberg, and who had taken pity on him for God's sake. It was a difficult task to guide the blind man up to these heights, but guardian spirits were with him and upheld him, or he would have slipped from the boy's weak hand a hundred times and down the steep and slippery path.

It is only from those who love life that God requires it; the wretch to whom death would be release may not die!

Again and again the boy was fain to stop, but the penitent was not to be persuaded to stay where a bird's call was still to be heard—where he could still lay his hand on fruitful soil. So, after long wandering, they had reached their goal—the last for which he longed—the realm of everlasting peace, where no sound of a human voice could pierce, where no slenderest thread could reach to link man to man. Here is the first circle of hell, cold and silent, here he might atone and die, and live above for ever.

The boy had contrived an indispensable shelter against the wind and rain under an overhanging rock, and then had left him; but from time to time he came to bring bread to the hermit. He was a strange boy, he came and went without the blind man's perceiving it, noiselessly and without a word, and Donatus was grateful to him for that. He would have felt it a desecration to break the sacred silence that bathed his soul like a sea which no profane sound might pierce.

Once every week his moss-bed was freshly made, and a fragrant loaf laid by the side of it; but he who brought it vanished as he came. Often it seemed to the blind man that it could be no boy of flesh and blood, but a friendly angel of death sent by God to guide him hither, and to support his existence until he were fit to die; and as the season advanced, and it became more and more difficult for any human being to find his way up the snow-covered path, he believed this still more firmly. What could prompt a strange and lowly herd-boy to such a fearful sacrifice? For what hope of reward could he do this? And what to him was the accursed outcast—the hapless wretch who could no longer give him even a blessing? Yes, it was daily clearer to his mind that it was a messenger from the other world; daily he felt more sure that here, with the earth far below him, he was nearer to the world of spirits. In the roaring of the storm, in the thunder of the avalanche, in the freezing snow-drift, in all the terrors of the wilderness, he felt with reverent awe the nearness of Him who rides the clouds and speaks in the thunder; and that which appals most mortals and fills them with dread, uplifted his soul which had triumphed over this life, in jubilant hope of redemption and release.

"Crush, mangle this body!" he would shout to the raging blast, to the falling rocks, to the torrents of heaven, when they whirled round him in wild uproar, and he kissed the invisible hand of the storm that lashed him, he thanked the pain that gnawed his numbed limbs—it all was penance, and penance meant deliverance; and then again when the tumult had subsided, when the last faint rays of the autumn sun shone from the once more peaceful sky, and all the air was still—then he felt as if a reconciled spirit hovered over him too—a divine something, for which he found no name. And then, indeed, a mood would come over him in which he would stretch out his arms to the vacant air, and a cry would escape his lips—like a bird freed from its cage —"Beata."

So near, so real, did her watchful spirit seem that he would fancy he heard her breathing and almost thought he felt her passing lightly by him.

"Beata—have you died down in the valley, and come up to watch by me till I may follow you into eternity? Oh, poor child, the son of perdition may not follow you—not even when he has shed this mortal husk, for you will soar upwards to the fields of the blest—and I must sink among the souls in purgatory," and then it seemed to him that the wind bore a soft cry to his ear. Yes, certainly—it was her soul—that mourned for him, that prayed for him with tears to the Saints. And could they withstand her prayers? In such an hour he felt as if a breath of salvation floated round him; here, up at the limits of the earth, on the brink of the other world, the very air was full of revelation. The two realms seemed to touch and mingle, and he learned more and more to understand their gentle ebb and flow.

Thus it grew to be winter and the chastening hand fell more roughly, and the fetters of death closed more tightly upon him; still he prayed and sang praises without ceasing, and as often as he found a fresh loaf by his couch and a warm skin to preserve him from the increasing cold, he received it as a miracle from God the Lord, who in days of old rained down Manna on his starving people. So long as God sent him nourishment, so long it was His will that he should live, and he relished the bread with a thankful heart, full of devout meditation as if it were the body of Christ—which no mortal hand might evermore present to him.

At last the supplies of bread ceased. He knew not how many days had passed, for him there was neither day nor night; but he perceived that it was longer than usual, for his meagre store had never been exhausted before the fresh supply came. Now it was exhausted, and the place where he was wont to find his bread was empty. Now he knew that the last trial was at hand. Nature inexorably asserted her claims, and gnawing hunger tormented his vitals; death was approaching in the form of starvation. He felt it—it was a cruel death, but he could thank the Lord for it; now the hour was come when, like the chamois, he must end in a hidden crevasse; he wound his rosary round his hand, and only prayed, "Grant, Lord, that I may bear the trial with honour."

He went out of his cave to seek a cleft in the ice so as to carry out his vow; something checked his steps—it was lying at his feet, and softly caressing his knee like a faithful dog. But it was not a dog, it clung to him and grasped his arm with a human hand. "Donatus," it whispered in a beseeching tone. "Donatus, forgive me!"

"Beata!" shrieked the blind man, staggering back against the cliff. He felt as if the mountain had fallen and had buried everything under it—man, and all his works and laws—as if he were left alone with Beata and with God. But that God was He who spoke, saying, "I am Love."

"Donatus, I could not help myself any longer—I can get you no more bread," stammered the girl. "For three days I have been trying in vain, but I can do no more—my limbs are frozen—the cold—I am dying. Oh, poor soul, what will become of you?"

"Beata! angel of my life—angel of my soul!" cried Donatus, rejoicing and weeping in the same breath. "Beata! blessed one, having overcome the world! You have been with me all the time, you have brought me food, have been by my side through snow and frost, in death and desolation? All-merciful God, why were you so long silent?"

"That you should not sin for my sake, nor drive me away—that is why I was silent! Forgive me for disobeying you—I could not, could not leave you."

"Forgive you—I forgive you, you messenger of grace." And with a strong arm the blind man raised the dying girl and carried her into the sheltering cave, and laid her on his bed, covering her with the warm skins that she herself had brought him in her indefatigable care. Then he flung himself down by the couch and covered her care-worn face and faithful breast, and her poor, frozen, little feet with innumerable kisses. He could say no more; only moans and inarticulate sounds of love and sorrow escaped him, and he held her in his arms, and rocked her and soothed her as a mother does her dying child.

And she clung to him in a perfect extasy of joy. "You see—now I am dying by your side—it has happened as I said"—she whispered in his ear. "And you have kept your word; you wanted to lead me to bliss—now I am indeed blessed."

The blind man was like one in the very whirlwind of a celestial revelation.

"Oh, sweet martyr! You have done what no man ever did. We, when we deny ourselves and subdue ourselves, we hope for a future reward and fear future punishment—but you have renounced all, and fought the fight without hope and without fear. You have sacrificed yourself freely and without compulsion, and have bled to death in silence. What is all that heroism and chastity have ever achieved in comparison with this deed? No—it is no power of the devil that has accomplished this. It is not with dying lips that the evil one seeks to tempt—nor with the kiss of death that he entangles his victims. It is a higher power—yes—now I see and know it! Beata, your death has released me from my bonds—there is a love, that is God—and we have loved each other with such a love, and for that love's sake we shall find mercy."

"Amen!" said the girl, and with a smile of rapture she clasped his head that had sunk upon her breast. And there was peace—the peace of God, in their souls. Her breath was now short and weak, but she clasped him to her with all her remaining strength. He pressed her to his breast and rubbed her frozen limbs, and breathed on her with his warm breath. He implored her with a thousand loving words.

"Do not die, my child, my wife—gift of God, stay with me. God who gave you to me, will let you stay with me one day—one hour, only one little hour that I may make up to you for all you have suffered!"

In vain! the cold hand could no longer stroke his head; it fell by her side.

"Beata!" he called in her ear. "I abandoned you in life, but in death I will not forsake you, I will die with you."

She still heard, a sigh of rapture answered him as from a happy bride—it was her last—then she bowed her head and slept, softly and peacefully, with a smile on her lips. She was gone like the night-moth whose fate it is never to rejoice in the light of the sun, that is snatched away by the first frosts of winter, without a sound, without a wail—out of darkness into darkness.

Donatus still listened for a while to hear if the stilled heart beat no more—not a breath, not a throb, all was over. Long, long did he lie so, the body clasped to his heart; then he rose, and saying half-aloud as though she still

185

could hear, "Come, my child," he laid the slender form across his shoulders like a dead lamb, and went out into the open air.

Snow was falling, softly and lightly spreading a white coverlet under his feet over which he glided inaudibly, feeling his way by the rocky wall. Whither was he going, what did he seek? He could not answer himself these questions, the time for thought was over; one feeling alone possessed him, and that was love. All seemed light to his blind eyes; a slight form rose out of the darkness, and floated before him with a sad but blissful smile. It was Beata's glorified spirit. She pointed out the way, and signed to him to follow with a look of unutterable love.

"Yes, I am coming, I follow," he cried, and hurried on as fast as he could through the snow—after her. Presently the sweet vision reached a spot where the rock ended precipitously, a perpendicular cliff of more than a thousand fathoms. She stood still and looked round. "Wait, I am coming!" he cried. Once more she beckoned, then she soared up and floated across the abyss up —away. By this time he too had reached the spot, and without a shudder he sprang after her; but his mortal body with its burden weighed him down. He slid into the abyss in a cloud of snow, and the loosened mass came plunging after him, a thundering avalanche that filled the air with an ocean of snow.

But just as the air that clings to a heavy body when it is plunged into the depths of the sea rises to rejoin its parent element in shining globules, the spirit of the engulfed Donatus rose from the deep to its eternal home.

The earth lay dead and dumb as if the sun could never rise again, as if love had perished for ever—and yet it will return, bringing softer airs, under whose quickening breath Heaven and earth shall once more be reconciled.

THE END.